They were alone now . . .

No guards. No handcuffs. Nothing was stopping him from touching her. "This is a bad idea," he whispered.

A shudder racked her softness and vibrated into the length of him.

He lifted his hand and fisted it into her hair, fingers sinking deep and tangling in the mass, the strands soft as silk against his rough palm. "You should tell me to go," he growled, fingers delving deeper, searching for the band to free it. She released a soft whimper as he found the thin elastic and tugged it free. The band snapped and broke and the mass of silky hair fell over his hand and arm, tumbling down her back.

Just like that, something snapped in him, too. The last invisible thread that had been holding him together.

"Last chance," he growled, thrusting his hips, letting her feel him, rock hard against her, letting her know exactly what was going to happen if she didn't tell him to get out of here.

By Sophie Jordan

Contemporary Romances
ALL CHAINED UP

Historical Romances
ALL THE WAYS TO RUIN A ROGUE
A GOOD DEBUTANTE'S GUIDE TO RUIN
HOW TO LOSE A BRIDE IN ONE NIGHT
LESSONS FROM A SCANDALOUS BRIDE
WICKED IN YOUR ARMS
WICKED NIGHTS WITH A LOVER
IN SCANDAL THEY WED
SINS OF A WICKED DUKE
SURRENDER TO ME
ONE NIGHT WITH YOU
TOO WICKED TO TAME
ONCE UPON A WEDDING NIGHT

ALL CHAINED UP

The Devil's Rock Series

SOPHIE JORDAN

AVONBOOKS

An Imprint of HarperCollinsPublishers

This is a work of fiction. Names, characters, places, and incidents are products of the author's imagination or are used fictitiously and are not to be construed as real. Any resemblance to actual events, locales, organizations, or persons, living or dead, is entirely coincidental.

AVON BOOKS
An Imprint of HarperCollins*Publishers*
195 Broadway
New York, New York 10007

Copyright © 2016 by Sharie Kohler
ISBN 978-0-06-242368-9
www.avonromance.com

First Avon Books mass market printing: April 2016

Avon Trademark Reg. U.S. Pat. Off. and in Other Countries, Marca Registrada, Hecho en U.S.A.
Avon, Avon Books, and the Avon logo are trademarks of HarperCollinsPublishers
HarperCollins® is a registered trademark of HarperCollins Publishers.

Printed in the U.S.A.

10 9 8 7 6 5 4 3 2 1

For Stacey Kade,
who takes my calls and helps make
everything click into place . . .

ALL CHAINED UP

ONE

*I*T LOOKED EVERY bit as intimidating as she thought it would. The broad, three-storied building was almost colorless beige. The minute the thought entered her head, she knew it didn't make sense. Beige was a color. In fact a lot of her wardrobe consisted of beige. Beige shoes. Beige slacks. Maybe a sad testament to her sense of fashion, but there it was.

Through the car window, all light seemed to end in the shadow of the building. As if the sun's rays could not quite reach past the electric fence with its coiling barbed wires and the looming watchtowers with armed guards. All light, all life, ended right before its walls. A small shiver scraped down her spine as one cold fact sank in. She was going in there.

They passed through the brick sally port and stopped at the gatehouse. Dr. Walker spoke with the guard on duty, handing him both their IDs. The guard examined them, his eyes lost behind the shiny lenses of his sunglasses. After a moment he looked up and scrutinized them inside the car. Briar tried for a smile, but it faltered at his impassive expression.

She caught a glimpse of her reflection in those gleaming lenses. She had tamed her unruly hair into its usual ponytail. At least at first glance she looked professional. Only from behind was the wavy mass even visible. She could almost forget that it was as coarse as a horse's tail.

The guard handed back their identifications. "Dr. Walker. Ms. Davis. Follow the signs around to the admin building."

"Thank you." Dr. Walker gave him a cheery wave and drove on, following the winding road as though they were on a country drive, and not entering a maximum security prison. Laurel said she was nuts for doing this. Briar was beginning to wonder if maybe her sister was right.

"You sure you want to do this, Briar?"

At the question, she blinked and tore her gaze away past the looming prison with its small windows that watched her like so many dark, soulless eyes. Dr. Walker glanced over at her, his gaze kind behind his spectacles.

"Yes. Of course."

He smiled indulgently and she felt like a child caught lying. He knew she wasn't being honest, but for whatever reason he didn't call her out on it. He was probably just grateful to have her help. She was the only nurse on staff to respond to his call for volunteers, after all.

He parked the car in the staff parking lot, and they stepped out into the sweltering heat. He pressed the lock on his key chain and the BMW beeped several times behind them as they made their way inside the prison, stopping outside a control room populated by two more guards.

Again they showed their IDs as Dr. Walker signed them in. A door buzzed and slid open. A ruddy-faced guard waited for them on the other side, his thumbs hooked into his heavy belt. "Welcome to Devil's Rock Penitentiary. I'm Officer Renfro."

He was fit, his barrel chest narrowing to a trim waist. The sight of him offered some reassurance. As did the keys, radio, cuffs, baton, gun, and other paraphernalia she couldn't even begin to identify attached to his belt. He looked ready for anything. She fought to swallow against the perpetual lump in her throat. *Unlike me.*

"I'll be escorting you to the HSU." At her cocked head, he explained. "The Health Services Unit." He gestured for them to follow. Dr. Walker fell in behind, his dress shoes tapping sharply in Renfro's wake. She brought up the rear, the tread of her tennis shoes silent on the concrete floor.

She'd chosen to wear her purple scrubs. They

seemed the least feminine. It was troublesome how many of her scrubs were pink or floral patterned. At least scrubs were thankfully shapeless. Not that she was rocking some siren's body, but this place was full of dangerous men who didn't see too many females. It was best that she not flaunt her gender. At least, that was her logic.

They were buzzed through two more doors. She glanced around as she moved forward, taking in everything. The strategically placed cameras in every corner. The blank stare of the guard that passed them in the long hallway. They stopped at a third door. Renfro punched several numbers onto a keypad that opened a heavy steel door. They stepped out onto a skywalk that stretched over a yard full of inmates wearing white uniforms.

She sucked in a small breath. It was like being on a film set of a prison movie. Except these weren't actors. And this was real.

She scanned the grounds below. Inmates worked out on several crude pieces of gym equipment. Some played basketball. A couple tossed a football. Some simply loitered around, smoking, talking in groups. Sitting. Standing.

Dozens of guards milled around, in addition to the guards watching from the surrounding towers. A trio of inmates sat on a bench, working a beat with their hands and feet. Their voices carried across the yard louder than any radio. A small audience gathered around them, nodding in rhythm to their rap.

"Aren't you concerned?" Dr. Walker asked as he slowed to a stop and pointed to the workout area. "Could they use the weights and other equipment as weapons?"

Officer Renfro glanced down. "The area is enclosed. Only a certain number are allowed in at one time. Warden Carter thinks inactivity is more dangerous."

Dr. Walker nodded. "Progressive man, your warden."

"You know what they say. Idle hands and all . . ."

"Indeed." Dr. Walker nodded.

They were noticed up on the skywalk. Even this far away, she felt the stares, the hot-eyed curiosity of the inmates. It was only a moment but it felt like it stretched on forever as they hovered there for the scrutiny of so many hard-faced, dangerous men. Sweat rolled down her nape and slid between her shoulder blades. Not even ten in the morning yet and it was already sweltering.

"Coming?" Renfro's voice grabbed her attention.

She jerked slightly and then moved ahead, quickly following the two men from the skywalk and into the building and the welcoming blast of air-conditioning. They turned down a corridor. She held her breath, half fearing they would walk through a cell block housing hundreds of inmates. But that never happened. Thankfully. They turned the corridor and arrived at another door, marked HEALTH SERVICES UNIT. Officer Renfro punched a code and opened the door.

The infirmary was a large airy room with big windows that looked out over a portion of the parking lot and faced the corner of the prison's west wing.

A white-haired officer stood near the door. He was older and didn't look nearly as fit or vigilant as Officer Renfro.

"This is Officer Murphy," Renfro said. "He's here most days. Different guards alternate nights in the HSU."

Dr. Walker and Briar took turns shaking hands with Officer Murphy. With his large belly, he didn't imbue nearly as much confidence as Renfro did, and she couldn't help wondering if maybe he wasn't past retirement age. He reminded her of her high school Spanish teacher. Students had made out in the back of Mr. Delgado's classroom. She was never sure if he knew and didn't care or was just oblivious.

She eyed his rosacea-splashed face, her gaze stopping on his swollen red nose, thinking of an antibiotic cream Dr. Walker might want to prescribe him.

A younger man wearing scrubs stepped forward, hand outstretched. He was thin with bright dark eyes. The fine lines around his eyes spoke to frequent laughter, and his resemblance to her brother-in-law, Caleb, put her at ease.

"I'm Josiah Martinez, the LVN here. We're so glad to have you both. Thank you for volunteering your time." He released Dr. Walker's hand and turned to shake Briar's. "We've been drowning since Dr. Pollinger took early retirement. There's only so much I can do on my own."

"We're happy to help." Dr. Walker shrugged. "Only one day a week, but maybe we can do some good until you find someone to take Dr. Pollinger's place."

As they continued exchanging pleasantries, Briar observed the room. It consisted of six beds and several utilitarian cabinets. A unit of shelves along the far wall held bedding, pillows, and other supplies. A cracked door revealed a restroom. She released a small breath of relief. She wouldn't even have to leave the infirmary until she was escorted out at the end of the day. She would have to tell Laurel that. It might make her sister feel better.

"I'll leave you in Josiah's capable hands," Renfro said, clapping the LVN on the back. "He and Murphy will run you through the protocols." He glanced to each man pointedly. "Yes? Be sure to discuss emergency procedures."

Josiah and Murphy both nodded. At the door, Renfro stopped as though suddenly remembering. "Oh.

Warden Carter had a meeting this morning, but he looks forward to meeting you both. He'll pop in today."

The moment the door shut behind Renfro, Murphy sank back down into a chair by the door. Somehow, she suspected he usually didn't move from that chair. Unless it was maybe for lunch. The older man smiled vacantly at her as he crossed his arms, tucking his hands beneath the stained armpits of his uniform.

"This way," Josiah murmured, a curl of humor to his voice as his gaze shifted from Officer Murphy to her. He motioned to the single desk in the corner that held a computer. "Hope you don't mind. Since I knew you were arriving today, I took the liberty of making appointments this afternoon. There are several inmates who have been coming in for a while with chronic complaints. I've opened their files up on the computer, if you would like to take a look at my notes before they start coming in."

"Very efficient of you." Dr. Walker nodded approvingly.

Josiah shrugged. "Dr. Pollinger's sudden retirement left us a bit in the lurch. I've been doing my best but we are very grateful to have your help."

Dr. Walker nodded as he moved across the room and sank down in the chair before the computer.

Josiah looked at Briar as Dr. Walker started clicking at the keyboard. "I thought you might like to explore the unit. Familiarize yourself with the supplies." He offered her a key that dangled off a rubber coil around his wrist. "Here you go. We keep all supplies locked."

She nodded. That made sense. She had an image of some scary yet faceless inmate overpowering her and getting the key that doubtlessly gave him access to all manner of things that could be used as weapons. Syringes, scissors, surgical tape. And then there were drugs, of course. A glance to where Murphy sat near the door, his eyelids drooping to half-mast, didn't help eliminate the image.

"Thank you," she murmured, turning for the cabinets lining the walls. "I'll take a look."

Josiah spoke quietly behind her. "They always put the older COs on duty in here. Murphy is one breath from retirement." Apparently he hadn't missed the direction of her concerned gaze.

"Not very comforting," she murmured, her sister's innumerable warnings ringing in her ears.

"Don't worry. We never see much action in here. When we get inmates, they're sick or injured. They want relief and aren't likely to bite the hand giving it to them. Even the appointments this afternoon . . . they've been waiting eagerly to see the doctor for weeks. And the more dangerous inmates that come from seg are always in restraints. Even if they wanted to cause trouble, they can't."

"What's seg?"

"Oh, that's what we call segregation."

She nodded, thinking about his words and deciding that she was acting like a wimp. She needed to get over her fears. Turning, she unlocked the mesh glass cabinets and began exploring the supplies. They were well-stocked. "Dr. Pollinger's retirement caught y'all by surprise, then?"

"Yeah. He wasn't planning to retire for another five years. No one blames him, of course. The stroke just made him decide to move things along faster."

"Life's too short," she agreed. "Hopefully he's recuperating and enjoying himself."

"Last I heard, he's improving his golf swing in Plano."

"Good for him."

"That's right. The rest of us schlubs gotta put in our time." He grinned good-naturedly.

"Well, hopefully you'll find a replacement soon." *And then she could stop coming here.*

"At this prison?" He snorted. "Not likely. We're eighty miles outside Sweet Hill and five hours from anywhere that serves decent sushi. It's practically the end of civilization. The Texas Badlands aren't exactly where a doctor wants to work. But at least we have you two coming in once a week. That should help."

Unease trickled through her. When Dr. Walker asked for volunteers, he made it sound like this arrangement would be temporary. A couple of weeks of making the hour and a half trip to Devil's Rock, at the most. She wouldn't have volunteered if she thought this was a permanent arrangement. She didn't get a nursing degree so she could work in a prison, after all. Bless those who did, like Josiah Martinez, but she didn't have it in her for this kind of thing.

She worked in a doctor's office in a small town where the biggest thing to happen was the arrival of Starbucks last year. If she wanted more excitement, she could move to Forth Worth or Houston or Austin and take a job at one of the hospitals there. On any given day, the most extreme thing she saw was a broken arm. On the scariest day, a case of meningitis.

So what are you doing here?

"Guess we better roll through those protocols," Josiah announced, clapping his hands lightly and rubbing them together.

Banishing that internal voice that sounded a lot like her sister, Briar forced a smile and paid attention as the LVN started explaining what to do in the event of scary-not-going-to-happen-in-a-million-years-situations. At least she hoped so.

TWO

"**D**ROP THE BISCUIT, asshole, or the next thing in your mouth will be my fist."

Knox tightened his hold around the other inmate's neck the barest amount. Not enough to kill him or even knock him out, but he knew the bastard had to be seeing spots.

"Fuck you," the guy wheezed.

Christ. He thought he was beyond this shit. He had spent the first year in here tasting blood. Every day, he fought. Protecting his back and his brother's had been priority number one. Still. Here he was. Throwing down over a biscuit.

It hadn't taken long for Knox to realize he and North needed allies, so he'd played the game. Made those allies—and kept them. For eight years he'd kept them. But that didn't mean he didn't have to fight anymore. He still had to crack a few skulls now and then just to hold his place in the pecking order.

Right now, for example.

The kid couldn't be over twenty, and he felt a stab of pity. That was how old he'd been when he entered Devil's Rock's hallowed walls. Twenty and scared shitless but determined to protect North and himself. Of course, this kid had enough swastikas and shamrocks covering him to crush any notion of youthful innocence. He was a full-fledged White Warrior, and given a chance, he'd shove a shank between Knox's ribs.

"Now don't crumble it," Knox warned. "I'm not eating any fucking crumbs off this floor, you hear?"

Knox knew it was just a biscuit. In another life, years ago, he'd probably left many a one uneaten on his plate, but this was a different life now. He couldn't let such a thing slide. Food was a commodity. No one gave it up without a fight. To do so would mark him weak. Not just him, but his brother, too. Hell, their entire crew.

And Reid wouldn't have anyone in his crew if they were weak. It didn't work like that in here. Eight years had taught him that. Hell, the first week had taught him that.

Reid was as merciless as they came. The scary motherfucker had been in here only a few years longer than Knox and North, but he ran one of the biggest crews. The day he let Knox and North into their midst had marked their survival. Only the strong ran with Reid.

Inmates gathered around Knox, spitting and growling like beasts hungry for blood. Guards would be on them any minute. His brother stood by, his deep brown gaze scanning the crowd, watching Knox's back, making sure none of the White Warriors decided to jump into the fray.

Reid and the rest of their crew looked on, too. No emotion bled from their stone-cold faces. In here, emotion got you killed. Or worse. And there was definitely worse than dead in Devil's Rock. If Knox had to live like some of these poor bastards, enduring what they did every day, he would gladly take a shiv to the ribs.

The scrawny skinhead writhed against the manacle of Knox's bicep, his brethren hovering close. One move from them and Reid would intervene. They knew it. Everyone did. The hatred between Reid's crew and the White Warriors was mutual and ran deep, but they weren't interested in dying today, so they held back.

Knox stretched out his hand. "Give it up."

Spit flew from the guy's lips. "Fuck you, man."

It wasn't about the biscuit. It was more than that. It was about Knox's continued survival in this prison. He couldn't back down.

This shit never changed. But it sure as hell got old. At least there was an end in sight. He'd already served eight years of his eight-to-fifteen year sentence for manslaughter. He wasn't granted parole at his first hearing four months ago—not with his frequent trips to the hole—but maybe in another year or two. If he didn't fuck up too much more.

When he and North went to prison for killing their cousin's rapist, their lawyer said it could have been worse. They could have gotten a more severe sentence. The jury had sympathized with them. Or more importantly, they sympathized with Katie, who had taken the stand and shared what Mason Leary did to her.

They killed a man. It hadn't been their intention, but they did it. Knox accepted that he deserved to be here, but it still didn't make it easy. Every day in Devil's Rock sucked a little bit more of his soul away.

With an inward sigh, he did what he had to do. Curling his hand into a fist, he crashed it into the guy's face, surrendering to the violence that governed his existence.

He felt a ripple surge through the crowd. A current of air behind him. Before he had a chance to turn, pain exploded in the back of his skull. He and the kid went down. Ears ringing, he shook himself, shoving away the pain as he pushed back up from the concrete.

Warm blood trickled into his eye as his gaze locked on another skinhead charging him, his face lost beneath a myriad of ink. The skinhead lifted a tray, presumably the one he'd already struck Knox with, ready to bring it down again.

Still no one intervened. Two against one were odds Reid expected any member of his crew to easily handle.

Knox sent a quick glance to his brother, telling him to stay with a warning look. If he didn't, North would intervene—screw what Reid wanted. Blood before all.

Knox lashed out, kicking the other inmate in the knee as he charged. A satisfying pop cracked in the air. The crowd hissed, knowing how much that had to hurt. The inmate went down with a howl. Knox snatched up the discarded tray and swung it into the face of the punk who first grabbed his biscuit and started all this shit in the first place.

Four bulls burst through the crowd, pulling up hard at the sight of the two skinheads groaning at Knox's feet.

Knox lifted both hands in the air, palms up, in an attempt to show he didn't plan on causing any trouble. Well, any *more* trouble.

Chester, one of the more brutal of the corrections officers at Devil's Rock, took one look at Knox and batoned him in the ribs twice. Knox could have guessed it was coming. The SOB loved taking down inmates. Whether necessary or not, he was all about cracking heads with his baton.

He bowed over, a whoosh of air leaving him as pain exploded in his side. That bastard really enjoyed his work. Guards came at Knox then, shoving him down to the concrete. He didn't resist, but that didn't stop Chester from dropping his knee and grinding it into his spine. He bit back a cry of pain, not about to give Chester the satisfaction of knowing he'd hurt him. Instead, he smiled as they cuffed him.

Yanking Knox to his feet, the guards shouted for everyone else to disperse. He caught a glimpse of his brother's scowl and sent him a shrug and a cocky grin meant to reassure him.

"Move it," Chester snarled, pushing him roughly after the other two inmates. Knox stifled a wince at the sudden movement. The prick had done a number on his ribs.

North nodded back at him, trying to convey that he would be all right, that Knox shouldn't worry. They knew the drill. Knox would get nothing less than a week in segregation for the fight. A week was nothing. He'd done longer stints in the hole. Weeks where he doubted his sanity within the gray, enclosed space.

Out in the hall, Lambert, the head bull on duty, looked them over with a bored expression.

The inmate Knox had kicked sniveled, unable to stand. Two guards supported him.

"What happened?" Lambert demanded.

Knox held his gaze, schooling his face into something blank and impenetrable. "We were just fooling around."

No one ever admitted to fighting. No one ever pointed fingers or blamed anyone. It was an unwritten rule, even among enemies. Fighting, whether one was the attacker or the victim, got you a longer stretch in the hole.

Lambert snorted. "That so?" He tapped the skinhead kid's knee with the tip of his baton, which only earned another howl. "Looks broken." He sent Knox a hard look before returning his gaze to the kid. "Callaghan do this to you?"

The guy brought his sniveling under control and lifted his chin, his expression under all that ink once again fierce. "Like he said, we was just fooling around."

Lambert rolled his eyes, clearly finished with them. "Fine. Whatever. Take them to the HSU. If that knee is broken, arrange transport to the hospital."

The skinhead's eyes lit up, broken knee and all. Out was out. God knew the food would be better in a hospital than the slop they ate here.

"C'mon, Callaghan." Chester prodded Knox in his already tender back, getting him to move after the other two inmates.

He shot a glare over his shoulder. It was all he could do. His restrained hands tightened into fists, his knuckles whitening around the raw and bloody scrapes.

Funny how he still felt this reaction. How some bull digging his knee into his spine or prodding him in the back and eyeing him like he was a piece of shit could still get a reaction from him. After all these years, you would have thought he wouldn't care anymore. That he would have given up all expectations for anything more. Anything better.

He should have accepted that this was simply his life.

THREE

$\mathcal{O}$F BRIAR WAS hoping for a quiet first day, it wasn't to be. Thirty minutes before their first appointment, the door to the unit buzzed open.

Four guards entered the room escorting three inmates in full restraints, hands bound in front of them. Murphy quickly patted them down, checking for any hidden weapons. The chains clinked at their wrists as they walked.

She stood up from the desk where she and Dr. Walker had been reviewing the files of the incoming patients, already making notes and potential diagnoses based on Josiah's assessments. They were hoping to see all the inmates Josiah had scheduled for today and maybe some additional cases, too. After glancing through the wait list and reviewing some of the inmates' complaints, Briar and Dr. Walker had exchanged looks. It was alarming how many of these men were walking around untreated with conditions that would have put them in the hospital in the real world. In fact, she suspected Dr. Walker was going to recommend immediate hospital transport for one or two of them.

The room suddenly seemed to shrink at the arrival of these menacing men in restraints. Dr. Walker and Josiah moved forward, directing the guards where to place the inmates, but her limbs froze. A dull beat started in her ears as she surveyed them. She couldn't move.

Two of the inmates were riddled with tattoos. They were scary looking men, ink covering every inch of their arms, necks, and faces. Her stomach churned. They were the type of men she would have crossed the street to avoid.

One of the convicts bled profusely from the mouth and nose, thick crimson dripping onto his white uniform. The other one hop-walked, supported by two corrections officers. Even though the tattooed pair were injured and it was her job to extend care, she couldn't stop the small shudder from rolling through her.

Yet even as alarming as those two skinheads appeared, it was the third man that gave her the greatest pause . . . who made her heart stutter and then kick into a hard hammer that shouted: *Stay away, stay away, stay away.*

He was tattoo-free, as far as she could tell anyway,

but that left the immense size of him and the harshness of his features to focus upon. His jaw looked like it could break granite, and his mouth was an unsmiling slash, bracketed by two short lines that could have possibly been dimples or smile grooves. Except she was certain that he never smiled.

A three-inch bloody gash at the corner of his forehead only added to the severity of his appearance. On someone else, it might have made him look weaker, but not this guy. He looked like a warrior unfazed and ready to plunge back into battle. She knew plenty of women were drawn to his type. A bloodied Viking. The Tarzan that dragged Jane into his hut and quickly made her forget that she was a good civilized woman. Raw and seething with power. He radiated danger. The edgy guy with intense, deep-set eyes and a shadow of stubble covering his square jaw. She could almost imagine brushing her fingers across that jaw. Almost. If she were crazy and into felons.

He stood a few inches over six feet, towering over everyone else in the unit. Even the guards, fully armed and so very competent-looking in their uniforms, seemed diminished beside him. She eyed the cuffs at his wrists, worrying if they were enough, if they would hold him.

"These beds here are fine." Josiah waved at three gray-blanketed beds. They were side by side, the heads butting one side of cinder-block wall.

The ink-free inmate made a move toward one of the beds, but a guard stopped him, his baton arcing through the air with a hiss and whacking him across the flat of his stomach.

It was no gentle blow, and Briar flinched. Everything inside her rebelled at the ease with which the guard delivered the hit. And, if she were honest with herself, the ease with which the inmate accepted it.

She had been so careful to construct a life free of violence. Violent people. Violent situations. She led a safe life. At least as much as she could control.

The inmate didn't even blink an eye. He merely stopped and turned a dead-eyed stare on the guard smirking back at him.

That same guard—his name tag read CHESTER— addressed Josiah: "I wouldn't stick these two anywhere near Callaghan. He might decide to finish the fight." He nodded at the inmate he'd just struck with his baton.

Callaghan. He held himself still, seemingly patient, but tension radiated off him. He reminded her of a jungle cat on one of those nature shows, ready to spring at any moment.

"Yeah. Not a good idea," Chester added, idly tapping his baton against his thigh.

So Callaghan was the reason the other two looked the way they did. Did he start the fight? As soon as the thought entered her head, she shoved it out. It didn't matter. It didn't make him any less culpable if he didn't start it. He was a convict. God knew what horrible thing he had done to land himself in this place. *Not a good idea* was the perfect sum of him.

"Okay." Josiah nodded and turned in a half circle. He waved at the bed in the far corner near the desk. "That one, then."

Nodding, Chester escorted Callaghan to the bed. The inmate sank down on it, still without uttering a sound. Not even a flicker of discomfort crossed his granite features.

Dr. Walker immediately started examining the whimpering skinhead with the hurt knee. Josiah squared off in front of the other skinhead, guiding him onto the bed. The doctor met her gaze and gestured to Callaghan. "You want to look at him, Nurse Davis? I'll clean up this one's face."

Hovering behind the desk, she was closest to Callaghan, so it made sense for her to examine him. But she hesitated, her feet rooted to the spot. He exuded danger, a threat she was reluctant to approach.

Chester rounded the foot of the bed, inching closer to where she stood. "It's all right, miss." He tucked his thumbs into his gun belt and puffed out his chest. "I'm here."

She had to stop herself from rolling her eyes.

Callaghan turned his head to look at her for the first time, and it was like being pinned in the crosshairs. Her lungs constricted, the air trapped there as he stared at her. She felt stripped of her skin. Like he was seeing inside her, assessing, weighing and measuring her. She had to resist hunching her shoulders and looking away.

The deep blue of his gaze was hard and flat. It reminded her of the cobalt glass her grandmother had collected. For years the little vases and bottles sat in Nana's windowsill, catching the morning sunlight. They had always mesmerized Briar. She'd felt safe in that kitchen, her legs swinging from her chair, not quite grazing the floor as she ate her breakfast. Not like she felt here.

Callaghan's top lip curled faintly in a knowing smirk, and she felt exposed. As though he knew all she had been thinking. Every low thought of him. Every fearful notion she had. Just as quickly as it appeared, the smirk vanished and his lips flattened, covering up his straight white teeth again.

Chester's voice snapped her to attention. "I can stay here and keep an eye on him, miss." He grinned at her with a cocky tilt of his head. "Make sure he don't give you no problem."

Her gaze flicked to Dr. Walker and Josiah, already attending to their patients. The other guards, with the exception of Chester, were leaving the room.

She squared her shoulders. She had signed on for this. No wimping out now.

"That's not necessary." She'd worked hard to put herself through college and become a nurse. She was a professional. It was her duty to care for the sick—not judge them.

She rounded the desk and grabbed some gloves from a box on a standing rolling tray of medical supplies. "You can go now, officer."

His cocky smile slipped slightly. He nodded slowly. He glanced at Murphy, awake from his nap and standing somewhat more attentively near the door. "Right, then. Don't hesitate to hit the panic button if you—"

"I won't. Thank you."

Chester's chest lifted on a breath. He walked over to Callaghan and tapped him on the shoulder with his baton. "Behave yourself, boy. I'll be back to fetch you later."

She watched the officer swagger off, the resemblance to her father uncanny. Not his appearance. It was his posturing. Her father was that same good old boy. On the surface he acted so good-natured and courteous. Everyone loved and admired him, the gentleman looking out for the fairer sex, when behind doors he liked to use them for his personal punching bag.

Shaking off those ugly memories, Briar moved on leaden feet, dragging the rolling tray of supplies with her and stopping in front of where Callaghan sat on the edge of the mattress.

Even sitting before her, in full restraints, he seemed . . . big. Intimidating in a way that he shouldn't be. He made her feel small. At five feet seven and a size twelve, that sensation had never plagued her. Besides, he was a prisoner. He lacked all freedom. Freedom to hurt her being paramount. That should take away his aura of power.

It should, but it didn't.

She eyed the gash on his forehead. "That's a nasty cut. What happened?" she asked before she could re-think the question. It was just habit. The thing she asked when she sat down with every patient. In this case, for a split second she simply forgot that he was *not* every patient.

At his silence, she lowered her gaze from his fore-head to his eyes. Her lungs tightened again as she fell into a sea of cobalt. She resented that—that he should have such stunning eyes reminiscent of a part of her childhood that was pure and untainted.

"Do you know where you are, honey?" The deep rumble of his voice felt like gravel rolling over her skin, and she blinked, confused by the question—and irritated by the "honey" designation. It was an en-dearment, but something in the way he said it made it feel like an insult.

"Of course I know where I am," she answered.

"Then you can probably guess what happened to me."

She flushed. "I'm sure it was a fight, but I was looking for more specifics." She dragged her gaze away and picked a cotton swab off the tray. Dousing it in astringent, she faced him again. She was careful to keep her attention trained to his wound and not his face—not those eyes.

Dabbing the swab against his forehead, she fought to keep her stare from dipping down. Wiping away the blood, she could see he was going to need sutures and said as much. "Dr. Walker is going to want to take a look at this."

A glance over her shoulder revealed Dr. Walker still examining the inmate with the injured knee. From his concerned expression, she knew he would send the man out to Radiology to get his leg X-rayed.

When she turned back to Callaghan, she found his unswerving gaze trained on her face. Her cheeks caught fire and she knew she was tomato red.

She sucked in a breath and shivered, rebelling at the idea that she was actually this close to an obviously dangerous criminal. Close enough to note the dark rings circling his irises. So close she could count the eyelashes framing his eyes. Dark lashes far too lush for any man to rightly possess. She held her breath, frozen for a long moment. Pinned beneath his scrutiny, watching him watch her, detecting the direction of his gaze, every inch of her face his eyes touched. Her eyes, nose, mouth, and hair. He missed nothing.

She tore her gaze away and finished cleaning his wound with unsteady hands. She reached for the butterfly strips, deciding to use them until Dr. Walker was able to suture. He didn't move as she carefully applied the strips.

Finished, she stood back, stripping off her gloves. "Why don't you rest back on the bed until the doctor can examine you?"

He stood up from the bed, presumably to center himself on the mattress, but the action brought him closer to her. She felt draped in his shadow, the great height and breadth of him falling over her like a blanket. The male scent of him filled her nostrils.

Briar stepped back quickly. Too quickly. She bumped the standing tray and sent it rolling several feet with a loud whir.

She chased after the tray, catching it with fumbling hands, then positioned it near the bed again, her hands trembling. *You're a professional, Briar. Act like one.*

He watched her with flinty eyes as he sank back down on the bed. She felt ten kinds of idiot. He was in steel restraints. There was an armed corrections officer twenty feet away. Cameras in every corner. A panic button six feet away. *Relax, relax, relax. Do what you would do with any other patient.*

He started to ease himself back on the mattress, and she couldn't help notice the slowness with which he moved. A wince passed over his face. It was so swift she almost missed it.

She stepped forward, forgetting her own nerves in the face of his pain. "What else is bothering you?"

He shook his head as he fully reclined on the bed, the pillow beneath his head, the white cotton stark against his dark cropped hair.

"You're moving slowly simply because of your head wound?" she pressed, unconvinced.

"I'm fine."

He was lying. She immediately knew that this big guy of few words was withholding something.

"Let me take a look . . ." She moved forward and began running her hands up his arms and over his shoulders. Beneath his shirt his muscles reacted and tensed, tightening under her questing fingers. It was a clinical examination. She had performed it countless times before, testing for injuries. Even if she wasn't oblivious to the hard cut of his body, she noted it all dispassionately, for the most part, keeping her inspection to cool observation. He was all lean lines and hollows. Not an inch of fat or softness anywhere on him.

She watched his face carefully, trying to detect if her touch hurt him anywhere. He held himself still, expression impassive. She gently probed his muscled pecs, skimming with her palms and then pressing down with the tips of her fingers. When she reached his left rib cage, the wince returned for a brief second before he masked it.

"Here?" She lightly prodded the area and a hissed breath escaped him.

Nodding, she lifted her hands from him and stepped back. "Will you please sit up and remove your shirt?" Her cool, efficient tone pleased her, reaffirming that she was business as usual. She wasn't frightened of him. Nor did his size, build, or above-average looks move her in any way. Not in the least. Not at all.

He stared at her, unmoving, his jaw set at a resolute angle. She frowned at him.

After a long moment he sat up and swung his legs over the side, apparently deciding to oblige her request. Thankfully, she didn't jump out of her skin at his movement this time. She stepped aside, giving him more room and waiting for him to remove his shirt, keeping her face coolly professional. A quick glance at Dr. Walker and Josiah revealed them both conferring over the inmate with the busted knee.

She looked back at Callaghan. He still hadn't removed his shirt.

"Your shirt, please."

He glanced down at his bound hands and then looked back at her with a cocked eyebrow. He needed help.

"Oh. Yes, of course." Bracing herself, she stepped forward and reached around him to grasp the hem of his white shirt. As she leaned forward, the aroma of some kind of industrial-strength laundry detergent seared the inside of her nose. But beneath that overpowering odor there was the scent of him. Male musk and a hint of clean sweat.

Briar tugged the shirt up, her knuckles grazing the smooth flesh of his back. He hissed a breath again.

"Sorry," she mumbled. "I'm trying not to hurt you."

His face was in the space beside her head, directly above her shoulder. A shiver raced down her spine as she felt his warm breath against her ear.

Anxious to put an end to their proximity, she became less careful with her movements and yanked the shirt up, pulling it over his head, the backs of her fingers brushing the dark cropped hair that hugged his scalp. She glimpsed a tattoo on his back, but he reclined back on the bed before she could properly view all of it.

She stepped away then, and her mouth dried at the sight of his body. A dragon tattoo wrapped around the side of his torso, evidently traveling from his back, crawling over his chiseled flesh like a living thing, its mouth open in a fearsome snarl across the front of his rib cage.

Here was the proof of what she had already felt. Hard sinew. Lean muscle. His was not a body given to leisure. Several white-ridged scars decorated his shoulders and torso, and she couldn't stop her eyes from dragging over him, counting each one. He must engage in knife fights regularly. She stopped counting at twelve.

"Looks like you visit here often," she muttered, her hand instinctively going to one angry-red scar slashing across his shoulder. The moment she touched the puckered flesh, she realized she had forgotten to put her gloves back on. Skin to skin, his flesh was warm against her bare fingers. Almost hot to the touch. She snatched her hand back.

He didn't respond, and she heard herself murmur, "Not much of a talker, are you?"

After a moment he shrugged one shoulder and finally answered her. "Often enough. Been here awhile."

That single announcement rattled around inside her skull like a loose marble. Even if he hadn't announced it, she knew. She sensed it. He must have done something pretty terrible.

She swallowed the impossibly large lump in her throat, her mind briefly touching on what some of those horrible things could be before she stopped herself. She didn't want to know.

They didn't lock people up for a long time for doing nothing. It was the only nudge she needed to remember what kind of man she was dealing with.

He stared blankly at her, unapologetic. There wasn't the faintest shame or regret in his expression over his admission. *Been here awhile.* He owned it like someone admitting to liking peaches 'n' cream ice cream.

"Are you afraid of me, Nurse Davis?" Her skin reacted at his faintly mocking tone, jumping alive with a thousand goose bumps at the deep timbre of his voice. *Nurse Davis.* Just the sound of her name laced with derision was enough to jackknife her pulse. Like he knew some secret about her.

Her gaze ate up his brutally beautiful face. And that wasn't right. Such beauty shouldn't be threatening. Or wild or dangerous. But she supposed many things were. She thought tigers were beautiful but she wouldn't dare touch one. And yet here she was, touching this man.

She looked down and examined the area that had made him wince and sucked in a gasp. The skin there was a deep red and already starting to bruise.

Ignoring his question, she wrapped herself in her professional armor and ducked her head for a closer look. "What happened here?" She shot him a warning glance. "What happened specifically?"

He shook his head like it was nothing. "Just the usual."

"Fists? Boots?" she pressed. As big as he was, she couldn't imagine a simple punch to the ribs doing this much damage.

"The usual," he repeated.

"It's useful in determining the severity of your

injury if I know what exactly happened. I assure you, it's not for my own perverse curiosity." She stared at him, waiting with a lift of her eyebrows.

"Baton," he supplied the single word.

A guard's baton.

Frowning, she looked down at his purpling flesh and touched him there, gently running her fingers over the sensitive area, testing it for signs of an obvious break. She didn't feel a protruding bone, but she knew the only way to know for certain would be to take an X ray. "You should comply with the corrections officers. This kind of abuse could result in some serious damage."

Something flickered in his eyes. She couldn't determine what it was. It passed so quickly, but a frisson of trepidation dripped through her. "Who said I didn't comply?" he asked.

She hesitated, her breath catching, and she didn't know why it should. The idea that seemingly good guys could be *not* good, that they could hurt someone when it wasn't needed, when it wasn't right . . . well, that shouldn't be an unfamiliar concept for her. Mean people came in all shapes and sizes. She knew that better than anyone. "Are you saying they used excessive force with you?"

He cocked his head, and for the first time his hard expression cracked. Disgust leaked out. "Are you for real? Where do you think you are, honey?"

Briar stiffened. "I know exactly where I am. If the guards used excessive force, you should report them—"

"First day here and you know so much," he murmured, his quiet voice no less deep or menacing. She felt her eyes widen as she realized the moment of her mistake. Her experience was not his, but she had presumed to *know* anyway. To understand. And then she dared to advise him how to live, how to exist in this cage. "You don't know fuck all about this place."

She flinched. He might as well have said *fuck off.* That's what she felt. What she heard. *What she deserved.*

Face burning, she turned and picked up the gauze, feeling like that stupid girl who bit off more than she could chew. The teenager at her first party slamming back a shot and then choking on the burn as it slogged its way down her throat. She plucked at the tape holding the roll of gauze together, knowing that whether Dr. Walker wanted Callaghan to have X rays or not, he would want his ribs wrapped. For Callaghan's comfort if nothing else.

Mostly she just needed to do something with herself after Callaghan's stinging words.

Her hands were shaking as she got the tape free and began unrolling a section. No matter how she willed them to stop, they wouldn't.

"Ah, what do we have here?"

Her head snapped up at the arrival of Dr. Walker. Relief coursed through her.

Renewed with purpose, she set down the gauze, stood aside and recounted Callaghan's injuries, feeling in control again. A professional. Not at all like the rebuked child of moments ago.

The doctor sank down onto the edge of the bed and examined the head wound first, checking Callaghan's eyes and asking the standard questions to determine if he had a concussion. He treated him like any other patient. Because that's what he saw. A patient. He didn't see the caged animal she did.

Anticipating his needs, Briar busied herself gathering up the supplies required for suturing the wound, retrieving items from the cabinets. She was glad she had taken the time to familiarize herself with the contents this morning so she didn't have to bother Josiah, who was now on the phone arranging transport to the local hospital for the inmate with the injured knee.

She offered Dr. Walker an anesthetic to help numb the area before suturing. "I don't need that," Callaghan said, his voice soft, but deep enough that she would have probably heard him from outside the HSU.

Dr. Walker smiled kindly, as though he wasn't dealing with a dangerous convict, and accepted the syringe from Briar. "It's nothing to be afraid of, son. It just hurts a moment, but you'll be grateful for the relief once I start sewing."

"I don't need it," he repeated in that quiet, un-shakable voice.

Dr. Walker stared at him a long moment before glancing at Briar, the hesitation clear in his eyes.

She shrugged. "If he doesn't want it . . ." She let her words fade away. As harsh as Callaghan had been to her, she wasn't particularly motivated to argue with him just so he could suffer less. If he wanted pain, then he could have it.

As soon as the uncharitable thought entered her head, she gave it a swift kick. Her profession called for her to offer comfort and compassion. In so short a time, this inmate had squashed that impulse in her. It made her feel small and ugly inside. So soon, this place was already changing her. She didn't like it, and right then she vowed not to let it happen. Part of the reason she went into nursing was because she wanted to be a good person. Nothing like her father.

"Very well, Mr. Callaghan," Dr. Walker declared. "I shall endeavor to use a gentle hand, but I can't promise it won't hurt."

Callaghan blinked, his lids dropping slowly over those blue eyes. He pulled back slightly, as if the *mister* before his name had somehow thrown him, and she doubted he had often, if ever, been extended that courtesy. At least not while he was in prison, and as he'd made clear, that had been a while.

Dr. Walker was good to his word, working quickly and efficiently. She stood at his elbow, handing him whatever he needed promptly, her gaze only straying once or twice to Callaghan.

The man stared straight ahead, his jaw locked tight, his expression reflecting none of his discomfort, even though she knew it had to hurt.

Was that what prison did? Killed one's ability to feel? The possibility left her a little hollow inside.

"There now." Dr. Walker slipped off his gloves. "Are you opposed to acetaminophen?"

After a moment of hesitation, Callaghan shook his head.

Dr. Walker smiled. "Very good, then. Nurse Davis will get that for you as well as an antibiotic cream to help with any potential infection." He lightly patted Callaghan on the shoulder like he was one of the old grannies that came to see him complaining of arthritis, and not a hardened convict.

"What about his ribs?" Briar asked.

"Ah, that's right. Let's take a look." Dr. Walker rubbed his hands together, warming his palms before placing them over the bruises on Callaghan's torso. "Possibly fractured," he said after a moment. "Maybe only bruised. How's your breathing? Any trouble?" Briar offered him a stethoscope, and the doctor placed it on both Callaghan's chest and his back, listening for long moments as he directed the patient to inhale and exhale. At last he sat down, looping the stethoscope around his neck. "Your lungs sound strong. Considering there is little to do to treat your ribs, I don't think it necessary to send you out for X rays. We'll bind you up, though. That should offer some comfort and help with the healing."

Callaghan nodded once, which she supposed was acknowledgment and thanks rolled into one. It seemed even this hardened criminal was not immune to Dr. Walker's generous bedside manner. The older man pushed himself to his feet just as the door opened.

Chester and another guard returned, entering the room in that swaggering way of theirs. "Any of these inmates ready?" Chester asked, his gaze falling on Callaghan, making it clear who he really wanted.

She tried not to let the fact that the guard clearly disliked him matter. If Chester was singling him out, it was just further evidence that Callaghan was a problem and probably deserving of such treatment.

"Thought we'd get them transferred to seg before our shift ends." He stopped and hooked his thumb in his belt, legs braced apart. "Save the new guards coming in the trouble."

Dr. Walker looked bewildered, his gaze seeking out Josiah, their interpreter in this strange new world.

Josiah pointed to the inmate with lesser injuries. "This one can be moved, but we've already called transport to take Rollins to Memorial—"

"What about Callaghan?" Chester strode closer to his bed, his manner almost possessive.

Dr. Walker blinked and looked down at the silent inmate. Even with his stitched forehead and his bruised torso, he looked formidable. Too big for the cot.

Briar's gaze dropped to his hands with the scarred knuckles. Her stomach clenched when she noticed they were curled into fists. Battle ready. She could almost imagine him bursting from his handcuffs like the Hulk. Her gaze shot to his face, locking with his eyes. Her chest tightened. He was dangerous. She knew it. And he knew she knew it, too.

"Him?" Dr. Walker queried. "He's not going anywhere."

Chester looked Callaghan over belligerently. "He looks fine. All stitched up, I see. Why can't—"

"He has a concussion and bruised, possibly fractured, ribs. He's not going anywhere for another twenty-four hours. At the very least."

Chester's lips fell into a mutinous line. He clearly wanted to argue, but knew better than to oppose the doctor. Especially a doctor who was so generously volunteering his time while they were short of staff in the HSU.

Dr. Walker turned back around and addressed Briar, a silent dismissal of the belligerent guard. "Why don't you go ahead and bind his ribs?" He glanced at the clock on the wall and shook his head with a grimace. "Hopefully, we can finally start on some of the appointments." With a sigh, he rubbed the center of his forehead. "I'd hope to get more accomplished today. Josiah, can we go ahead and send for the first two appointments?"

Josiah nodded and moved to the phone.

Briar lowered her head, hiding a small smile as Chester swung around in clear displeasure at being dismissed by the diminutive man. He barked at the inmate who was well enough to leave. "On your feet!"

She knew Chester likely put up with all manner of abuse day in and day out on this job, but he struck her as a bully. She had never liked bullies.

The door buzzed open and shut as Chester and the other guard left the room with the inmate between them.

Soon, two new guards entered the room to escort the second inmate for transport, assisting him into a wheelchair. Josiah and Dr. Walker moved over to supervise, and Briar was left with Callaghan. She still needed to bind his ribs.

She reached for the gauze and unrolled it a fraction. Gripping it between her fingers, she faced the inmate, her tone all business. "If you wouldn't mind sitting up again."

He obliged without a word, lifting long arms corded tightly with sinew out in front of him so she had room to wrap his torso. She began circling the gauze around him, leaning in and out, in and out, repeatedly. Her hands stroked the cotton, making certain it lay smooth against his firm flesh, without wrinkles or bunching. "It needs to feel a little tight," she murmured, "but let me know if it's too uncomfortable."

His breath fell in a steady cadence near her ear. She trained her gaze on his body. Not his face. Not the eyes that she felt moving over her. Touching him like this, being this close, she dared not look up.

Because his body was unnerving enough.

She held in a snort. Just barely. His body was ridiculous. Honestly, there was nothing about him or this situation that did not unnerve her. The hard wall of him made her skin feel too tight. Too hot and itchy.

"You don't want to be here," he said so quietly it was practically a whisper in her ear.

Her breath caught. Her eyes flicked to his. She couldn't help it. She had to take a quick peek. He was watching her like a hawk as she worked. She pasted a brittle smile on her face, her heart racing faster than a jackrabbit in the face of his scrutiny. "Why do you say that? I'm here, aren't I?"

Was she putting out an I-don't-want-to-be-here vibe? If that was the case, she hoped Dr. Walker wasn't picking up on it. Of the eight nurses that worked under him and the other three doctors at the practice, she was the only one who volunteered to join him in this latest charity project. She wanted to be essential to the doctor and the practice. Especially since Nancy, the senior staff nurse, was retiring next year. Briar was gunning for that position, and she knew that having a good attitude was crucial.

Satisfied she had wrapped enough gauze around him, she snipped off the end and taped it into place. With a final pat, she moved back from the bed. "I'll get you something for pain."

She didn't wait to hear if he thanked her. Eyeing the clock on the way to the supply cabinet, she told herself she only had a few more hours to go until she left this place. Then another week until she had to return. A week of normalcy. Back to her safe job with promising chances for advancement. Her comfortable town house. Her freezer full of Cherry Garcia and a DVD chock full of her favorite shows. That was the life she had created. This place didn't fit into that life.

By the time she had to return here, Callaghan would be gone. She probably wouldn't have to see him again. Who knew? Maybe they would find a full-time physician in the next week and she and Dr. Walker wouldn't have to come back at all.

Glancing around the grim room with its gray walls and gray-blanketed beds currently occupied by one fierce-looking inmate with hard eyes that tracked her every move, that was just fine with her.

FOUR

$\mathcal{E}$IGHT YEARS, TWO months and six days.

That was how long it had been since a woman voluntarily touched him.

The nurse wasn't the prettiest woman Knox had ever seen, but he could safely say he had not seen anything as attractive inside these walls. Ever.

Even though she downplayed her looks, she had a curvy body under the scrubs and so much hair his hands could get lost in it for days. The brown mass was shot with gold and russet streaks. All that hair exploded out of a tight ponytail that looked ready to bust out of the elastic band. Yeah, she had her assets.

His gaze followed her as she moved around the room, never once looking at him. And she wouldn't. Not unless she had to. He knew that much about her already. She was a good clean girl who wanted nothing to do with a filthy convict like him.

She had treated him civilly, but he knew what she

thought of him. Her distaste was written all over her face, in the purse of her lips and the wrinkle of her nose. In the way her hands shook when she had to touch him.

He tried not to let it get to him. After eight years, his skin was made of thicker stuff than that. What did he care what one narrow-minded woman thought of him?

He forced his gaze off her. Inmates soon started arriving in a steady flow. Two at a time. After their initial frisk, the nurse talked to one and took his vitals while the doctor conducted an examination of the other.

She was nervous. Her movements as fidgety as a cat in a room full of rocking chairs. He felt his lips pull into a frown. That would be her downfall. In a place like this, you needed composure. At least pretend you were fine.

The others sensed her nervousness, too. Their hard faces watched her. Hunger avid in their eyes, animals that had gone too long without meat. Even old Hatcher, who had spent the bulk of his life in here and walked with shuffling steps, his back stooped over, watched her like she was his next meal.

Knox's eyes drifted back to her. He observed her from where he lay in the bed, tension coiling inside his gut. News of her would travel fast. Like blood in the water, it would attract more of them.

A few women trickled in and out of Devil's Rock over the years. Personnel and staff. There had been that counselor, Dr. Sheppard, who interviewed him and a bunch of inmates, trying to get them to open up and talk about the things they had done that put them behind bars. Sheppard had been over fifty, but other guys requested meetings with her once they heard she had nice legs. Hood rats and skinheads alike, everyone suddenly wanted to pour out their hearts for a chance to check her out and catch a whiff of her perfume.

Not Knox. Those meetings had been a misery for him. All that talking. Why did he do what he did? Did he regret it? Would he change his actions if he could?

Christ. He didn't need that shit. He knew why he had done what he did, and yeah, he regretted it. He'd hurt a lot of people. He felt bad about that, but there was no going back, so why talk about it?

There was only moving forward. Surviving this place. Day after day after day. The end goal was to get himself and his brother the fuck out in one piece. That was the present. The past didn't amount to shit.

His gaze traveled back to the nurse. Her features were scrunched up in concentration as she fiddled with a package of swabs.

He'd had his fair share of ass on the outside. His

high school girlfriend had been a cheerleader. The one that did the splits on top of the pyramid. Yeah. Those memories had helped sustain him. When he was hard up, the memory of Holly riding him in her cheerleading skirt served well enough. Or Jasmine. He'd been dating her when he was arrested. She had a penchant for miniskirts. He used to slip his hand beneath . . .

Shit. He hauled in the train of thought. Now, stuck inside this infirmary, staring at the first female he had seen in weeks, wasn't the time to daydream about sex.

Jasmine had visited him twice after he got locked up, even hinting about them getting married. He shut that down fast. He told her to stop coming. That first month had been the hardest. He didn't need her making him long for what he couldn't have for another eight to fifteen years. And it wasn't fair to string her along and expect her to wait for him either.

Not that the rest of them—the dregs of humanity that populated Devil's Rock—wouldn't fantasize about Nurse Davis. Once word of her got around, the infirmary was going to be under siege. She was young. Younger than him. Although he felt ancient, older than everyone else in the world even if he was only twenty-eight. He inhaled sharply and caught a lingering whiff of her. Her hair smelled like pears, for fuck sake.

Closing his eyes, he actually wished that they had let Chester take him to the hole.

IT WAS DARK by the time they left the prison. Briar was grateful that Dr. Walker drove them today. She was exhausted in a way she never had been at the end of a workday at the clinic.

"I really appreciate your help today, Briar," Dr. Walker announced as they drove the hour and a half back toward town, the sleek nose of his car cutting through the inky night. The desert mountains of the badlands rose up on either side of them, darker even than the night sky. "I know it's not the job you signed on for and certainly not a requirement."

She nodded against the headrest. "Well, they're clearly understaffed. It's generous of you to offer your time."

"One day a week hardly seems enough," he murmured, frowning.

She nodded in agreement.

After several moments of mulling silence, he added, "I know I usually take Fridays off, but I'm thinking I might go back tomorrow and take care of some more of those long-standing appointments."

"Oh." She held silent for a moment, staring into the vast desert night, suddenly feeling an uncomfortable weight on her chest. A car flew past in the opposite lane. There wasn't much traffic out here. Not much of anything at all. Just wilderness. Wide-open mesas and stark mountains. She fiddled with the strap of her handbag. "I suppose I could accompany you again—"

"You don't have to do that, Briar," he quickly cut in.

"I don't mind," she heard herself say, and then wondered who she had become. She could almost hear her sister calling her crazy again.

He glanced at her before facing the road again. "If you're certain. That would be much appreciated. Bless you, Briar. You'll receive full wages again, of course."

She nodded, and waved a hand as though it didn't matter, but of course it did. She was saving to buy a house. A home of her own. The house was part of the dream she was working toward. Just one piece of it. The other piece was advancing in her career. Would she have volunteered to accompany Dr. Walker if she wasn't angling for that promotion? Especially considering how uncomfortable she felt working at the prison? Doubtful. Her less than altruistic motives didn't make her feel particularly proud of herself, but then it was the reality. She grew up watching her father mistreat her mother day in and day out. Why would she want to surround herself with men like him?

The rest of the drive passed in relative silence, and Dr. Walker was soon pulling into the parking lot of the clinic. "I'll pick you up here at seventy-thirty again."

She nodded her thanks and stepped out of the car. With a small wave at her boss, she slipped inside her car and started the engine. Dr. Walker waited until she had her seat belt on before driving away.

She followed him out of the parking lot, turning in the opposite direction. Dr. Walker lived in a big house outside of town. Her town house was five minutes away.

She appreciated living in close proximity to work, especially as bone-tired as she felt. She just wanted to kick off her shoes, curl up on her couch and devour the leftover lo mein waiting for her. As much as she enjoyed puttering around her kitchen and cooking, tonight was definitely not a night to stand over a stove.

All the parking spots in front of her building were taken and she had to park a couple buildings down. It was a nice complex. Not luxury living, but then, there was no luxury housing in Sweet Hill. At least not among the apartments and town houses. Still, it was one of the nicer complexes in town. The tan stucco was clean. Cacti and Mexican heather served as most of the landscaping.

She was on the second floor. A fact she'd hated when moving in two years ago. Well, mostly her brother-in-law hated it, since he was the one who lugged all her furniture upstairs with the help of his brother. She wouldn't think of asking her dad. She didn't want his help with anything.

She was fumbling for her key when the door across from hers opened. Children's voices crowded the air.

"C'mon, Noah, get your flip-flops on," Shelley ordered, holding her three-year-old's hand as she waited on her five-year-old. "No, those are your brother's flip-flops. Do they look like they fit you? Get the camo ones."

Shelly looked up and caught sight of Briar. "Hey, there. How was your day? We're going to get something to eat. I'm in the mood for nachos. Want to join?"

Briar shook her head. "I'm beat. Maybe next time."

Noah finally stepped out into the hall in the appropriate flip-flops, and Shelley locked the door behind them.

"Beebee." Tyler rushed forward and hugged Briar, wrapping his chubby arms around her legs and nearly knocking her over.

She patted the boy's head. "Hey there, sweetheart."

"C'mon, Tyler, don't knock over Briar."

The toddler looked up at her, a big grin creasing his plump apple cheeks. Shelley peeled one of his hands from Briar. "Come on, buddy. Let's go eat." Her gaze locked on Briar and she stepped closer before Noah tugged her away. "I want to hear all about your day at the prison. I'm sure it's better than anything I've got on DVR."

Briar rolled her eyes. "My life is not that interesting." An image of Knox Callaghan flashed across her mind. She'd read his file. Knew all about his medical history. He was twenty-eight years old. Six feet two. Two hundred pounds. Healthy. Surprising, considering the number of times he had visited the HSU over the years. All the result of fighting. "Trust me, it wasn't like *Shawshank Redemption*."

"It's more interesting than cleaning people's teeth." Shelley was a dental hygienist at one of two dentists in town. The other dentist? Her ex-husband. It made for interesting stories. She stabbed a warning finger at Briar as she moved to the stairs with her kids. "I mean it. I want to hear everything."

"We'll catch up this weekend," Briar promised.

Once inside her apartment, she dropped her bag and keys on the side table and headed for the shower. After washing away the day, she slipped into an oversized T-shirt, claimed her lo mein, and settled in front of the TV. For an hour, she lost herself in mindless television.

When her sister Laurel called, she didn't answer, not wanting to justify yet again why she'd volunteered to work at Devil's Rock. Nor was she in the mood to endure her sister grilling her for a recap of today. Tomorrow would be soon enough to give her an abbreviated version.

Shelley, on the other hand, didn't need an abbreviated version. She could handle all the details . . .

including listening to Briar confess how uneasy the entire experience made her. Especially interacting with a certain steely-eyed inmate. *You don't know fuck all about life in here.* Her cheeks flamed at the memory and she shivered. Yeah. Her sister would freak if she shared that tidbit with her. Shelley always listened. Without judgment. Laurel was another story.

By ten o'clock she was crawling into bed. She double-checked her alarm as she settled into her pillow, her mind drifting again to Knox Callaghan. Her mind tracked over all those scars, big and small, riddling his hard body. She marveled at all the battles he must have fought to earn so many. Not for the first time, she wondered what he had done to end up at Devil's Rock.

She glanced toward the dark outline of her laptop sitting across the bedroom on her desk. A quick online search could answer that question. It was a matter of public record.

She started to push herself up on the mattress but then stopped. Sinking back down, she rolled over so she couldn't see the dark shape of her laptop, deciding there were some things she didn't need to know.

She stared at the dark wall of her bedroom, surprisingly awake, still thinking about her day. What drove men to do horrible things that ended with them getting arrested and locked up? Even if they didn't care about hurting someone else, who wanted that life?

Finally her mind relaxed enough and her muscles went limp. She drifted into a troubled sleep, only to wake up gasping in the predawn light, her chest aching hard with ragged breaths. She dragged a hand down her clammy face.

She had been running through a dark, unending tunnel, passing cage after cage of monsters, all snarling through the bars for a piece of her. At last the tunnel ended and she reached a cement wall. No going forward. No escape. She spun around, her back colliding with the cold wall, her breath crashing wildly in her ears.

A great, hulking shape advanced on her, hunting her, his face cast in shadows, his long legs eating up the space between them. Her fingers curled into the wall behind her, nails cracking from the force. He reached for her, clasping her shoulders, covering her quaking skin with his hard hands. He pushed his face close until she finally had a glimpse of him. Until his cobalt eyes devoured her, touching her everywhere.

Thankfully, she woke before anything else could happen, but she remembered it with such clarity that she could still taste the fear in her mouth. And something else. An unidentifiable emotion. It was weird. She rarely remembered her dreams.

Rising from bed, she started to get ready for work and tried to forget those eyes and the sensation of those hands on her,

She tried to forget that her impulse, in that moment, had not been to scream.

FIVE

SHE WAS BACK.

He'd overheard yesterday that she and the doctor were only supposed to come here on Thursdays. And then not at all once they had a new doctor working full-time on staff. The fact that they were back the very next day had to be the doctor's doing because she didn't look happy to be at the prison again.

One look at her pinched expression as she moved around the infirmary said it all. She never looked his way as she assisted the doctor through the steady stream of patients. As far as Knox was concerned, her absolute refusal to look at him only indicated the opposite. She was acutely aware of his presence. People didn't last hours in the same room without glancing at each other once or twice.

He, however, had all the time in the world to look at her. He probably shouldn't, but there wasn't anything else to do. He counted the different colors in her hair, stopping at seven. He wondered what it looked like, what it felt like, out of the tight ponytail, sprawling across her pillow. Her skin captured his imagination, too. Her cheeks reminded him of peaches, so soft and fresh. Like nothing inside here. It added to her air of innocence.

Martinez arrived at his side to check on him, carrying a tray of food with him. Grateful for a reason to no longer torture himself by checking out the nurse, Knox focused on the LVN. He was a decent guy. A different breed from most of the guards in this place.

"This might not even scar. Much," Martinez remarked, eyeing Knox's forehead.

He snorted as he finished his food, certain that Martinez was cracking a joke. At this point, what did he care about scars? He wasn't entering any beauty contests.

Martinez took Knox's empty tray and left him alone again. Refusing to watch the nurse anymore like some salivating dog, he tried to doze, but every time he was about to nod off he caught a whiff of pears when she passed too close and he tensed with alertness.

Any hope for sleep was obliterated altogether when she approached his bed, dragging the rolling tray after her, its wheels whirring on the cement floor. "Sorry."

He cracked open his eyes to slits.

She did look sorry as she stared down at him,

her features drawn almost too tight from the severity of her ponytail. She looked like she wanted to be anywhere else in the world than here. Talking to him. "Dr. Walker wants me to check your vitals." She held up a monitor as if offering proof that she wasn't coming around him to simply chitchat. She actually had a job to do. "Would you mind sitting up, please?"

He smiled slightly at her polite tone. So proper. He wondered if she ever let her hair down. Ever loosened up? Was it just him and this prison that had her so on edge or was Nurse Davis always this tightly strung? Was there a husband that knew how to make her laugh? She wasn't wearing a wedding ring. Was there a boyfriend, then? A guy that knew how to drive her wild? Whose back she clawed and hair she pulled when he went down on her?

Christ.

"Hold out your arm please. A little higher. Thank you." She placed the cuff around his bicep, her fingers cool against his flesh. He watched her as she went about the task of taking his blood pressure, pumping the bulb several times. She was close enough for him to smell pears again, and even though her hands were cool, her body radiated warmth. The cuff released with a hiss of air. "Good BPI," she murmured, moving to type his numbers into the laptop sitting on the nearby stand, her gaze trained on the screen, focusing with such intensity that he knew she deliberately avoided looking at his face.

It was a wonder his blood pressure wasn't through the roof, considering the dirty direction of his thoughts. His pulse thrummed at his neck and his skin suddenly felt like it didn't fit his body.

She turned back to him, this time holding out a thermometer. "Open your mouth, please."

He parted his lips and tried not to jerk when he felt her thumb brush his bottom lip as she placed the thermometer inside his mouth. Her face flamed bright red and he knew touching him sure as hell wasn't deliberate on her part. They both held still, two frozen statues as they waited for the damn thing to finish its reading.

It beeped and she quickly pulled it out from his mouth. "Ninety-eight point two."

Again, as hot as he was feeling from his interaction with her, it was a wonder he wasn't running a fever. He really had a problem being this close to her, which only made him think about every other poor bastard she came into contact with here. All the others who struggled with low impulse control. Which was essentially everyone.

"Couldn't get enough of this place, you had to come back so soon, huh?" he asked softly. Her hands shook a little as she presumably typed in his temperature.

She was still frightened. Of him. This place. Maybe both? He didn't know and the source of her fear didn't matter. Fear was fear. "Why are you here?" he demanded, inexplicably angry but wise enough to keep his voice low. He would feel a whole lot better if she quit. Not that it mattered how he felt. Not that she cared.

Her gaze snapped back to his face. Flags of red stained her cheeks. He'd never seen a woman blush so much. Even before prison, girls were always comfortable in his presence. *You weren't a criminal then.*

Yeah, there was that.

"You don't want to be here." He sent a quick glance around the infirmary as if assessing their surroundings. "God knows I wouldn't be here if I could help it."

"*Couldn't* you help it?" Briar quickly countered, suddenly finding her tongue. "I mean, you made whatever decision that landed you in here. It's about choices, isn't it?"

He shook his head and felt a flash of annoyance. She didn't know him or what he had done. Or maybe she did. Had she gone home and nosed around on the Internet? His crime was no secret. It was open for public consumption. He swallowed back a snort. He was giving himself too much credit. She probably went home and had sex with her boyfriend without giving him another thought. She was just a judgy little shrew. Nothing more, nothing less.

He shrugged as that bitter pill washed down his throat. "Self-righteous little thing, aren't you? Gotta tell you. It's been a long time since anyone thought I was worth the trouble of a lecture."

There went that blush again. "Forget it. It's not my place." She inhaled. "In answer to your question, I'm here because it's my job. And speaking of my job," she said pointedly. "Can we get back to the matter at hand?"

God, she was so correct and proper. She had the stern nurse act down to a T. And it hit him like a punch to the gut. Who knew he liked that type? That he would ever think it was so fucking hot? She held up a light and checked his eyes. Her breath mingled with his. It would be so easy to lean forward and take her mouth, taste her. *Christ.* He was sick. As if she wanted anything to do with scum like him.

"How's your head?" she queried.

"Fine."

"Any dizziness?"

"No."

"Headache?"

"A little. I've had worse."

She made a noncommittal sound and returned to type some more into the laptop.

"You can't be a nurse anywhere else?" He jerked his head toward the doctor. "He blackmailing you into doing this or something?"

That nose of hers went up a notch. "Not everyone is a criminal."

The kitten had claws. He stared at her for a moment, studying her stoic face with the faintly pink cheeks. She blinked and looked down at her laptop again, clearly flustered.

"Why are you so nervous?" he asked.

"I don't hang out with a lot of felons. I don't know how to act."

She was cute. Annoying, but cute. And not because she was female and there was a decided shortage of those in his life. She was cute, he decided, because she was cute. Feisty. He scanned her in her purple scrubs. Hard to tell for certain, but there was a banging body under there.

The door buzzed open. Chester and another bull entered the room.

He exchanged words with the guard near the door, his cagey, squinty eyes looking beyond the old man to survey the room. His gaze landed on the nurse and he actually licked his lips. Something ugly curled up inside Knox knowing that assholes like him could stare at women like her all they wanted. He could lick his lips and hit on her and be his general asshole self and it was okay. The world was okay with that. And that just summed up what a screwed-up planet they lived in.

As if sensing his stare, the guard looked his way.

Chester's lips twisted into its usual sadistic shape. Knox released a breath, knowing his time in the HSU was up.

Suddenly the nurse was at his side. Her brown eyes snapped with fire as she stood between him and the bed, facing the advancing bulls like some kind of gatekeeper.

Chester did not look troubled. He swaggered forward, holding out both hands as though calming some fractious colt. "Now, now . . . it's been twenty-four hours. That's all you said you needed."

Her gaze shot to the clock on the wall. "Twenty-two hours, actually. It wouldn't hurt to have him under observation longer . . ." She turned in the direction of the doctor across the room, as though seeking aid from the man who was busy examining some old inmate's gnarly foot.

"C'mon. This ain't no place for bleeding hearts." Chester stepped closer and touched her shoulder. A bitter taste coated Knox's mouth at the sight of those bloated sausage fingers covering her shoulder, flexing slightly, getting the feel for her. "Don't let him fool you into thinking he's sick."

Knox tensed at the implication that he was faking illness to stay out of the hole. After eight years he knew how to take a stint in the hole.

Enough of this. Swinging his legs over the side of the bed, he announced, "I'm fine. Ready to go."

Chester dropped his hand from her shoulder. "See there." The bastard smiled at her. "Nothing to worry about. Callaghan knows his place. Right, boy?"

Knox grunted as he reached for his shirt draped over the end of the bed. He'd kept it off ever since she bandaged his ribs.

He pushed both arms into the sleeves and winced as he pulled it over his head, the action pulling on his tender ribs.

Suddenly Briar's hands were there, grasping the hem of his shirt to help pull it down. The back of her fingers grazed him and his stomach muscles quivered. All of him quivered. *Shit*.

He stepped back, severing the contact. Yesterday had been bad enough with her hands all over him. Even as impersonal as her touch was, it had been too long since he felt a woman's hands on him. He didn't trust himself not to react.

"We'll need him back in a week to remove the sutures," she instructed.

"Yeah, sure," Chester said, grabbing hold of his arm.

"And if the ribs worsen, Mr. Callaghan, be sure to alert one of the guards that you need to return."

Chester laughed. "*Mister* Callaghan. Ain't that nice. Like you're a real gentleman."

Yeah. A piece of scum like him didn't deserve such a courtesy title.

Knox gazed coldly at the guard, not rising to the bait. He'd long since learned to feign deafness. To react would land him in trouble and prolong his sentence. In six months he would have another parole hearing. North was due for another hearing around then, too, and given the comments made from the board during his last hearing, North might be getting out this time around. Who knew? Maybe he had a shot, too. He sure didn't need to mouth off and jeopardize his chances.

Nurse Davis's face flushed and it gave him some satisfaction knowing she didn't care for the guard any more than he did. The idiot didn't realize he was insulting her as much as Knox by laughing at how she chose to address him.

As he was led from the room, he looked once over his shoulder.

She was still standing beside the bed he had occupied. This time she had no trouble staring at him. A frown marred her smooth features, probably left over from her displeasure with the guard.

"C'mon, Callaghan. Move it." As soon as they were out in the hall and the door to the HSU shut behind them, Chester pushed him against the wall and elbowed him in his bandaged ribs.

He bowed over from the force of the blow, the air leaving him in a great whoosh as fiery pain burst in his side. He lifted his head slowly to gaze at his abuser, smiling because he knew that would only piss him off more.

The bull pushed his red sweaty face closer, hissing at Knox in a stink of stale coffee breath. "You think a nice girl like that cares about a piece of shit like you?"

Knox trained his expression into blankness.

The guard grinned then and stepped closer. He spoke, the words puffing against Knox's cheek. "I think I might take her out this weekend. You see, sweet pussy like that isn't for the likes of you. You're stuck in here, sucking cock with the rest of them."

Knox's hands curled into fists at his sides. He clenched his jaw so hard his teeth ached.

Chester laughed once in a heavy breath. "Huh. Don't like that?" His gaze raked him up and down. "What are you going to do about it?"

The cocky son of a bitch grinned, waiting. Knox would love to see this guy on the outside, without his uniform to protect him. Or better yet, on the inside without his uniform to protect him. Let him know what it felt like.

"Nothing, *boss*," he said, treating the title to heavy disdain.

A muscle ticked near the corner of Chester's eye. "That's right, prick. *Nothing*. Now let's go." Chester pushed him forward. The two guards fell into step behind him, following him back into hell.

SIX

AFTER FRIDAY, BRIAR'S life resumed its familiar routine. She breathed a little easier knowing she had almost an entire week before she had to return to Devil's Rock.

She spent her Saturday doing laundry and grocery shopping. Sunday morning she went to church and then drove to her sister's place for an early dinner. Laurel lived forty minutes away in the slightly bigger town of Fort Stockton. Briar enjoyed playing with her nieces and nephew. And she loved her sister even if she didn't love her prying.

"I don't understand. Why *you*? Can't anyone else go with him?" Laurel bounced the baby on her lap as her other two kids played loudly on the play set a few yards away. Her husband Caleb stood over the sizzling grill, flipping burgers.

"No one else was exactly jumping to volunteer," she explained. Again.

"Well, go figure." Her sister cocked her head and rolled her eyes.

"Laurel," Caleb chided, clearly disapproving of her sarcastic tone. He sent Briar a sympathetic look as he took a long pull on his beer.

Her brother-in-law was a saint. A truly gentle man who loved her sister and worked hard, putting in long hours of overtime to provide well for Laurel and the kids. Everything he did, he did for them. In looking for a life partner, Laurel's goal had been simple. Find the polar opposite of their father. She had succeeded in that.

"What?" Laurel blinked her big eyes. "Am I not supposed to say anything when my baby sister puts herself in a dangerous situation?"

Caleb sent Briar a look that said: *Score one for big sister.*

Briar bit back the thought breezing through her mind. *You had no problem leaving me alone with Dad. You got out as fast as you could.* Of course, she wouldn't say that. Laurel had left home and married Caleb as soon as she graduated. Briar had been fourteen. She had four more years of Mom and Dad without Laurel for company. The fighting. The tears. The slaps she wasn't supposed to hear. No, she couldn't blame Laurel for getting out of that house as soon as she could. If the situation had been reversed, she would have probably done the same.

"Laurel, it's one day a week." Briar wasn't about to tell her she had gone twice last week. "And I'm in the infirmary. With a guard and cameras and a panic button. It's not like I'm walking the cell blocks."

Laurel snorted and rubbed circles over the baby's back, clearly unconvinced.

"And the inmates we see are usually sick, you know," Briar added. "They just want relief. They're not inclined to bite the hand offering to help them."

Laurel shook her head, her short red curls tossing around her. "I don't like it."

"Have you talked to Mom?" Briar asked, deciding to change the subject before she became truly annoyed.

Laurel stood, propping the baby on her hip. "Not lately. But we're supposed to have lunch next week. I'm going in to get the potato salad."

She disappeared inside the house, sliding the glass door shut behind her.

"That's one way to get her to stop talking," Caleb said as he placed burgers in a square tin.

She smiled at him. "Never fails. Bring up Mom."

"Or your father."

Briar's smile slipped. Even she didn't talk about him. She maintained a superficial relationship with her mother. Phone calls. Texts. Occasionally they met for a meal. Not Dad. Never Dad. If she was lucky, she wouldn't have to see him ever again.

"Laurel is worried about you, Briar. And she's

questioning your motives for working at the prison. I can't say I haven't been wondering myself."

Briar stared at him for a long moment. "Like what? That I'm attracted to violent men? I'm drawn to them and want to be around them?" Her stomach turned at the notion. Laurel hadn't been around in those last years. When her father drank more. When he hit more. Laurel had no idea how bad it really got.

Shaking her head, she stared at her adorable niece and nephew as they clambered up the faux rock wall of the play set and slid down the slide with happy squeals. A pang punched her in the chest.

Laurel had built a beautiful life with Caleb and her children. She'd turned her back on the past. Moved on. Forgotten it—or simply refused to look at it anymore. When was Briar going to do the same? Why wasn't it as easy for her?

"I'm not attracted to violent men, Caleb." Far from it. Whenever she was in that prison, she could hardly breathe.

Her brother-in-law shrugged, and that irritated the hell out of her.

"I'm not." *I'm not like my mother.* "I'm not going there for kicks."

For some reason, Knox Callaghan's face flashed across her mind. He put her on edge. Something about him. The tension she felt coiled tightly inside him, just beneath the surface. He was a storm waiting to break. She just hoped she was nowhere near him when that happened.

"So," Laurel proclaimed as she returned, baby and a giant bowl of potato salad in tow. "Did Caleb tell you about his boss's nephew?" She waggled her eyebrows. "He's a partner at a big accounting firm. Single, of course. Balding but attractive. He's got that Bruce Willis thing going for him. He's very open to being set up. He's just coming out of a bad relationship."

"Isn't Bruce Willis like sixty now?"

Caleb snorted back a laugh as he set the burgers down on the table. Laurel glared at both of them. "I didn't say he *was* Bruce Willis. And I meant Bruce Willis like in his *Die Hard* days."

Briar grinned and took a sip of her iced tea. Laurel plopped the baby in Briar's lap and started fixing the kids' burgers. "C'mon. When was the last time you went on a date with a nice guy?"

Briar couldn't remember.

"Say yes," she commanded in that bossy way of hers.

"Maybe," she hedged.

"I'll give him your number."

"Laurel," she warned.

"What? Is it so wrong I want you to meet a nice guy? Have you dated anyone seriously since college? Since Beau?"

Beau. Her stomach bottomed out. No. There hadn't been anyone since him. Not really. She'd dated off and on a little in college after they broke up, but no one serious. Her father and Beau had pretty much killed her faith in the male gender. Neither were exactly stellar examples. After them, who wouldn't swear off men forever? Of course, she had never told her sister the full story regarding Beau. Laurel had been pregnant with Addy at the time, but that wouldn't have stopped her from coming after him with a shotgun.

"Let's eat." Briar clapped her hands and bounced little Tyler on her knee. Her sister wasn't the only one good at pretending the past had never happened. Sometimes she wondered if she pretended enough, maybe she could forget it all.

IT WAS THE darkness that got to Knox the most—that found its way under his skin like a parasite digging for home.

The unending stretch of hours. The smothering silence that only came with darkness. He tried to sleep at night when the dark was the worst, the deepest, the most impenetrable . . . desperate to escape that smothering tar, but the hole was a tricky place.

In the hole, even the daylight hours were dark. Well, *gray.* Paltry light crept out from the small slit where they delivered food to him and where prisoners stuck out their hands to be cuffed. Like a weed growing out of concrete, the light fought its way in, trickling onto him where he sprawled on the cot. He held his hand up to that ribbon of light, turning it over, letting it flow over his fingers as though it were something tangible. Something he could *feel*.

Men went crazy in here. Tear-out-their-hair, see-the-ghosts-of-their-victims, and cry-for-mommy kind of shit. He clung to sanity by building a regimen and dedicating himself to it. That was the key to keep from going nuts in segregation, to keep the demons at bay.

Out of the hole, there wasn't a day he and his brother didn't break their backs exercising. He and North worked out both in the yard and in the privacy of their cells. It was one of the first things Knox established when they got to the Rock. A permanent workout routine. They didn't need a gym. They stayed fighting-strong working out and pushing past the pain. Anything and everything to make themselves formidable amid a cesspit of punks and killers and men that would jack up their own grandmothers for a C-note.

A stint in the hole changed nothing. If anything, he amped up his workout. He kept at it, pushing though his injuries, training his body to the point of exhaustion. Push-ups. Lunges. Sit-ups. Jogging in place. By Monday he added jumping jacks, ignoring the tenderness in his ribs. There was no room for tenderness in the Rock. He killed all softness from his body, using the wall for a punching bag, toughening up his fists.

If, during the nights, the darkness ever got too much and pushed at his carefully constructed walls, he just closed his eyes and fell into the colors inside his mind. Peach skin and hair a dozen different shades. He imagined he was somewhere else, with someone else.

Dipping into a pool of make-believe, he dreamed up sunshine. Air that smelled after-rain fresh. Grass all around him. And a woman beneath him.

He stroked himself off, pulling hard at his cock, pretending it was a female's heat, her softness milking him, her creamy thighs spreading wide in welcome. If, at the end, her face resembled the nurse from the HSU, if her mouth cried out sweet, dirty things as he fisted her hair, then so be it. It was just a fantasy to get him through. No harm.

Someday he'd be out of this hellhole and then he could stop losing himself in impossible dreams and start living again. Someday, when he and his brother were free of this place, he could finally have a life worth living. He wouldn't need to jack off to the image of a girl who thought he was a low-life bastard.

SEVEN

"**O**H, THAT HEALED up nicely," Briar announced, glad to hear that her voice was crisp and efficient as she hovered over Callaghan—especially considering her pulse was hammering at the skin of her throat in a way that made her want to press her fingers there.

Stop it, Briar. Get ahold of yourself and be professional. He was an inmate. Forget about his body and how big it was . . . how it could break anything. Forget about the way his skin smelled like man, and clean sweat and something else entirely. Probably pheromones. Seriously, he could bottle that stuff and sell it for a fortune.

She'd been working with a surprising degree of productivity since she arrived this morning. Working side by side with Josiah and Dr. Walker, she fell into a rhythm treating patients, almost forgetting they were criminals. Until Callaghan arrived and she remembered everything that had made her uncomfortable about this place in the first place.

She felt the warmth of Knox Callaghan's breath near her chin and quickly stepped back, putting space between them as she resisted the urge to rub at her face.

He hadn't touched her. He had hardly spoken at all, but it was still there—that undercurrent of something dangerous and unpredictable radiating off him, curling around her and making her chest tight and uncomfortable.

She turned for the tray of medical tools. "I'm sorry, but this may not be that comfortable." She tugged on the requisite gloves and picked up the suture scissors.

"It's all right," he answered, the first words he'd spoken since he was escorted into the room.

Nodding, she began snipping at the sutures, thinking that his way of life wasn't one of comfort. She glanced only once at his stoic features. He hadn't shaved in several days and stubble dusted his strong jaw. "You look a little pale," she murmured. "Are you feeling well?"

"No sunlight in the hole."

She paused at this, imagining some dank little cell with no window. "You've been in there since last week?" For some reason, she hated thinking about that. Her mind conjured a dark, terrible dungeon right out of some horror movie. No one deserved being stuck in a place like that. *But then you don't really know him. Maybe that's precisely what he deserved.*

"They're letting me out today. After here."

Silence fell as she worked, tugging at a particular stubborn piece of thread that had decided to stick to his flesh. He didn't show the faintest reaction.

Feeling the need to speak into the space of silence, she supplied, "That will be nice."

His blue eyes flicked to her face then, like he couldn't help himself from looking at her when she uttered such a perfectly stupid thing.

That will be nice.

As though he would be attending a picnic or a baseball game. She heard his voice all over again telling her she didn't know *fuck all about this place.* Her face burned at the memory.

For a split second the corner of his mouth twitched. Her hand started to shake a little and she had to pause to regain her composure and adjust her grip on the scissors. With him this close to her, she felt certain he was examining the pimple on her chin. She was twenty-six but still had the occasional breakout. Stress didn't help and there was no denying that working here stressed her out.

Pulling the last bit of thread from his skin, she released a shuddery breath. "There, now." Taking a step back, she deposited the trash and tools onto the tray. Moistening a little antiseptic on some gauze, she lightly patted the wound where fresh blood trickled out.

"I don't think it will be too deep a scar. Maybe I can give you some Mederma to help minimize—"

"That's okay," he cut her off, and she flushed. Of course, he wouldn't care about a new scar. That was for people in her world who cared about things like their income tax and whether they would get that upcoming promotion.

"Okay." She rubbed her hands on her thighs, mostly for something to do with them. "I'll call for a guard to escort you." She gripped the edge of the rolling tray, wanting to flee but knowing she wasn't done. She had a job to do and she wasn't doing it right if she only did half of it. Deep breath. "Why don't I check your ribs again?"

He hadn't mentioned they were causing him any problems, but she told herself she was just being thorough before releasing him back into the general population.

He stared at her blankly for a moment, his face as hard and implacable as stone. Almost like he didn't understand her.

"Are you still wearing the bandage?" She reached for the hem of his white uniform shirt, ready to assist him. The fabric hung past his waist, so her fingers inadvertently brushed his thigh.

His hand shot out and locked around her wrist. She stalled, freezing at his grip on her. Her heart lurched into her throat at his viselike fingers.

"It's fine," Knox said, his voice thick and gravelly. Their eyes held.

"I already removed the bandage," he added.

Briar moistened her lips and shivered as his gaze dropped to her mouth. "And you're not in any pain?"

He shook his head once. "I'm fine." His fingers unfurled from around her wrist, slipping away.

"Let me check," she insisted.

Something flared in his eyes and her skin shivered, breaking out in goose bumps. It occurred to her that he was probably not the kind of man accustomed to being ordered around by a woman, unless, of course, it was a female corrections officer.

He seemed like the kind of man that took charge. Her gaze skimmed the immense breadth of his shoulders, the broadness of his chest, the way his biceps bulged. She had a sudden image of him with a woman. In a bedroom. Well, on a bed. She snapped her gaze off his body with a mental curse. So. Wrong.

Her gaze fell to his hands. They were big, blunt-nailed with long tapering fingers, his wrists solid with a light spattering of hair on the backs. She could visualize those hands, guiding, demanding. She blinked, forcing the disturbing image away.

There couldn't be too many people ready to oppose

him, but this wasn't a world where he was free to take charge.

Fortified with that reminder, she moved in for his shirt again, but then stopped, watching him. He arched an eyebrow at her, clearly questioning her pause. Firming her resolve, she gripped his shirt and tugged it up. He lifted his arms so she could pull his shirt over his head and drop it down beside him.

He brought his hands onto the bed beside him, palms flat on the mattress, sitting bare-chested in front of her. His body was ridiculous. Even bearing bruises, he looked like a well-honed warrior.

She was a nurse. She'd seen him like this before. He was a prisoner. A criminal. He shouldn't affect her. In that moment, she vowed to take her sister up on her offer. She needed to go out on an actual date with a man. It had been too long since she actually kissed anyone. Even longer since she had sex. This was simply a case of a starving libido.

She narrowed her eyes and studied his body with what she hoped was clinical analysis. She shook her head at the dark bruises discoloring his ribs. Bringing her hands up, she ran her fingers over his smooth, warm flesh. "Still tender? You shouldn't have removed your bandages." He gave a small grunt as she pressed a fraction harder.

"They inhibited my movement."

"You get to move a lot in segregation?" she countered.

"I like to stay busy." A corner of his mouth kicked up. He was mocking her.

She lowered her hands from him and handed him his shirt. "You should take it easy for a few weeks. No strenuous activity."

His lips smirked like she had said something amusing.

"Why do I sense you're not going to take my advice?" she asked.

"I wouldn't dream of disobeying you, Nurse Davis." He shrugged back into his shirt, still smirking, still mocking. Shirt fully on, he slid off the bed and dropped to his feet. "Are we done now?"

She stepped back. "Yes. I guess that's it. I'll send for a guard."

"Thanks."

Pushing the tray ahead of her, she sent a glance over her shoulder. No one was ever in a rush to leave the HSU. She had learned that much already. Everyone was happy to linger on one of the gray-blanketed cots, preferring it to hanging out in the general population. But Callaghan seemed almost anxious to get out of here. Maybe because he would be returning to the masses. Maybe because he didn't like being around doctors. Or other sick people.

Except he wasn't the squeamish sort. No. She had the strongest sense that he didn't like *her*. That he was trying to get away from her. Which was ridiculous. A scary guy like him wouldn't be afraid of anything or anyone.

Least of all her.

KNOX LIFTED HIS shoulders and rolled them in a small circle as he entered the yard, inhaling the outside air. Hopefully he wouldn't have another visit to the hole or the HSU for a while. He knew better than to waste time wishing he would never return to seg. It was an eventuality. A reality in here that he couldn't escape—especially as a captain of Reid's crew. Reid had amassed one of the biggest gangs in the Rock, with as many connections inside as outside, but that meant anyone that wasn't one of them wanted to tear them down.

Above all he was a realist. But hopefully he wouldn't have to visit the HSU again and suffer Nurse Davis's hands all over him. He'd rather go straight to the hole over that.

He inhaled, relishing the sweat-laced air and open space of the yard, trying to ignore the hint of pears still clinging inside his nose.

He could breathe again without a sense of the walls closing in on him. Even if he had to constantly watch his back out here he preferred this. It was better than being stuck in a smothering, airless room, his sanity ebbing away bit by bit.

He did a quick sweep of the yard, taking in everything at a glance. He could never let his guard down. A newer guy, wanting to make a name for himself, could always try to take him out. It wouldn't be the first time someone tried to slip a shiv between his ribs.

His brother spotted him through ribbons of undulating heat and started toward him in his easy, long-legged gait, resembling a rangy wolf, all hard lines and sinew strolling across the yard. Knox released a small breath. Whenever he was in the hole, a part of him always worried about North. Whether he was doing okay. Whether he was safe. Whether Knox not being around, not looking out for him, would be the one factor that got his brother killed. He'd lost so much already. He couldn't lose his younger brother, too.

North was nearly as tall as Knox, standing a little over six feet, but to Knox he would always be the kid brother he had to keep an eye on. The one that used to chase after him and his friends, pleading with them to wait up. The one that spied on him when he was making out with Gina Bagdanelli.

They looked each other over as the distance between them closed, and he realized it was the same for his brother. Every moment they were apart, North worried about him, too.

His brother wasn't the only one studying him. Knox felt the eyes on him. Hard men assessing for vulnerabilities, trying to see if he was still injured, if his stint in the hole had somehow damaged him. Weakened his mind or body. Not a day went by that he didn't have to look strong, hard. Unbreakable.

Stopping before him, North held out his knuckles to connect with his. "Hey, man." He eyed the fresh scar on his forehead and then looked over the rest of him, clearly searching for other injuries hidden beneath the white of his uniform. "You all right?"

Knox nodded. "Yeah." He motioned to his head. "It's nothing. Takes more than a tray to crack my skull."

North grinned, his teeth a flash of white in his tanned face. It always surprised Knox—his brother's ability to smile. He was still good-natured. Even after eight years in this shithole.

Knox scowled at him and North sighed, killing the grin. Knox had told him enough times to cut out the smiles. Others might think him too soft. And then there was his kid brother's face. He was too good-looking, and grinning just advertised the fact. Knox knew he wasn't bad looking—he'd had his fair share of girls before prison—but North belonged on the cover of a magazine . . . or on a billboard advertising cologne. They had the same dark hair, but his brother's eyes were a deep brown. There was a warm light in those depths despite all he had been through.

The first month in the Rock had been hell for both of them. They barely managed to protect each other. They had been hanging on by a thread when Reid took them in. Maybe he'd watched them fight long enough and hard enough and deemed them worthy. Or maybe he just felt sorry for them. Young, pretty boys never held up well.

Knox knew it put him in Reid's debt, and he accepted that. Fortunately, Reid had never asked either of them to do anything he was intrinsically opposed to. If that day ever came . . . Well, he would deal with it then.

"The skins are pissed but not making any moves."

Knox snorted. "They're not going to do anything."

North nodded as they crossed side by side to where Reid and a dozen of their guys played basketball.

"Everything's been pretty quiet. Well, except the two fish. They've stirred up a little noise."

"Yeah?" he murmured, stopping at the edge of the game. Reid, the big motherfucker, was shirtless. Sweat gleamed off his tan muscles as he dribbled the ball effortlessly, eyeing the players on defense.

He was surprisingly graceful as he wove between them, his elbow shooting out and colliding with another guy's nose in a move that would have gotten you thrown out of any other game in the civilized world. Blood spewed and the player dropped. Reid didn't pause in his drive, dunking the ball and sending the rim into loud vibrations.

"Yeah," North continued, "word is they hatched this crazy-fuck plan to hijack the HSU."

Knox swung around, all of him locking tight. "What?"

"Yeah. Everyone's been talking about this new nurse in there. You must have seen her. Old Smitey couldn't stop talking about her. Hell, everyone's suddenly claiming they've got food poisoning to get in there and check her out . . ."

The rest of his brother's words faded. A roar of blood rushed to his head. He turned around, scanning the yard, searching for the two new fish his brother was talking about. He remembered them. They talked too much and spent the better part of their time getting their asses handed to them. Skinny guys, both in for armed robbery. Repeat offenders, they were in for life this time.

"Where are they?" he demanded.

His brother looked at him oddly, his dark eyebrows drawn tightly together. "They both faked sick. Made themselves puke and everything. Guards took them about twenty minutes ago."

He must have just missed them.

The roar in his ears faded to a dull ringing. Cold seeped over him as he thought of Nurse Davis in there with those two bastards. His cousin's face flashed across his mind. All her youth, all her innocence, destroyed. In its place had been only a ravaged shell with soulless eyes.

Shaking his head, he faced his brother. "Fuck me up."

"What?"

"Listen to me. I need you to hit me. Make sure you do some damage."

"Fuck that. I'm not hitting you."

He grabbed his brother by the shirt, gripping fistfuls of white fabric. "I need in that infirmary. Either you send me there or I pick a fight and let someone else fuck me up."

North's gaze drilled into him. "You're serious?"

"Make it look good." He released his shirt and backed up a step.

His brother studied him a moment longer, his eyes full of questions. Knox knew he wanted an explanation, but there wasn't time. She was in there now. With them.

His brother trusted him enough to do as he asked. North also knew he would get someone else to give him a beating if he refused. If that happened, there was no telling what kind of injuries he could sustain.

"Do it," Knox barked, his pulse throbbing wildly in his neck. "Make me bleed."

North clenched his jaw with resolve. His dark

eyes glinted, reading Knox's urgency. "All right." He shrugged and cocked back his arm. "What are brothers for?"

Knox braced himself for the blow, sorry his brother might get a brief stint in the hole for this, but there was no help for it.

He had to get to her in time.

EIGHT

THE MOMENT THE two new inmates arrived, unease bubbled like acid in the pit of Briar's stomach. *God.* Working here was going to give her an ulcer. Would she never get used to it? Hopefully, they would find a full-time doctor soon and she wouldn't have to.

Wiping a loose tendril of hair back from her forehead, Briar eyed the newcomers over the laptop where she worked as they entered the room with all the boisterousness of two people arriving at a party. Like this wasn't a prison. Like they weren't inmates at all—or sick, for that matter.

Her disquiet deepened as one of them leveled his gaze on her and elbowed his companion. As Murphy frisked them, they looked her over from across the room.

Finished searching them, Murphy returned to his chair. The wood legs creaked beneath his settling weight. Josiah motioned them to a set of beds nearest the door. They moved with all the swagger of young men who owned the world.

The skinny one with a ponytail talked to everyone in the room—not just his companion. He called out to the guard. Josiah. The approaching doctor. Even Briar. He talked even if no one answered him back.

They were different than the others who came through here, who were mostly subdued because they were hurting or sick. They were hyped up almost like they were high. A definite possibility. There were drugs in prison. She'd watched enough prison movies and *48 Hours* episodes to know that. But their eyes weren't dilated. Simply wild and shifty. Like the raccoons her father used to catch for their pelts down by the creek. Sometimes she would sneak out before sunup and set them loose from their traps. Even though she was trying to help them, the animals had tried to take a chunk out of her hand on more than one occasion.

These guys made her feel that same sense of wariness.

Ponytail bounced on the bed lightly, testing it out as though it was a Holiday Inn and he was settling in for a long stay.

Josiah paused near her elbow.

"They hardly look sick," she murmured.

"Well, they must be. The guards don't bring them in here unless they show some signs of illness or injury."

She nodded, still not entirely convinced and *still* keeping an eye on Ponytail. For some reason, she couldn't take her eyes off him. It was like with Knox Callaghan . . . but different. Knox made her uncomfortable for different reasons. Reasons she hated to admit were wrapped up in his good looks and nonstop muscles. It was perverse of her, but nonetheless true. These guys simply creeped her out.

Dr. Walker settled on a stool between their two beds and began conversing with them in his low, calm voice.

Briar sighed and set her hands on the edge of the table, ready to push up and see if he needed assistance. No matter how uncomfortable it made her, this was her job and why she was here.

Josiah looked down at her and patted her shoulder. "Why don't I take this one?"

She smiled up at him and eased back on her stool. "You know I'm growing to love you, right?"

He winked. "Just pay me with bagels tomorrow. I like strawberry cream cheese from the Bagel Stop in Sweet Hill."

"Done."

She tried not to feel guilty as she settled back into her chair. She was a nurse. She shouldn't suffer such qualms. If she did, she had no business being here. Ignoring her guilt, she concentrated on the computer screen in front of her as Dr. Walker and Josiah conducted examinations of the new patients, telling herself she was working, too. Someone had to organize patient files, after all. They hadn't even removed inmates from the system who'd died ten years ago.

A half hour passed before the door buzzed and two more guards entered. She blinked at the sight of the inmate between them. *Un-flipping-believable.*

She rose to her feet and crossed her arms, glaring as Murphy patted down Callaghan. He was bleeding from the mouth and nose. He had just been released from segregation today! Couldn't he stay out of trouble even for an hour? Disappointment washed through her at the sight of him. He was back again, and judging from the restraints, he was somehow responsible for his current injuries.

His eyes collided with her across the distance and she felt sucked into that ocean, lost in the dark blue depths. She quickly shook off her disappointment. It wasn't hers to feel. He was a dangerous criminal. Should she have expected any less of him?

"Hey, man!" Ponytail called from the bed. "You fucked those skins up last week!" He gleefully slapped his knee while his friend nodded. "What happened to you today? Looks like we missed a helluva fight!"

Without comment, Callaghan was led to a bed across from the other two inmates, his hands bound before him, the chains of his cuffs clanking slightly.

"Watch your mouth, boy," one of the guards

warned as he attached Callaghan's restraints to the loops at the sides of the bed.

Callaghan didn't look particularly proud of the other inmate's praise. He was stoic as always, staring back at the two inmates without a flicker of expression on his face. Shaking her head, Briar wondered what it would take for him to crack, to let emotion bleed out. Did he even have it in him or was he simply without feeling?

Ponytail glared at the guard, his lips compressed in a flat line as though he was fighting the urge to mouth off. His eyes flashed with something that made her shiver. Clearly he didn't handle authority very well.

The two additional guards departed, and they were left with Murphy snoozing by the door again. For a moment she had the wild impulse to call them back.

Callaghan looked the ultimate savage sitting there shackled, blood running from his lip. A quick glance confirmed the doctor and Josiah were still occupied. There was no choice. She had to attend to him. Steeling her spine, she marched over and stopped several inches from his bedside. "Back again?"

He hardly spared her a glance. Just stared straight ahead with frightening intensity. A nerve ticked at the corner of his eye. She followed his gaze to the two inmates, wondering if they had something to do with his altercation today and they just didn't realize it. Barely checked violence radiated from Callaghan as he sat propped on the bed.

She moistened her lips, reluctant to get any closer. Her skin broke out in goose bumps. "What happened to you?" she asked carefully, mindful to keep any judgment from her tone.

"You need . . . to go."

He uttered the words so quietly she thought she misunderstood him at first. She leaned forward slightly. "I beg your pardon?"

His gaze snapped to her for a moment and then away, focusing again on the other two inmates. "You heard me. You need to get the fuck out of here." She flinched at the ugly words. "Go. Now, Briar." She started at the sound of her name on his lips. Of course, he must have heard the doctor or Josiah address her as Briar before . . . but to hear him call her by her name, and in such a rough manner, rattled her.

She pulled her shoulders back and reminded herself that he was the inmate shackled to the bed. She was the free woman here . . . and a professional. He needed to be reminded of that. "How dare you—"

His gaze shot to her face, and the intensity there struck her like a slap. The blue was bright and fierce, scraping the skin back from her bones. "You need to get out of here before it's too late."

She backed away at the threat, uncertain, but full

with the knowledge that this man was dangerous. That *she* was in danger. Restraints or no restraints, he was close to erupting. She crossed the room back to her desk, eyeing the bright red panic button. Something told her to push it—an instinct that her logic fought against as too extreme.

"Aww, how come I get the guy? Hell, there shouldn't even be guy nurses. That's just fucked up!" Ponytail's loud complaint drew her attention as Josiah took his vitals. The inmate caught her gaze and winked. "I want the pretty girl to kiss my boo-boos."

Briar frowned. He so did *not* look sick. Had they fabricated some illness just to get out of the general population and visit the HCU? The possibility of that hinted at a deeper cunning than she wanted to credit them with. If they were capable of fooling the guards, what else were they capable of?

Murphy, in a rare show of awareness, stood up from his chair and inched away from the door. His footsteps clicked on the concrete as he approached the beds. "Enough of that, you hear? You show respect."

"C'mon. Who would you rather have tending your wounds?" Ponytail motioned across the room to Briar. "A pretty piece of ass or some guy?"

Murphy blustered, his hand moving to his side. She wasn't sure if he was reaching for his mace, the radio, or baton.

Ponytail exchanged a look with his fellow inmate on the bed beside him, and that's when she knew. Everything inside of her squeezed tight. Prickles broke out over her skin and her nape tightened. She'd felt this way countless times at the dinner table. When her mom said the wrong thing. Used the wrong tone of voice. Served the wrong thing for dinner.

It was like that moment when you trip. Those seconds before you land on your face. When you're on your way down and you know pain was all that waited.

Murphy sputtered, his swollen hands finally clasping the radio at his belt, presumably to request backup. Unhooking his radio, he brought it to his lips, grumbling, "Maybe a little time in seg will teach you to watch your mouth."

Something sank and twisted inside her. Murphy made the wrong choice in that split-second decision. He should have gone for the mace. Or baton. A weapon, at the very least. Not his radio.

Ponytail's sideways glance and the flick of his hand were subtle. If you weren't looking for it, it was easy to miss. Josiah didn't miss the gesture, however. He pushed back from the rolling stool and sent it crashing into a neighboring bed.

"Murphy!" he warned as he quickly backed up. "Watch out!"

It was too late. Ponytail surged up from the bed

and latched onto Murphy like some kind of jungle monkey. He wrapped his arms and legs around him and held on tightly, arms locked around his neck.

Briar lunged the two steps she needed to get to the panic button and slammed it down. The alarm peeled out across the room and beyond, but it didn't matter. Too late. Ponytail had Murphy's gun from his holster. He jumped off the guard's body, the gun clasped in both hands, his eyes wild, a crazed smile creasing his sweating face.

Murphy held his hands up, shaking his head fiercely, senseless words tripping from his lips as he clumsily backed away.

"Gronsky! No!" Josiah shouted, holding out a hand as if that could somehow stop the inmate from firing.

Two bullets punched the air. Briar jumped at the loud pops. Murphy jerked as he took the hits. She covered her mouth with both hands, stifling a scream.

Murphy's heavy weight dropped to the floor with a rattling groan.

She trembled, her breath escaping in violent pants. _Oh God. Oh God._

She took a staggering step toward Murphy where he sprawled on the floor. Suddenly, Josiah was at her side, stopping her, pulling her away and tucking her behind him.

"That's the alarm," Josiah warned Gronsky, his

gaze steady on him, still holding up one hand as if that would be enough to hold him off.

"Yeah, motherfucker, I can hear it." Gronsky closed the distance and turned the gun sideways in Josiah's face. "But I don't really care. No one's storming in here." He stabbed the gun closer. "Not while I've got the four of you at my mercy."

From the corner of her eye Briar glimpsed the other inmate yanking Dr. Walker from where he sat shell-shocked on his stool. She winced as he threw the older man to the floor like he was nothing more than a rag doll.

She tried to lunge around Josiah to reach her boss, but Josiah held her back, not letting her go as the other inmate started kicking the doctor.

"Stop!" she pleaded, watching helplessly as Dr. Walker curled into a small ball, crying out sharply from the blows. "He's not fighting back! Stop it!"

It didn't seem to matter to the inmate. He continued kicking and kicking, his breathing harsh with excitement.

"Please," she begged over Josiah's continued attempts to reason with Gronsky. "You're going to kill him!"

"Pritchard," Gronsky snapped. "Enough. Can't you see you're upsetting her?"

She swallowed a sob. Still keeping the gun trained

on them, Gronsky marched over and snatched the doctor up from the floor.

Briar's heart lurched at the sight of his bloodless face. The inmate dragged Dr. Walker to the corner of the room and grabbed him by the chin, forcing him to look up into the camera where she knew officers in the control room were watching.

"You want him to live? You want anyone else to die? Then go ahead and come in this room," he called up into the camera, pressing the barrel of Murphy's gun to the doctor's temple. The move forced Dr. Walker's head far to the side, and she bit her lip to stop the whimper that threatened to escape her. "That bull won't be the only one to die, I fucking promise you! The HSU belongs to us now. Got it?" Gronsky pointed the gun toward the camera and shot off another round, blasting it to pieces.

She cried out. Bitter fear coated her mouth. It was insane. She felt like she was trapped in some crazy movie. *This didn't happen in real life. Not my life. Not me.*

Except it was happening.

It was happening right now to her.

Her fingers gripped Josiah where he still stood before her. She glanced around the room, as though searching for a way out. Her gaze jerked to a stop on Callaghan, sitting so calmly, bound to the bed, his face void of emotion. He didn't even care. He dealt in violence. Saw it every day. Committed it. What was happening in this room didn't faze him. Disgusted and glad that at least he was restrained, she returned her gaze to the inmate with a gun.

Finished with the camera, Gronsky forced the doctor to sit on one of the beds. The slighter man immediately slumped over, holding his ribs, and she felt true fear for his injuries.

The other inmate, Pritchard, removed everything else from Murphy's belt. Murphy gave a small groan, indicating he was still alive, and she uttered a small prayer. Until she realized he wouldn't be alive for long. Not without medical care. Blood pooled around him like thick dark syrup.

Dr. Walker must have had the same thought. He lifted his head and gestured to the guard, his voice a weak wheeze as he said, "He will die. Let me see to him—"

"You think I care about some pig?" Gronsky demanded. "Maybe I should go ahead and shoot him? Put him out of his misery."

"You kill him and it won't go over easy for you," Josiah warned, his hands palms out once more, as though he was trying to placate a wild animal. Which was essentially the scenario.

"You think I care? I'm in for life! They're not letting me out again."

There was a heavy pause. Just the soft wheeze of Dr. Walker's breaths and a faint gurgling sound from Murphy as he bled out.

"How long do you think you can hold us in here?" Josiah asked, his voice surprisingly even and calm. "Before they force their way in?"

Gronsky shrugged. "Don't care. Might as well have some fun while we're here." His eyes drifted to Briar then and a cold finger scraped down her spine.

Josiah's hand gripped her hip, tucking her even farther behind him. "No."

It was a single word, but it held a wealth of meaning. Over the nonstop blare of the prison alarm, Gronsky understood what Josiah meant. The smile deepened in his perspiring face. He understood and he didn't care.

Gronsky shared a look with Pritchard, who released a small huff of laughter and rubbed a finger against the long line of his nose, considering her where she cowered behind Josiah.

Terror filled her and her stomach heaved. She was going to be sick. These men had already lost everything, she realized with a sinking sensation. They didn't care what they did. They didn't fear consequences.

And they wouldn't accept no.

Josiah turned his head to look back at her. The bleakness reflected in the dark depths of his eyes struck her hard. Made her feel more alone. As though this entire situation was hopeless. As though she was already lost.

Josiah's lips parted and he uttered quietly, for her ears alone, *"Run."*

NINE

BRIAR KNEW SHE would never reach the door. She'd never make it. But the desperate look in Josiah's eyes and the rocks sinking in her stomach told her she had to try. It was her only chance.

She broke away and lunged for the door, her arms pumping, shoes slapping over concrete. She prayed to God she at least got the door open before either one caught her—or worse, before a bullet tore into her back.

Scuffling erupted behind her. *Don't let it be Josiah. Don't let him get hurt.* She didn't pause to look, though. Josiah had given her this chance, and she wouldn't waste it by taking a second to look over her shoulder.

She was almost to the door when a hard hand grabbed her by the hair and swung her around. Agony burned through her scalp. Screaming, she clutched her ponytail at the base, certain she was about to lose every strand on her head.

Gronsky tumbled her against him, one arm wrapping around her while the other one held her prisoner by her hair. Over his shoulder she could see Josiah fighting with the other inmate. A series of punches to the gut followed by a savage backhand sent him crashing to the floor.

"Please, please," she begged, not even recognizing the sound of her voice. She sounded far away. Like someone else. *Like her mother.*

The realization jolted her. Looking up, her gaze locked with the inmate's wild eyes. He made a shushing sound, his cruel fingers digging into her hair, forcing her neck back, arching her head at an uncomfortable angle.

He walked her backward, still shushing and crooning at her like she was some skittish colt. Her legs collided with one of the beds, and then she had nowhere to go. His weight was pressing her down and she was falling.

There were other sounds, too. The screaming alarm. Dr. Walker shouting, pleading, begging. Josiah crying out as Pritchard brutally beat him.

The room whirled and buzzed as she struggled on the narrow bed against the weight bearing down on her. There was a dizzying flash of ceiling tiles and the inmate's leering face over her. She turned her head sideways. His wet mouth landed on her cheek. A rush of stale breath filled her nose.

Her gaze landed on the single motionless figure in all of this nightmare. Knox Callaghan sat a few beds over, observing everything as if life and death wasn't being played out around him.

Gronsky continued to nuzzle at her cheek. Bile surged in her throat. She raked her fingernails down the side of his face. He lurched back, fingering the scratches. "Bitch!" He cuffed her upside the head. Hard. She held still for a moment, stunned and out of breath, her ears ringing.

He seized her chin and forced her to face him. "This can go two ways. You fight me and I hurt you. Or you don't fight. And I won't hurt you."

Apparently he didn't consider raping her the same thing as hurting her.

"Either way," he continued, readjusting his weight on top of her so she could feel the hardness of his erection at her thigh. "We're going to take what we want from you."

She pressed her lips together to suppress her sob. She wouldn't break down. She'd seen and heard her mother cry enough over the years. It had never helped. Never did any good.

So there would be no tears from her. She wouldn't give this animal the satisfaction. She couldn't. She *wouldn't*. And she wasn't going to make it easy on him no matter how much pain he dealt her. Every moment counted. If she fought him long enough, maybe she could stall him. Maybe help would come in time. Help had to be coming. It *had* to.

She lifted her head off the bed and spit in his face.

"Fucking bitch," he snarled, and then his hands were clawing at her, fast and angry, trying to get her out of her scrubs. Fabric ripped and she screamed and fought and struggled to escape. He was too strong. It was happening too fast.

"Pritchard," he shouted to the other inmate. "Get over here and hold her."

She twisted wildly, glancing around and spotting Josiah prone on the floor. *Please not dead. Please not dead.* There was no help coming from him.

Pritchard moved beside the bed. Grabbing her hands, he pinned them above her head on the mattress so hard she thought he would snap her wrists. She thrashed her lower body as Gronsky worked at the drawstring of her pants. Impatient curses flayed the air as he fought to undo the knot. She squirmed and twisted and worked her hips and legs. He flattened his body over her, digging an elbow deep into her abdomen and she cried out.

He gave a triumphant cry as the knot finally unraveled. Cool air wafted over her hips as he yanked down on her pants.

God. No, no, no.

"What about me?"

Everything inside her locked tight at the sound of that deep familiar voice.

Gronsky jerked his head around, his ponytail whipping on the air as he looked across the room.

She lifted her head, peering over the inmate's shoulder to where Callaghan sat on the bed. The lines and hollows of his face still revealed nothing. As though the chaos and violence didn't touch him at all.

"What about you?" Gronsky demanded, but his tone was different. Less edge. As though he recognized one of his own in Callaghan.

Callaghan angled his head and stared the other inmate down. It was remarkable. He was restrained to a bed while these two violent criminals had free rein of the infirmary, but he still managed to be scarily intimidating. He parted his lips and spoke words she couldn't have imagined in her worst nightmares.

"I want a piece of her, too."

A cold blade of fear scraped down her spine. *No.* She whimpered. Now, for some reason, the tears felt close. She was on the verge of breaking down. Knox Callaghan wanted to hurt her. He wanted to do this terrible thing to her.

Gronsky hesitated and sent a long look to his friend hovering above her. Pritchard's hands flexed around her forearms above her head, each finger bruising her tender skin.

"What do you think, man?" Gronsky muttered in a low, conspiratorial voice, nodding in the direction of Callaghan. "He's part of Reid's crew."

She looked up, watching Pritchard's face. He glanced down at her and then back up to Gronsky. Grinning furry teeth, he gave a wordless nod.

"All right." Gronsky released her and dropped down on the ground, spreading his arms wide with flourish. "Sure. Why not?" We're all brothers in here, right?" He moved over to Murphy and collected the keys off his body before turning to Callaghan, unlocking his restraints and freeing him from the bed.

Her heart beat so fast her chest actually ached. Callaghan rose to his full height, towering over Gronsky and looking so big and formidable that something inside her withered a little bit at the sight of him. If the other two inmates had wrought so much damage, what would he do? This man who was capable of so much more? Who exuded power and strength and menace His cold eyes fastened on Briar as he rubbed at his wrists where the cuffs had been.

"Go ahead, man." Gronsky gestured to her, his manner deferential. "We'll let you have first crack at her." He laughed dumbly and fingered the scratches on his face. "I like them a little softer anyway. Maybe you'll fuck some of the fight outta her."

With one hand still massaging his wrists, Knox leveled an empty stare at Gronsky.

The inmate's laughter faded in the face of his stony gaze. Gronsky shrugged. "Well, go on. Knock yourself out, man."

Callaghan turned back to face her. "I'll do that."

She dragged a shuddering breath into her lungs, everything inside her, *all* of her, shriveling up as he approached, his steps thudding over the concrete, each one jarring and striking fresh fear deep into her bones.

She shrank back on the bed, her gaze fixed in horror on him. She'd always known that Callaghan was dangerous, but she had somehow imagined him above this. Which was ridiculous. He had said it best. She didn't know fuck all about this place. Or him, for that matter.

He stopped at the foot of the bed, towering over her as she cowered, arms still pinned above her. Bitter dread washed over her as he did a quick scan of her body, and she hated him right then. As scared as she was, she despised him for making her feel like this, for betraying her. She had treated him. Cared for him—at least physically. And now he would do this to her.

Her pants were still pulled partially down, trapped below her hips, revealing her underwear. Sensible underwear. Pale pink cotton panties, but she had never felt so exposed and humiliated.

He grabbed her feet and jerked off her tennis

shoes, not bothering with the laces. He tossed one shoe over his shoulder, then the next one followed. His gaze lowered to her panties, resting there for an agonizing moment, his square jaw granite. A muscle feathered along his cheek.

His hands curled around the loosened waistband of her scrubs, the backs of his fingers warm on the tops of her thighs. She jumped as though singed by a white-hot poker.

"N-No," she choked.

His cold gaze shot to her face and held her stare for a long moment. Those blue eyes ensnared her, effectively trapping her more than the hands pinning her arms.

He looked away, shutting her out as he dragged her pants down her legs in one swift motion, stripping her of everything except her panties and top.

Something died inside of her as she lay there, splayed before these prisoners in only her underwear and a shirt. This was really happening. *Not a nightmare. Not a movie.* She swallowed back a sob, thinking of her sister and all her well-meaning advice. She should have listened to her.

Gronsky groaned in approval, more animal than man, his features rapt on her, reminding her of some beast set on devouring her. He crowded close to Callaghan. "Fucking hot."

Callaghan sent him an annoyed look. "Back off."

She squeezed her eyes tightly shut, wishing she could shut her ears to their voices, too. To everything. To all of this.

A squeak escaped her when his hard hands circled her ankles, wrapping easily around their width. Her eyes flew open again as Callaghan dragged her down the bed and stepped between her knees. He ran his big hands up her bare legs, over her knees and the tops of her thighs. Gulping back a sob, she sucked in a breath. His gaze lifted to her face. That sea of blue could drown a small city. Astounding, really, that such cruelty lurked in those eyes.

Gronsky hovered a little behind him, shifting his weight on each foot, his face contorting with excitement as he watched Callaghan's hands roam over her.

"Knox," she pleaded, hoping that using his name might reach him, might break through and affect him. Remind him that she was a person. Not an object to be used and destroyed. "Please."

He didn't seem to be looking at her anymore, though. His gaze flicked up to the inmate pinning her arms to the bed and then sideways to Gronsky.

"C'mon, man," Pritchard growled. "We ain't got all day and I want my turn, too."

Annoyance cracked the stony mask of his face, but he obliged, coming over her, flattening his hands on either side of her head. She sucked in a sharp breath, certain she was about to start hyperventilating. Or pass out. Maybe that was best . . . so she wouldn't be present for what was about to happen to her.

He was so big she felt smothered, even though he hadn't dropped his full weight on her body. Ducking his head, he brought his mouth close to her ear. "Just lay still," he whispered.

She swallowed back a sob.

She had chosen such a careful life. Safe. How could this be happening . . . ?

She blinked suddenly burning eyes, the air still crashing from her lips harshly.

Maybe it was such thinking that got her here. Thinking that she somehow deserved better. That something like this could never happen to her if she made smart choices. If she didn't want it to. If she didn't *let* it.

"Shh." He placed one hand on her forehead while the other hand gripped her waist, a tactile reminder that he was not about kindness or tenderness. He was about ruining her. Hurting her. "It will be over soon."

Oh. God. She shuddered, bile rising to her throat at his hushed utterance.

She turned her face away, stared toward the windows, trying to disappear inside herself. Something glinted through the glass, catching her eye. She squinted, noticing it again. It flashed in the sunlight from atop the neighboring building.

Then suddenly Callaghan surged. Lightning fast, he sprang. She flinched, expecting pain, but it never came. He didn't touch her.

His hands dove for Pritchard—grabbed him by the throat and hauled him off the bed. Simultaneously, he lashed out and kicked Gronsky in the face in a smacking crunch of shoe on bone that launched the other inmate halfway across the room.

Suddenly free, she sat up, gaping at Callaghan and Pritchard. They fell to the floor in a pile of wrestling limbs and flying fists. Gronsky staggered around with his hands cupping his nose, blood streaming through his fingers, obscenities flying from his mouth like bullets.

"Run!" Callaghan shouted as he fought with Pritchard, grunting as the inmate landed a blow to his bruised ribs.

The sound of his bellowed command reverberated through her. *He was helping her? He was on her side . . .*

Snapping out of her astonishment, her gaze swept the room, landing on the gun several feet away. She jumped off the bed and scrambled toward it, but Gronsky was on her, his hand clamping down on her calf and bringing her down on the ground with a sharp cry.

She twisted and started kicking at him with the heel of her foot. He howled, blood flowing more freely from his face, but he didn't release her. He clawed up her body with digging fingers. She struggled against him, scrabbling and scratching, desperate to carve out a piece of him.

He spat hot curses as he cocked back his fist and nailed her in the face with an iron fist. Pain and fire erupted in her cheek, radiating outward to her jaw. She was going to be sick. She went limp, blackness edging in on her vision.

Dimly, she heard a roar, and then Gronsky was gone. His weight off her. Wheezing for breath, she rolled to her side, holding her face and fighting off nausea.

She blinked several times, bringing her vision into focus. Callaghan lifted the inmate up off his feet with a growl that sounded like it was wrenched from the depths of him—then slammed him back down onto the concrete. Gronsky's head struck the floor with a sickening smack. He collapsed there. Stunned. Maybe dead. She didn't know.

Chest heaving, Knox staggered one step and stopped before her. She gazed up at him, feral and wild, blood dripping from a fresh cut to his mouth. She pushed unsteadily to her knees. He reached for her arm, helping her to her feet.

"Are you okay?" he asked.

She nodded, a sob threatening to break loose

from her chest. She pressed her lips tight to deny it, but then a rush of movement behind him made her scream.

Knox whirled around as Pritchard charged them. Knox shoved her back. The collision propelled her into a bed. Gasping, she arched away, her fingers clutching the edge of a mattress behind her. Before she had time to react, to search for the gun again, a flash of reflected light hit her in the face.

A pop of gunfire shattered the world in an explosion of glass.

A man screamed. Then there was another pop.

Knox tackled her, wrenching her to the floor. "Stay down!" he shouted.

"What's happening?" she croaked.

She lifted her head to see what was going on, but he slapped a hand on her head and forced her back down. "Damn it, they're shooting!"

In that brief glimpse she saw that half the windows lining the wall were gone, presumably the result of a sniper positioned on the building across from them. Someone was moaning not far from her, but she couldn't see who.

Suddenly, the room erupted with the arrival of black-vested men holding rifles, shouting directives that she couldn't understand. She couldn't find her voice. She couldn't move. Couldn't think. She could only stare into the pair of blue eyes boring down into hers.

Even as he was hauled off her and dragged away, she felt connected to those eyes, that face, that man.

Knox Callaghan had saved her life.

TEN

"ARE YOU SURE you don't want to stay the night? You've been through quite an ordeal, Briar," Dr. Walker said from where he reclined on his hospital bed. His wife sat beside him, holding his hand, the worry still etched in the gentle lines of her face.

Briar inhaled, the smell of antiseptic and industrial strength laundry detergent sharp in her nose, reminding her of the two semesters she completed her hospital rotations. Some people hated hospitals, but they comforted her. They were where the broken were made whole again. Most of the time at least.

Given the beating Dr. Walker took, they wanted to keep him overnight for observation. Fortunately, nothing was broken, but he wasn't a young man or particularly strong either. Josiah was lucky, too, resting comfortably in a room down the hall. She'd already paid him a visit after being released from the ER.

It was a miracle the three of them were alive.

Murphy, on the other hand, had been rushed into surgery and they had yet to hear word.

"I just really want to crawl into my own bed and sleep for like three days." She'd endured the ER examination and answered all the questions from the prison personnel who immediately besieged them. It was almost midnight now, and today was officially the longest of her life. She just wanted to go home.

"Well, don't think of coming in on Monday. Or Tuesday. Take the week even. Maybe you should see a therapist before returning—"

"I'm sure I'll be fine. Just need a little down time. Don't worry about me." From the concerned look in his eyes, she knew it was pointless. He was going to worry.

"Briar. You've been through a trauma." Mrs. Walker covered her husband's hand, wincing as she eyed Briar's face. Briar knew she looked like a train wreck. The CT scan confirmed nothing was broken in her face, but it would be a while before the swelling went down and she no longer resembled a prize-fighter fresh from a match. "Are you sure you don't want us to call your parents?"

Briar hated being pitied and viewed as something broken. That's why growing up she had let the world think her dad was the greatest guy. She worked hard all her life not to let anyone know that her home life was essentially an after-school special.

"Thank you, but no. I'll be fine. Really. It could have been so much worse. I'm just grateful we're all okay."

Dr. Walker nodded and said the name that had been circling around in her mind all night. "Callaghan," he marveled. "He saved us. He saved you from—"

"I know," she cut in. Not because she didn't want to discuss Callaghan but because she didn't want to give voice to what had almost happened to her. She actually *did* want to talk about Knox.

She wanted to make certain he wasn't in any trouble. When he had been dragged from the HSU, there didn't seem to be any distinction made between him and the other inmates. She had hammered that point exhaustively to prison officials when she was interrogated about the attack—that Knox Callaghan was not only innocent but responsible for saving their lives.

"You spoke to the people from the prison?" she asked.

"Have no fear, I was quite vocal regarding his heroics."

She sighed with relief. She had given a full accounting as well, but she was hoping the doctor and presumably Josiah's testimony added weight. The image of Callaghan being dragged away burned through her mind. She hated the idea that he could be stuck in segregation again . . . or punished in any other way.

"How are you getting home?" Mrs. Walker asked.

"I called my neighbor. She's waiting out in the hall." No way would she have called her sister. Hopefully, Laurel would never have to know what happened.

"You get lots of rest, dear." Mrs. Walker gave her that pitying smile again.

"Thank you." She turned back to her boss. "Take care of yourself, too, Dr. Walker."

With another smile that made her face ache, she ducked out of the hospital room. Shelley waited in the corridor where she had left her.

"Sorry. That took longer than I thought. They practically wanted to admit me overnight."

Shelley frowned, pushing off the wall as she eyed Briar's face. "Are you sure you shouldn't—"

"Not you, too. I need a shower and my bed. That's all."

Shelley nodded, her dark eyes still bright with concern. "Have you eaten anything? Want me to stop and pick you up some food—"

"No, I can eat something at home." Not that she had much of an appetite anyway. "Thanks for coming to get me. Who's watching the kids?"

"Mrs. Gupta from downstairs is with them."

Briar nodded distractedly. "That's nice of her."

"She doesn't mind. She loves the kids."

The night was considerably cooler than when they'd arrived by ambulance to the hospital. They walked outside to Shelley's car in the parking lot. Thankfully, her friend held her peace on the drive home, not prying into the day's events beyond what she had already been told.

Clearly, she sensed Briar's need for silence. That was why Briar had called Shelley. She was easy. No judgment. No pestering. Dread washed over her at the thought of Laurel ever learning of the day's events. Briar didn't relish hearing her say: "I told you so."

Soon Shelley was parking in front of their building and they walked together up the second flight of stairs to their doors.

"Sure you don't need anything?" Shelley asked, pausing with Briar outside their doors. "If you don't want to be alone you could stay the night with us. The kids would love to wake up and find you there. I can make pancakes in the morning."

Briar shook her head. Right now the empty solace of her apartment beckoned. She wanted to close the door and lock herself away from the world. "No, I'm okay, really."

"All right. Touch base with me tomorrow so I don't worry about you, okay?" Shelley stepped forward and hugged her, patting her on the back several times before letting her go.

Once inside, Briar collapsed against the length of her door for a long moment, reveling in the humming silence. She was home. She was safe and in one piece. Thanks to Knox Callaghan. Knox Callaghan, who clearly possessed a noble streak and happened to be still locked up in that prison. It seemed vastly unfair that he was still in there with men like Gronsky and Pritchard.

Pushing off the door, she hurried to her bathroom and stripped off her scrubs. She kicked them in the corner, positive she would never wear them again.

She hesitated in front of her floor-length mirror, her gaze traveling over her ravaged face before slipping down, fixing on the bruises on her arms. Four perfectly delineated fingerprints marked each forearm.

Her face crumpled. Tears broke free from her burning eyes. She couldn't hold them back any longer. Naked, she slid down the wall, watching her anguished reflection in the mirror. She wrapped her arms around her knees and wept, wiping at her wet cheeks and snotty nose. She cried for what had happened, for what she had almost become today. A victim. Just like her mother.

And she cried for Knox Callaghan still locked up in that prison.

ELEVEN

KNOX STEPPED INTO the room, not fully understanding what was happening. The room was familiar, as were the people sitting behind the table, staring at him and making him feel like he was something being examined beneath a microscope. He'd been brought to this same place four months ago for his first parole hearing, where they had resoundingly rejected his release.

A week had passed since the lockdown. If he was in trouble for what went down in the HSU, they would have already acted and enforced whatever consequence they deemed fit. He wouldn't have been walking around like business as usual.

He knew he had saved Nurse Davis from rape and maybe even worse. Maybe they would have killed her. Or killed Martinez. Or the doctor. Turned out they hadn't killed the guard. An oversight for them. They hadn't been about mercy that day.

Still, it didn't mean that the powers in charge wouldn't find him at fault. He squared his shoulders and took a careful breath. He wasn't fool enough to think his actions had earned him any points. He was no hero in anyone's eyes. Chester had conveyed that message clearly enough at the first opportunity.

After they hauled him from the HSU, they'd taken him to the hole. Chester had stopped by to taunt him through the door. "So I hear you played Superman in there," he sneered. "Is that what you think you are now? Some fucking hero?"

Knox had held silent. He knew well enough that no one cared about what he had to say. He learned more keeping his mouth shut anyway. And sure enough, Chester kept on talking.

"You got that doctor fooled telling everyone that you saved them . . . but not me. Don't think this is going to change anything for you. You're still scum, Callaghan."

Ironically, he had been released from seg an hour later with no explanation. Apparently the doctor had succeeded in persuading the powers that be that he wasn't involved in the attack. He liked to think Briar Davis had a hand in that, too. That she had found her voice to speak on his behalf. It shouldn't matter. It shouldn't have been a hope, but there it was.

Gazing at the suits behind the table, he realized Warden Carter sat behind the table, too. Knox had never had occasion to speak to him before, but he was seated at the center of the table, two men on both sides of him.

"Knox Callaghan." He gestured to the empty chair across from the table. "Have a seat."

After a moment of hesitation, he stepped forward and took a seat. There wasn't really any choice. There never was.

"What you did last week was remarkable," the warden began.

Knox stared, uncertain how to respond to that.

"Dr. Walker has not stopped singing your praises." The warden glanced to the left and right of him before looking back at Knox. "What do you have to say for yourself?"

So he was expected to speak. "I'm glad the doctor and his staff are all right." *Her.* He was glad *she* was all right. Because he had done it for her. He couldn't say for sure, but he doubted he would have gone through so much trouble had it not been for her.

Was she all right? She had looked so wrecked at the end. Barely clothed, her eyes huge and haunted in her pale, battered face.

Before he was hauled from the room, their gazes had locked and something passed between them. A silent exchange beyond words. She was shaken but not broken.

Her eyes had been enormous in a face that was

the same shade of gray as the concrete floor. Dark smudges marred the skin under her eyes, reminding him of bruises. He was sure she had those, too, and not just what he saw on her face. Bruises all over her body. But they would fade. Probably already had. And so would that day. It would dull to memory for her.

She would put this place and what almost happened behind her. She was lucky that way. Lucky to be able to go on with her life. No scars. She wouldn't jump at the sound of every man's voice. There would be no nightmares she couldn't shake, driving her to swallow a bottle of pills.

But it could have been that way. If he had just been one day longer in the hole. Or if his brother hadn't mentioned anything to him . . .

Panic swelled up inside him before he pulled back. But it didn't happen. It didn't go down like that. She was okay. Nothing like his cousin.

"They are alive and largely unharmed thanks to you," the warden continued. "A fact the good doctor won't let us forget." His eyebrow arched in a way that made Knox think he would have liked to forget it. He would have liked to move on.

Warden Carter sighed and looked down, treating Knox to a view of his shiny bald head as he opened a folder in front of him. He scanned it for a moment, turning one page as he said, "You were denied parole at your first hearing."

Knox nodded. He hadn't particularly cared. As North had been denied parole at his previous two hearings, Knox wasn't expecting to get out at his first one. The courts had found him more culpable. It had been his idea to go rough up Mason Leary that night. He was in for eight to fifteen. North was in for only seven to twelve. It wouldn't have felt right, leaving this place before his brother.

The warden closed the folder with a snap. "We've decided that you've satisfied your sentence. Given your heroics last week, we can expedite the process for you."

Knox blinked and leaned forward slightly in his chair. "My next hearing isn't until—"

"Consider us convening now, Mr. Callaghan." The warden motioned to the gentlemen on either side of him. "Right at this moment."

Knox stared. He hadn't counted on being released at least for another two years. And definitely not before his brother. His gaze moved from the warden to the other men at the table. One of the suits actually smiled at him. As though he was bestowing a gift.

"Am I . . ." He couldn't finish the words. A mixture of elation and guilt warred within his too tight chest. The possibility that he was free after eight years collided with the nightmare of leaving his brother behind. His baby brother. Who wouldn't even be here if he hadn't dragged him along on that long ago night.

The warden nodded. "You're paroled, Mr. Callaghan."

LOOKING AROUND HIS CELL, Knox couldn't think of a single thing to take with him. He didn't possess much. Nothing special. The only thing he wanted to take with him was his brother.

North sat silently across from him, gripping the edge of the mattress.

"I'll visit—" Knox started to say.

"Don't. Don't come back here. I'll be out soon enough. My rep was never as bad as yours. You're the one considered a troublemaker." He flashed Knox a grin. "They sounded like they would probably let me go at my next hearing. You'll see."

Knox grimaced, sure North was exaggerating to make him feel better.

North continued, "I'll be on my best behavior . . . make sure they don't have a reason to keep me around."

"You watch your back," Knox warned, tightening the drawstring of his sack, knowing he didn't have much time before a guard returned for him. He looked his brother over, viewing him objectively. North wasn't as brawny as Knox but he was still solid sinew and muscle. His little brother was bigger than most guys in this place, super fast on his feet *and* well-versed in kicking ass. Still. That face was too pretty. Too many guys wanted to make him their bitch.

"Always do," North said.

"Stick close to the crew."

"Man, I can handle myself. Now get the fuck out of here. Go get laid. Find that nurse who you had to play fucking hero for."

He snorted even though something twisted inside his gut at the idea of seeing Briar Davis again. On the outside. "Right."

North arched a dark eyebrow. "Don't act like you don't care. You risked your ass for her. She got her hooks in you. Maybe you should get yours in her."

Reid chose that moment to enter the cell. Several others of their crew accompanied him, hanging back outside the bars. Knox and North fell silent at his arrival. It already felt tight with the two of them crammed inside the cement box, but now it felt claustrophobic with the six-foot-four guy in their midst.

"It's true, then," Reid said. "You're out."

Knox nodded. "Didn't plan on it. I expected to be in here couple more years." He stopped, a lump clogging his throat he fought to suppress. Emotion was weakness. "North was supposed to get out of here first."

"Yeah, well, life never goes the way it's supposed to. Does it?"

Knox nodded, thinking fast. He'd learned that lesson at twenty. When he'd buried his seventeen-year-old cousin. When he kissed his freedom good-bye.

He stepped forward and held out his hand. Reid stared at it for a moment before taking it. Clasping it hard, he hauled Knox in for a quick guy hug, clapping him once on the back. "Don't ever fucking come back here, you understand?" he said roughly close to his ear.

A shudder racked Knox at the unexpected display of affection. Reid wasn't a hugger. Not hardly. The guy was a few years older than him, and he'd been in here since he was nineteen. He was all hard edges and pale eyes without mercy. And he was never getting out. Reid was a lifer.

"I'll never come back," Knox promised. "At least not as an inmate. I'll visit North—"

"No," his brother bit out, coming up off the bars he had been leaning against as Knox and Reid talked. His brown eyes flashed darkly. "You won't. Save yourself the trip. Don't visit me."

"Bullshit," Knox snapped out. "I'm not going to just forget about you in—"

"We stopped Uncle Mac from visiting—"

"That was different. Seeing us in here was killing him." Knox wasn't going to let himself think about how hard it would be to sit across from his brother still locked up. It didn't matter what hurt him. He was the reason North was in this place. He would suffer in silence on those visits to his brother, but he *would* come.

"Yeah, well. I'll be out soon enough. You don't need to come back ever. Understand? You got something to tell me, you call me. We can talk on the phone."

He stared hard at his brother, mute frustration warring inside him. He had seen his brother every day for the last eight years—excepting the times either one of them spent in the hole. How could he just walk out of here and not see him again for months? Maybe even longer? There was no way he could forget about North stuck in here. Living, fighting, surviving without Knox.

"Hey, man," Reid inserted as though reading his thoughts. He clapped Knox on the shoulder. "We got his back. Like always."

"See." North grinned again, all cockiness and swagger. He jabbed a thumb in Reid's direction. "I got a fucking babysitter."

He nodded, mostly because he didn't want to spend his last moments with North arguing. The fact of the matter was that nothing would keep him from visiting North. "Fine."

"Good. Now let's get the sappy shit over with. They got a new shipment in the commissary." His brother stepped in for a hug that was longer and harder than the one he'd just shared with Reid.

North's fingers dug deep into his shoulder blades. "I'll be out soon. Don't worry. And don't forget . . . look up that little nurse while you're out."

He stiffened and stepped back. "Yeah, not a stalker."

"Whatever. You saved her life. She just might want to thank you properly for that."

He rolled his eyes and reached for his bag. "I'll settle for one of the regulars at Roscoe's. Maybe look up an old flame that isn't married with a few kids yet."

"Man, you're making me jealous. Go eat some chicken fried steak and mashed potatoes at Millie's, too."

Reid snorted and waved his hand. "I'm outta here. What a lifer doesn't want to hear about is all the chicken fried steak and ass you're about to score." Before he departed, he leaned in close to add, his light-colored eyes, a color caught between green and amber, scanning Knox's face meaningfully, "You need help when you're outside, I've got people. Just say the word."

"Thanks, man." Knox nodded, but hoped it would never come to that. He knew some of those guys. A few had served time with them in here. They weren't men that would ever be clean, and Knox was planning on doing just that. He was going to walk a straight line. Take care of his family. Never fuck up again.

Alone with his brother, the enormity of what was

happening pressed down on him. Emotion thickened his throat. "I'm sorry, bro."

"For what?"

"For landing you in here. And now leaving you."

"Man, you didn't put me in here. We did that together. That night . . . you weren't leaving me at home. I wasn't having it. I was there beside you every step of the way."

He wasn't going to argue with his brother that it had been his idea. His plan. He should have thought to the future and what could come of going after their cousin's rapist. The outcome seemed so obvious now. He should have considered what going to jail would do to his aunt and uncle, and to Katie, who was already so fragile after the assault. He should have thought of Mason Leary's family. They didn't deserve the grief his actions put them through. Only he hadn't thought. He'd been young and angry and stupid. And he would pay for it all his life,

A guard appeared at his open cell door. "Let's go, Callaghan."

He looked a final time at his brother. He didn't move in for another hug. They'd said all they needed to say. No use dragging this out. For either one of them.

The pretty bastard grinned that smile of his. The one that was still disarming and full of life—that said he wasn't beaten and that wasting his youth in this place hadn't ruined him. "See you on the other side."

He nodded, the lump in his throat preventing him from saying anything more. Turning, he walked out of his cell with his small bag of items, every one of which he would probably burn once he was free of this place.

He passed a blur of steel bars and faces as he left the cell block. Only one face crystallized from all of those staring at him.

Reid watched him from a table on the bottom floor surrounded by the usual crew. Reid's words played over in his head: *Don't ever fucking come back here, you understand?*

An ugly sensation twisted through him as it sank in that Reid would never have that. He would never get out. Sure, he had done bad things. He was a bad man. No one was really innocent in this place. Reid deserved to be in here like the rest of them, but Knox knew that without Reid, he and his brother would have been fucked from the very beginning. In every meaning of the word. As far as he was concerned, Reid was blood.

Reid nodded and sent him a wave, his lips lifting in a half smile of derision that told him he was at that very moment thinking about the chicken fried steak and ass he thought Knox would be getting.

Knox sent him a single nod, knowing this was the last time they would ever see each other.

The guard led him out of the cell bock, buzzing

him through doors and down halls until he was in the admin wing and moving through the same processing room he had first arrived in eight years ago.

"Good luck," an officer he had never seen before said blandly as she directed him to sign his name on the bottom of several release papers. Her expression was bored as she inquired, "You need transportation?"

He hesitated, thinking of his uncle. He hadn't seen him in five years. They only talked on the phone these days. He and North had demanded that his uncle quit visiting them because he'd hated seeing the old man's face . . . the lost look in his eyes as he sat across from him. He'd made the demand as much to spare himself as his uncle. No doubt the same reason North was doing it now.

"Bus station's not far," he commented. "I can hike it."

She grunted, clearly not caring one way or another. He doubted he was the first guy to leave these walls without a ride waiting.

She scratched at her chin and slid him his release papers and parole information. He gave it a cursory glance before taking it. Reading material for the bus ride. There would be rules, of course. As guilty as he felt for getting out before North, he didn't intend to screw up and lose his parole.

"Here's your account balance." She slid him an envelope. He peered inside. He had over nine hundred dollars accrued. Some of it was money Uncle Mac or Aunt Alice sent him—despite him asking them not to. The rest was from eight years of bartering.

He shoved the envelope into his bag and moved on. His heart started hammering faster in his chest as he was buzzed through another door.

He was finally escorted outside. He stepped into rippling waves of sunlight. August in Texas was no joke. Especially in the badlands. He felt his pores open wider, desperate for breath. For air that wasn't so sweltering hot. His T-shirt stuck to his back like a sweaty hand he couldn't shake off. It seemed even hotter than in the yard. The sunlight glinted off the cars in the parking lot, waves of heat undulating over the metal hoods and asphalt.

"C'mon. Walk you to the gate."

Squinting against the bright day, he followed the guard down the path and through the sally port. He could already detect a difference in the guard's manner. He didn't look over his shoulder to eye him. He wasn't worried that Knox was going to get the jump on him. Guess not too many inmates jumped a guard as they were being led *out* of prison.

He showed his papers to the guards on duty at the sally port. With a quick cursory glance at his face, they handed him his papers and nodded for him to go.

He turned and faced the final gate, waiting as it rolled open. He didn't so much as blink. His eyes watched as the gate parted, the gap to his freedom ever widening, yawning open to reveal the world outside. The life he had been denied for eight years. Freedom. It was his now. The gate slid home and came to a jarring stop.

With a deep breath, he stepped over the line.

BRIAR ENTERED THE HSU along with Dr. Walker. She had more butterflies in her stomach than knots of apprehension—which, considering the last time she'd visited this place, was really messed up. It had been two weeks, but she should have been filled with all kinds of panic and trepidation. Bad memories could cripple a person, but she could only think about seeing Knox Callaghan again. Telling him thank-you. Staring into his intense blue eyes and seeing what she had seen in those cobalt depths when he was dragged away. That sizzling connection between them . . .

Shaking her head, she told herself to stop. There was no future in weaving a hero-fantasy around an inmate. That could only lead to nowhere.

Thank you. That's all she wanted to say. What she had to say. Two simple words and nothing more. She couldn't allow herself to feel more than gratitude toward him, and yet she did.

She viewed him differently now. What he had

done—at risk to himself—changed him in her eyes. *Everything* had changed. He didn't scare her anymore. The appreciation she had felt for his body, his face . . . it almost felt okay now. He wasn't some evil person. He was a hero.

Josiah was already there. He rose from behind the desk to hug her. She hadn't seen him since that night in the hospital, and it felt good to touch him, to reassure herself that he was all right. Murphy had pulled through the worst of it, too, and was offered early retirement. Full pension. A new corrections officer stood at the door. A woman in her thirties. Briar couldn't help thinking she appeared both more alert and fit than Murphy ever had.

"Josiah." Dr. Walker reached out to shake his hand when they finished hugging. "So good to see you again."

"Thanks for coming back." Josiah grimaced. "No one would blame either one of you if you didn't."

"The same could be said of you," Dr. Walker reminded him.

Josiah shrugged. "I've been here for ten years. Wouldn't know what else to do with myself if I wasn't clocking in."

"An LVN as qualified as you could always find work elsewhere, but this place is lucky to have you."

"Well, I heard the warden is interviewing new potential staff today . . . a PA that served in the army.

Guess what happened in here really shook him up and made him take action."

Dr. Walker brightened. "That's excellent news."

Something inside Briar sank. It was just a fleeting sensation, but she couldn't deny it. She should have been glad her time here was coming to an end, but in that split second Knox Callaghan's face flashed through her mind. No doubt he would visit the HSU as regularly as before, but she wouldn't be here to see him . . . to put her hands on that big body that had filled her dreams and made her all jumpy inside. She wouldn't hear his deep voice roll across her skin.

She sucked in a deep breath and pressed a hand to one of her heated cheeks. Dr. Walker caught the sound and sent her a concerned look. "Are you all right, Briar?"

He meant was she okay to be here. He had thought it too soon for her to come back to the prison—he'd even suggested she not come anymore at all—but she insisted on joining him his first day back.

She nodded. "No, I'm fine. Should we look over the patient files for the day?"

Josiah nodded and motioned to the desk. "I have them pulled up right here."

Dr. Walker moved ahead of them. Josiah followed at a slower pace, looking her over carefully. "You sure you're all right to be here? You know, no one would blame you for not coming back."

She nodded again, maybe a little too vehemently. "Really, I wanted to come." *I had to come back.*

Dr. Walker sank into the chair behind the desk and started clicking through files open on the laptop. He adjusted his glasses on the bridge of his nose in that way he did when he was concentrating.

She crossed her arms over her chest and slid Josiah a glance. Attempting for subtle, she asked, "So, any word on what happened to the inmate that helped us?" *As if she didn't know his name.* "He didn't get in any trouble, did he?"

Josiah turned to stare at her. "Oh, Callaghan? No one told you?"

Dr. Walker looked up from the computer. Apparently he wasn't concentrating so hard he wasn't paying attention. "I forget to mention that to you, Briar. He was paroled for his actions that day. Isn't that nice? Something good came out of that horrible day, at least."

Her stomach dropped. "Paroled?"

"Yes, well it appears he was eligible months ago, but denied parole. After a conversation with the warden, they agreed to move his next hearing up and approve his release."

She stared at the doctor's smiling face before turning to face Josiah. He nodded at her. "That's right. They released him a few days ago."

"Oh," she murmured dumbly, hoping she didn't

appear as shocked as she felt. "That's . . . good news."

Dr. Walker's gaze drifted back to the screen. "The least of what he deserves for saving our lives."

"Of course," she whispered, wondering at the emotions tripping through her. Displeasure that she would never see him again. Happiness that he was no longer locked up in this place. Hope . . . *excitement* that she might see him again on the outside. The last emotion, she swiftly crushed.

There was no way she would see him again. He probably wasn't even local, and even if he was, it wasn't as though she would go looking for him. Nor would he look for her. That would just be creepy. She probably wasn't even an afterthought for him.

She glanced at Josiah and met the weight of his stare. His all too knowing stare. She blinked and forced a smile that hopefully conveyed blandness . . . that she was not reeling from the news that she would never see Knox Callaghan again.

That she was not disappointed to learn he was gone from her life for good.

TWELVE

SLAMMING HER FRIDGE SHUT, Briar walked back to her living room and plopped down on the couch to glare at the television. It was a Friday night. She didn't have to get up for work tomorrow. She didn't have to do anything, really.

She had already refused Shelley's attempts to drag her out to a bar. The kids were staying at their father's for the weekend and Shelley wanted to cut loose. Briar, not so much. She hadn't felt like doing much of anything since her gig at the prison ended over a month ago. They brought in an additional part-time nurse to help Josiah and a full-time PA. Dr. Walker—or she, for that matter—were no longer needed.

Truthfully, she was relieved not to go back there. It reminded her too much of Knox Callaghan. Too often she found herself thinking about him. She wondered where he was. What was he doing? Was he abiding by the law and living a decent life? Was he back in the arms of some girlfriend? Or lots of girl-friends? She punched her elbow several times into the couch cushion to her left, trying to get it just right to rest her arm.

Eight years in prison. He had a lot of time to make up for. Lots of hot wild sex. Her skin flushed just thinking about. Hell, maybe he had a wife. She didn't even know.

A text beeped on her phone. She plucked up the phone from her coffee table and glanced down at the message from her sister. *Caleb got that promotion! Thinking of celebrating with a bbq.*

She typed back: *Congrats! Sounds great. I'll be there.* ☺

Setting the phone back down, she stared blindly at the TV until she couldn't ignore the growling in her stomach. The cheese quesadilla she made for dinner felt a long time ago. She'd gone to the store yesterday and had a fairly well-stocked fridge and freezer, but somehow she had forgotten to buy ice cream, and that was the only thing she was craving.

It was a guilty vice for certain. One she shouldn't let rule her, but watching reruns of *The Big Bang Theory* without a pint of Ben and Jerry's Cherry Garcia seemed somehow criminal. The two went to-gether like pot roast and Sunday.

Slipping into a pair of flip-flops by her door, she

grabbed her keys and purse. She hesitated and sent a quick look down her body.

She was braless, but going back into her bedroom to don a bra seemed like a lot of work. It was much easier to grab the soft cardigan hanging on a hook by the door and put that on over her T-shirt.

Outside, the evening was much cooler than when she entered her apartment at five o'clock, but they'd had a rare rain shower so it was humid enough that the air sat on her skin like vapor from a sauna. It might be fall in the rest of the world, but this corner of Texas hadn't gotten the memo. Things wouldn't really start to cool off until Thanksgiving.

She hopped in her car and drove the three minutes to the corner store. She parked in front, at the far end, distancing herself from the trio of teenage boys hanging out, smoking cigarettes. One was holding a burrito and sucking down a big gulp. He eyed her over the cup that was bigger than his head.

She eyed them without turning her head to look. A trick she'd learned from working in the HSU, she realized. Tugging the cardigan closed in front of her, she hugged herself as she walked, regretting now that she had not taken the time to put on her bra. Covered up in her cardigan, she knew no one could tell, but she felt vulnerable and exposed anyway.

"Hey," one guy called out in greeting, flicking the ash from his cigarette. He went on to say something else to her, but she ignored him and pushed through the chiming door.

The cashier sent her a cursory glance before turning his attention back to his phone. She walked down the candy aisle and paused, considering the assortment of chocolate bars. Tempting, but ice cream was indulgence enough for one night.

She kept going until she made it to the freezer chest of ice cream. Opening the lid, she picked out the Cherry Garcia and turned back down the aisle.

A man stood right there in the candy aisle where she had been contemplating Snickers or Twix only a few moments before. She froze, her lungs seizing tight and shoving out all air.

She couldn't see his face yet, but there was something about him. The set of his shoulders. The way his dark T-shirt rested against his shoulder blades. The narrowness of his waist. She knew that back. Recognized the hint of sinew shifting beneath soft-looking cotton. Remembered the torso beneath that she had touched on more than one occasion. So many times actually that she dreamed of it. Of *him*. Even without the scratchy white cotton uniform, she knew that body. She knew she was staring at Knox Callaghan.

She blinked and pressed her fingertips to her eyes, squeezing them shut. She was losing her mind. Why would he be here? It had been two months. Certainly he had left the area. She dropped her hand and opened her eyes again.

He turned in that moment, his fingers looped loosely above a six-pack of beer. In his other hand he held a bag of M&Ms.

His eyes collided with hers. And that's what it felt like. A bone-jarring collision.

Her lungs hurt but she couldn't breathe as they stared at each other. There was no ease to the pressure in her chest. It was like someone had pushed a pause button. Neither moved. Or spoke. He was even hotter than she remembered. Memory had somehow dulled the deep blue of his eyes, the sharp lines of his face, the well-sculpted lips. Just like in prison, a few days' worth of stubble lined his jaw, adding to his edgy good looks.

She couldn't blink. He looked her up and down, but she couldn't tell what he was thinking. The stretch of silence got to be too much. The tension . . . too much. Someone had to move. Or speak.

"Hey," she finally blurted.

"Hey," he returned in that deep voice that fell like rain on sun-parched ground.

She drank it up, lapping it greedily inside herself. Okay. So she wasn't insane. It really was *him*. He was here. And this was okay. The two of them staring at each other, talking to each other was okay. There was no prison caging them in. *Caging him in*. No alarm was going to go off. No guards would rush in.

Now what?

"I heard you got out."

He cocked his head, his blue eyes glinting beneath the bright fluorescent lighting of the convenience store as he studied her.

"Congratulations." Oh, sweet Jesus. Had she just congratulated him on getting paroled? Like it was his college graduation or something?

"Thanks."

Her gaze flicked over him. He looked good in regular clothes. The dark T-shirt and worn denim did amazing things for his body. Hell. Who was she kidding? She had seen him without his shirt on. He would look amazing in just about anything. A burlap bag with armholes wouldn't detract from his body or looks. "How are you doing? You look well. I mean . . . are you well?" Awesome. Apparently she forgot how to talk.

"I'm good."

"You're working?" She winced. Now she sounded like his parole officer.

He angled his head, his eyes narrowing slightly as he nodded. "Most nights. I'm helping run my family's place. Roscoe's."

She'd driven past the roadhouse bar just outside of Sweet Hill before. Rows of bikes were always parked out front. She knew it was an institution in these parts, but it had a rough reputation. It wasn't the kind of place she would hang out. Not that she frequented bars in general.

"Good." She nodded dumbly. It dawned on her then that she could say the thing she had wanted to say that day she showed up in the HSU and learned he had been paroled. The two simple words.

"Thank you." There. She said it.

He simply stared at her. Looking at her so blankly, so stoic. The same way he had looked at her when he was inside the prison. Hell, maybe he didn't even recognize her. That was a kick in the face. Frustration bubbled up inside her.

"I said thank you," she repeated, her voice a little clipped.

He nodded slowly. His hair was a bit longer. Still short, but the dark cropped hair did not quite hug his scalp anymore. "I heard you."

He was still cold. A damned robot. Was that all he would ever be? All he was? Disappointment bubbled up in her chest. She thought she had seen something in him . . . when those bullets had ripped through glass and he had thrown his body over hers, she thought there had been something between them. A connection that ran deep.

A man didn't do that for just anyone, right? She had been so certain she had seen something more in him. Heat in his gaze as he was hauled away from her in the HSU.

She had thought he would say something in that moment if he could have. Touch her. Claim her like some warrior after a near miss with death . . .

God. She was reading too many romance novels to have such fanciful thoughts. This was reality. Not fiction.

She swallowed back against the hot lump clogging her throat. "I just wanted you to know that."

"Okay. Sure." He turned then and headed for the cash register, dismissing her like she was no one. Just some stranger. Not anyone that he had a bond with. Not anyone who mattered.

Watching him walk away felt like a slap in the face. Yeah, he was free now. Why would he want to waste time on her?

It took her a moment to make her feet move again. He was walking out of the store, not a glance over his shoulder for her as she stopped at the counter and paid for her ice cream.

The guys were still loitering in front of the door when she exited. Their gazes fell on her. The one that had tried talking to her earlier was ready for her. He pushed off one of the cement posts he had been leaning on. "Whatcha got? Some ice cream? I like ice cream."

Rolling her eyes, she turned to head for her car.

She definitely wasn't in the mood to suffer some delinquent's awkward attempts to hit on her.

Her eyes burned and she wished she had just stayed home. She wished she had never seen Knox Callaghan. Her last memory of him in the infirmary had been better than the memory of him turning his back on her at a convenience store. Almost to her car door, she fumbled with her keys to push the unlock button.

"You shouldn't stop at convenience stores so late at night."

She jumped and swallowed back a squeak, dropping her keys. She hadn't even seen or heard him approach, but Knox was at her side, towering over her.

He glanced behind them and she followed his gaze, noticing that the boys were closer, the burrito-wielding guy who claimed to like ice cream hovering at the lead. They'd actually been following her toward her car, and she hadn't noticed. She was too upset over her run-in with Knox to even pay attention.

The boys stopped and looked between her and Knox.

Knox adjusted his stance, bracing his legs and looking even more imposing. He nodded once at them. "S'up?"

The leader of the group eyed him. "Nothing, man."

"Yeah? Then turn around and keep walking."

Knox stared hard at him, his blue eyes flinty, his jaw locked tight.

The boy sank his teeth into his burrito almost defiantly and turned around, walking stiffly back to his post at the front of the store, his two friends sticking beside him, casting shifty glances at Knox.

Knox faced her then and she realized they were standing really close. Closer than they had ever stood before. The top of her head barely reached his chin. "Uh, thanks. I'm sure I didn't have anything to worry about, though. This is a pretty safe neighborhood."

His lips twisted. "Never know what you'll run into late at night at a gas station." His head dipped a fraction closer and she felt his breath on her cheek. "You could even run into a dangerous felon."

She arched an eyebrow. "You trying to tell me I should be afraid of you?"

He released a short huff of laughter as if that was the dumbest question in the world with the most obvious answer.

She lifted her chin. "Well, I'm not."

The laughter faded from him. His gaze flicked over her face, taking in all of her features, scrubbed free without so much as lip gloss. "You should be, Nurse Davis." Yeah, he was definitely annoyed with her. "I'm still that guy you knew behind bars."

"Yeah. I remember you. I remember what you did

for me in there, too." She moistened her dry lips and her stomach tightened, clenching as his stare dropped down, watching the slide of her tongue. She was suddenly tempted to take the ice cream she purchased and roll it down her overheated throat.

He moved in suddenly and the air sucked out of her in a hiss. Until she realized he was only bending to retrieve her keys. Not to touch her. Not to do anything else.

He held her keys out for her to take. "Don't confuse me with some hero. I'm as tarnished as they come."

She opened her hand, palm up, and his fingers brushed her skin as he dropped the keys into it. He started to turn to go.

"Why did you do it?" she whispered so quietly she wasn't sure he heard her. "Why did you save me?"

He stopped and turned back. Another huff of laughter. "Hell, who knows why I did it? Just a whim. Who's to say I'd even do it again?"

"Liar," she challenged, something prickly hot spreading through her chest. She didn't like his words. She refused to accept them. Refused to believe that they might be true and she was wrong about him. "You'd do it. For me. For Josiah and Dr. Walker. For anyone who was working in the—"

"No. You're wrong." His eyes drilled into her, moving left and right as they stared into her eyes, and he inched closer, invading her space, the immense size of him eating up all the air between them and filling her up with his heat. "I did it for you."

Then he was gone. A stinging curse burned on the air in his wake. He left her gaping after him, her heart pounding like a drum in her chest.

She stalled from sliding into her car, the small carton of ice cream sticking to her fingers. She adjusted her grip slightly, feeling brittle sheets of ice slide between her skin and the cardboard carton. It was cold in her hand but she felt so hot and achy that it felt good. She was actually tempted to roll the carton against her feverish cheeks, her throat . . . lower.

Panic welled up in her as she watched his retreating back. She shifted on her feet, certain that if he left now, she would never see him again. No. She couldn't have that.

Sucking in a thick breath, she called out to him, "Knox!" Her voice rang out louder than she expected, and even to her ears there was a hint of desperation to it. Need and want. Her face burned hotter.

He stopped several yards away, not quite to the gas pumps yet where he had left his pickup truck. He turned to face her, his deep-set eyes almost black across the distance.

His expression revealed nothing. Impassive as ever. But just this sight of him—that hard warrior body that seemed to belong to another time, when men wore chain mail and armor and knocking heads was a part of every day—pulled at something deep in her belly and gave her all the encouragement she needed.

She had seen him in action. Quick and deadly as a viper. Fighting to defend and protect her with a searing intensity that she had never seen before. Or felt. And she had *felt* it. Felt him. Just as she did now. His gaze felt like a physical stroke over her body. Heat rippled over her skin.

She couldn't forget that day. It wasn't the horror that stayed with her. It was the memory of *him*. His raw power. His brutal beauty. The way his entire body had been a weapon. She wanted that weapon. She wanted him to turn it on her. To unleash himself on her.

She didn't even know if he thought about her that way. If desire for her even entered into this *thing*—whatever it was—between them.

Tugging her cardigan tighter over her T-shirt, she held out the carton like it was some kind of proof, evidence that she was merely asking for something safe and innocent. Like sex was the farthest thing from her mind. She clung to it like the excuse she desperately needed it to be. "You like Cherry Garcia?"

THIRTEEN

YOU LIKE CHERRY GARCIA?

She voiced the question so innocently, as though she was asking him over for ice cream on a Sunday afternoon. Like he was some loafer-wearing choirboy from her church youth group with nothing on his mind beyond first base. It had been years since he stepped inside a church. He would likely go up in flames if he even tried.

He stared at her in front of the open door of her car and read the mortification gleaming brightly in her big eyes. She shifted on her feet, waiting for his response. It took everything in her to ask the question. He knew that right away, but he still couldn't bring himself to answer her immediately.

It was a game. The question was whether he would let her play it. Let her pretend asking him over for ice cream wasn't any invitation to fuck.

He didn't do games.

Knox eyed her in her baggy T-shirt, her toes curling self-consciously in her flip-flops, wondering if maybe, in fact, she didn't know what she was doing. Maybe she didn't realize that he was the wolf and she the lamb. That inviting him over meant he was going to devour every inch of her.

He studied her wide eyes and shifting feet and decided, yeah. She didn't know. Not fully. She couldn't. She couldn't fathom what she was inviting on herself. She probably thought they might kiss. Make out a little. As though that would be enough to satisfy the hungry beast prowling inside him, pawing at the gate, ready to be unleashed so that he could do all the dirty things burning through his mind.

"Yeah," he heard himself answering, even though he had no idea what flavor Cherry Garcia was. "I like it."

He couldn't *not* go. He wasn't that good or honorable. He wasn't that strong. If she wanted to play with a wolf, then that's what she would get.

The cold truth was that he had gone too long without a woman.

He had turned down other women since he got out. Working at Roscoe's, he'd had plenty of opportunities. At the end of a work week, everyone was looking to blow off some steam with a quick, meaningless fuck. But no one had tempted him. No one felt right. After living in a drought for almost a decade,

he didn't want to feast on a crummy P&B sandwich.
He wanted steak.

And Briar Davis was that. She'd filled his thoughts
since the first time he saw her. This unattainable gem,
too bright, too expensive, too good for the likes of
him. Even when he got out of prison he had thought
about her. He still fucked his hand like he was stuck
in that concrete hole with visions of her running
through his head.

Turning the corner and seeing her in that convenience store aisle had been like entering the seventh
circle of hell. Seeing her. Confronting the one thing he
had convinced himself he couldn't have. It wasn't supposed to happen. Even though he was a free man, he
wasn't free enough to have her. He'd never be that free.

She bit her bottom lip and something exploded in
his gut. A deep, visceral reaction that made him want
to leap across the distance and take that lip with his
own teeth. Take *her*. He steeled himself with a hard
breath, clenching his hands into fists at his sides.

"Would you like to come over for some?" She
held out that damned ice cream again and nodded in
direction of the town house complex he had passed
before stopping for gas.

He nodded once. Before she changed her mind. Before he changed his. Good girls like her didn't invite
felons over for ice cream. Apparently she missed that
memo.

"Great," she said all breathy and with forced brightness. "Um. Just follow me."

He watched her for a moment as she got into her car and reached for her seat buckle. Then he turned and made his way to his pickup, climbed inside and started the engine. It almost felt like a weird out-of-body experience. Like he was watching someone else follow this nice clean girl back to her apartment. Killers like him didn't get invited over for ice cream.

But she knew what he was. A smart girl like her, she had to know. She knew his hands were dirty, his thoughts dirtier. Even if she only guessed at a fraction of his thoughts when it came to her, that was enough to send her running in the opposite direction.

But she was still inviting him over.

He flexed his hands on the steering wheel and waited a moment before shifting into drive. He followed her onto the road and turned left, then waited as an electric gate slid open for them. She must have a remote opener in her car. They passed through a brick entrance and around several buildings until she parked in front of a rock fence. This late, most of the parking spots directly in front of the town houses were occupied. People were snug on their couches, watching reruns. He had to park several spots down from her car. She waited on the sidewalk for him, holding her small pint of ice cream that had to be softening in the warm night.

She still wore that smile. The sweet one that looked strained and uncertain. It almost made him turn around and leave. Almost. If he wasn't such a selfish bastard.

She led him up a set of stairs and his gaze fixed on the shape of her legs in her skintight yoga pants. Her loose T-shirt and cardigan drifted up enough that he could see the bottom of her ass and the upside down V of her inner thighs meeting her crotch.

His mouth dried and he bit back a groan when she reached the top of the stairs, taking the sight away. Her baggy scrubs had always covered her up. Except that day those fuckers tried to rape her, ripping off her pants, and he had seen all that peaches and cream skin . . . including those little panties and the shadow of hair beneath the pale pink cotton that hid her sex.

He shoved the memory away. It felt wrong to remember her like that, in that moment. That knowledge of her, the sight of all that skin and the soft texture of her thighs under his rough hands, was a stolen thing. He didn't have a right to that. It was tainted.

He hated having seen her like that, but he couldn't unsee it. He couldn't fully chase it away or keep the memory from bursting in on him like a flash of light in the darkness, an unwanted intruder as he stroked himself off in the shower or his bed at night.

She let him inside her home, gesturing at the cozy space with a wave. She'd left the television on and a show he didn't know played on the flat screen.

"Have a seat." She nodded to the couch. Slipping out of her cardigan, her hands shook a little as she dropped it on the back of the sofa. "I'll make us some bowls."

It was his turn to feel uncertain as she left him alone in her living room full of nice things and entered the kitchen. He rotated in the small space, the wood floors creaking under his weight as he noted the soft, clean colors. Pewter-framed photos of some cute kids sat on a wood media table beneath the flat screen attached to the wall.

Knox stepped closer to examine the images, noting the parents standing proudly behind the children. The mother was a bit heavier than Briar, but she was young and bore a strong resemblance to Briar. He guessed they were sisters. They had the same fresh girl-next-door-faces and curly hair.

He heard the sound of a cabinet closing and the clink of glass. "Would you like a drink, too?" she called out. "Water . . . I have beer, but I don't guess that actually goes well with Cherry Garcia."

He followed her voice, moving silently into the kitchen. She was scooping ice cream into bowls on the counter, her back to him. He studied her for a moment, the soft skin at her nape and the copious amount of coppery-brown hair piled into some messy concoction on top of her head.

He approached, stopping an inch behind her, not touching, but she stilled anyway, sensing him at her back. She didn't turn around, but he heard the change in her breathing. The shallow rasp. Like she couldn't get enough air.

His chest tightened as he absorbed her warmth. Even this close, it was like a current connected them. All of him felt coiled and ready to snap like a contracting spring.

She lifted her head and stared straight ahead into the cabinets, waiting. Was this it, then? She had invited him over here on the pretext of ice cream, but the first move was his?

He closed the final distance and braced both hands on the counter, leaning in, letting her feel all of him against the trembling line of her body.

He spoke into her ear and caught a whiff of pears. Just like all those times in the HSU. Except they were alone now. No guards. No handcuffs. Nothing was stopping him from touching her. "This is a bad idea," he whispered.

A shudder racked her softness and vibrated into the length of him.

He lifted his hand and fisted it into her hair, fingers sinking deep and tangling in the mass, the strands soft as silk against his rough palm. "You should tell me to go," he growled, fingers delving deeper, searching for the band to free it. She released a soft whimper as he found the thin elastic and tugged it free. The band snapped and broke and the mass of silky hair fell over his hand and arm, tumbling down her back.

Just like that, something snapped in him, too. The last invisible thread that had been holding him together.

"Last chance," he growled, thrusting his hips, letting her feel him, rock hard against her, letting her know exactly what was going to happen if she didn't tell him to get the fuck out of here.

He pulled back on her hair and another one of those little sounds escaped her as she arched her throat for him and he pressed his open mouth to the flushed skin at the side of her neck, directly beneath her ear.

She pushed back against him in response, rocking her ass into his hardness.

She might come to regret it, but he had his answer.

SHE WAS ON FIRE. She arched her neck, guided by the hard hand in her hair. She pushed back against his erection, grinding her bottom into him, moaning as his wet mouth found her neck. Her eyes fluttered shut and she bit her lip to stop from crying out so loudly.

Was it possible to orgasm with your clothes on?

She felt like she was seconds from coming. And he hadn't even kissed her yet.

And God, she wanted him to do that. She wanted that mouth on hers. She wanted to taste him with an ache that went bone-deep. Despite all his tough edges, that mouth had always looked so beautiful, hinting at a tenderness in the well-carved shape.

She inhaled a ragged breath, trying to get it together and calm her nerves. Desire rushed through her like a high-speed train. She hadn't been on a date in over a year. And that date had ended in a handshake. She hadn't been kissed in closer to two years. And sex? Forget it. She couldn't even remember how long it had been since Beau. Maybe it was abnormal, but she had never cared. Never missed it. Not in these many years had her lack of sex life bothered her. Until now.

Until she had confronted someone she wanted so badly her body ached and hummed. He felt so good against her it was frightening.

With a frustrated choke, Briar turned, squeezing between him and the hard edge of the counter. He looked down at her, so much taller, bigger, the blue of his eyes almost black as he gazed hotly at her.

He still braced his hands against the counter's edge, caging her in. He ate up all the space in her small kitchen.

"Knox," she whispered, a thread of wonder in

her voice as she flattened a hand against his chest. She stopped just short of begging him to give her his mouth. His heart beat hard against her palm, but surely hers beat harder. She felt so awkward. Almost like she didn't know what to do next, which was silly. She'd done this before even if it was a long time ago. Even if it had never been with anyone like him.

Maybe that was just it. It had never been with anyone like *him*. Her hand smoothed its way up his shirt, stopping at the hard curve of his shoulder. She rose up on tiptoes and pressed her mouth to his exposed neck. He tensed as she feathered tiny kisses along the bristly edge of his jaw until she reached the corner of his mouth.

Air shuddered from her at arriving there—at the mouth that rarely smiled. At least before. In the prison. Here, it was different. Everything was different. They were alone and she could have him. She could touch her mouth to his. See for herself if it felt soft or hard, cold or warm.

She stretched higher on her tiptoes and slanted her mouth across his more fully. His lips were soft. Firm and dry. Her chest squeezed with a desperate desire for him to kiss her back. For her to do it right so that she pleased him.

She started to sink back on her heels, disappointment pumping through her at his lack of response. And shame. Shame that she had thrown herself at him and he didn't want what she was offering. She didn't arouse him.

His head dipped then, swiftly catching her mouth before she was fully gone from him.

"Where are you going?" he growled against her lips.

He snatched her by the waist with both hands and picked her up and plopped her onto the counter before she could draw a breath. The motion positioned them more evenly, brought their lips level. He settled one hand at her waist, gripping her there while his other hand sank into her hair, his fingers curling around her skull and pulling her in, drawing her closer until their mouths were fused.

She gasped and his tongue entered her mouth, slicked over hers in total possession. She leaned in, moaning, tangling her tongue with his, tasting something faintly lemon on him and wondering what he had eaten. He tasted so good. Lemon, a faint saltiness, and man. Sex. She tasted sex on his tongue and the pleasure to come. She curled both her fingers into his shoulders, clinging to him and pulling him closer.

He made a deep sound in his throat and kissed her deeper, his fingers clenching tighter around the back of her head. She touched his face, the bristle of hair on his cheek a delicious scrape that ran right through her. They kissed and kissed and kissed. She didn't know kissing could be like this. So drugging. So addictive. Simultaneously endless and not enough.

His hand on her waist moved up and palmed her breast over her shirt. Sensation shot through her and Briar moaned into his mouth, pushing into his big palm.

"Christ," he muttered against her lips, pulling back. His hand left her hair, too. She whimpered at the loss of him, but it was only temporary. He grabbed the hem of her shirt. Seizing it, he yanked it over her head, leaving her naked from the waist up on her counter. No bra. *God, why hadn't she worn a bra?*

His eyes went to her chest. "Fuuuck."

Her hands instinctively dove for her breasts, but hard fingers circled her wrists, exerting only the slightest pressure, but she was fully aware of his power, the strength in his big hands as he tugged her hands down.

"Don't," he commanded. "I want to see you."

Knox shook his head once, his blue eyes dark and intent on her, moving from her face and down the slope of her throat to her breasts again. Trembling, she didn't know if it was more from his gaze or his words. The deep sound of his voice spiked her desire higher, twisting it into something almost painful between her legs. She felt her nipples tighten under his stare.

He slowly eased his hands away from her wrists, and this time she didn't try to cover herself. She held up her chin, closing her fingers around the edge of the counter, clutching tightly to stop herself from covering her body up again.

She tried to block out her embarrassment and focus on him. It worked. She was so busy watching him watch her, reveling in his stark beauty, the intensity of those deep-set eyes on her, the brutal slash of his sexy mouth, that she didn't at first realize what he was doing with his hands. One of his hands reached for the nearby bowl. He dipped two fingers into the melting Cherry Garcia, scooping a small amount and carrying it to one of her nipples.

She gasped at the wet coldness.

His deep voice rippled through her. "Tonight these are mine . . . you're mine, Briar."

She could only nod senselessly as he rolled both fingers over her rigid nipple. Back and forth, back and forth, toying with the peak, making the point grow harder with every swirl of his slick fingers.

She made a choked sound and dropped her head back on her shoulders, thrusting out her chest.

"Fuck, that's hot," he growled.

Then she felt him at her other breast, rolling more ice cream on that rapidly hardening nipple. "Wh-what are you—" Her voice died on a squeak as he pinched her slippery nipple. She felt a rush of wetness between her legs and she squirmed on the countertop, desperate for relief, for an end to the ache growing there.

He looked at her from beneath heavy lids. "This is how I like to eat my ice cream," he said thickly, and then she felt him there, his hot mouth closing over the wet, chilled tip of her breast like he was starving and she the long denied feast.

She cried out as his warm tongue sucked her nipple into his mouth.

She grabbed the back of his head, urging him closer. Everything in her tightened and squeezed, pleasure centering where his mouth fed on her, his tongue swirling wildly. Her sex pulsed, clenching in agony.

"Knox," she pleaded, crying out again as he suddenly turned on her other breast, sucking hungrily, licking every bit of ice cream off her, not even missing the sticky sweetness that rolled down the sides.

Her sounds were wild. Embarrassing little pants that verged into full-on wails. Especially when his teeth scraped one stiff nipple and his fingers pinched down on the other one.

The pressure inside her built, twisting into something that she couldn't stop. She actually did try to resist, digging in her heels, too alarmed at the intensity, too terrified at the new sensations. Shudders began to overtake her. "Oh, God, God, God . . ."

He spoke against her nipple, his words muffled as his tongue played on her flesh. "That's it, baby. Let it happen. Come for me."

Was that what was happening? She was actually about to have an orgasm?

She shook her head. She felt out of control. Too wild, too removed from her own body.

"Let yourself have it," he said, his voice darker, harder. His hand delved between her splayed thighs then so that his fingers could rub over her crotch.

She gasped, heat flaming her face at the truth he felt there. Even through the layers of her panties and leggings he felt it. He knew.

"Oh, baby. You're so wet. You must be hurting." Those firm fingers of his rubbed up and down her and the friction was unbearable, the pressure so sweet, especially when he grazed her clit.

Just like that, she exploded, coming apart with a shriek and surging against his chest.

She was still shaking, gasping, stars blinking behind her eyes as he picked her up and carried her out of the kitchen like she was a feather in his arms. She couldn't form coherent speech as he walked them into her dark bedroom, his body tense and pulsing all around her—a direct contrast to her. Lethargy pulled at her, making her muscles limp as noodles.

He set her on the middle of her queen-size bed and stood back, stripping off his clothes. His eyes glittered at her in the near dark. The only light in her room spilled through the open bedroom door and the thin spaces between the slats of her blinds.

She blinked lazily, appreciating what she could see of him—the amazing chest and ridged abdomen. She wished she could see more, in better lighting . . . wished she could shake off this fog of postorgasm bliss. Her gaze traveled down his thin happy trail, stopping at his hands yanking open his fly. He shoved down his jeans and briefs in one move. At her first glimpse of him, her eyes flared wide and her sex reawakened with a swift pulsing clench. He was enormous and standing straight out, ready and eager to penetrate. To claim.

A faint tremor of nervousness skated down her spine. He fished a condom out of his wallet and came over her as she inched back warily on the bed.

"I'm not sure that's going to fit," she breathed.

He prowled up her body, his hands walking up either side of her. "You felt it, too. This thing between us. Didn't you?" he asked roughly.

She nodded, unable to deny it. It was the truth. On some base, primal level Briar had always known. Her body knew before her mind ever understood. She was his for the taking.

He seized the elastic of her leggings and pulled them off her in one smooth move, reminding her so much of the predator she first thought him to be in the prison.

She trembled under him in nothing but a pair of panties. He flattened a hand over her abdomen, fingers splayed wide, the base of his palm directly over her sex, cupping her mound so that she had to bite back a moan.

He looked up the length of her body, his heavy-lidded eyes snaring hers. "This is where I want to be. Where I've wanted to be since you first put your hands on me."

The inner muscles of her sex squeezed as though in agreement. It wanted him there, too, but she still felt a stab of apprehension. "You're too . . . big."

He rotated his hand until his fingers where diving down along the seam of her, the only barrier the thin cotton of her panties.

She choked back a cry, arching her spine slightly at the sliding pressure of his fingers against her. "I belong here," his deep voice said so confidently. "We're going to fit together perfectly." He knuckled aside her underwear and slipped a finger inside, spearing her deep. She came off the bed at the penetration.

"God, you're tight." His words came in quick pants as he continued to move that finger, thrusting in deeply, steadily, curving upward until he found that spot she never knew existed. He worked in a second finger, stretching her, readying her for him. She knew that, and she took him, wanting every bit of pleasure he was giving her. Wanting what was to come and wanting it to never end.

She started to shake as another orgasm welled up inside her.

"Oh, no. Not yet." His fingers slipped out of her. She felt a tug and heard the slight rip of her underwear. But she didn't care. She writhed on the bed, at a loss for the sudden emptiness inside her.

There was the crinkle of the condom wrapper and then she felt him. The broad head of him parting her, entering her just a fraction.

Her hands instinctively groped for something to hold onto, grabbing his tense biceps on either side of her. He was bigger than his fingers. Bigger than anything she'd had inside of her, and she tensed.

"Hey," he whispered. "Look at me."

She found his gaze in the dark. His eyes glittered, and for once she read emotion there, a desperate need that mirrored her own, and something else. Something vulnerable she had never seen in him before. He was waiting for her, holding himself back for her.

Even though his jaw was clenched tight and she knew it was killing him to restrain himself, to wait, he was doing just that. He cared about her comfort. Her pleasure. This man wasn't what everyone said he was—what the world thought. And in this moment, he was all hers.

She reached up to touch him. She dragged her thumb over his lips and leaned up, kissing him. He kissed her back. Hard and hungry, desperate even.

He pushed a little deeper inside her and she gasped into his mouth, her inner muscles stretching, burning. Not exactly uncomfortable. He eased back out and she released a little sigh of relief.

"Fuck," he groaned. "You've done this before, right?"

"Yeah," she panted. "It's just been a while . . . and never anything like—" She gasped again as he pushed in more, going deeper, and a growl vibrated from his bare chest into hers.

He threw back his head. "You feel so good." A sense of feminine power swelled within her with the knowledge that she brought this man pleasure. Everything melted and softened inside her. She slid one hand down his back and gripped his taut ass. She dug her nails into the tight skin and he choked, "Don't, Briar . . . I can't go slow when you . . ."

She pressed feathery kisses on his jaw, his cheek, moving to his lips. "Don't, then. Take me like you want to." She licked his mouth and then bit his bottom lip. "Fuck me harder, Knox. I won't break."

Before the last word even left her mouth, he rammed himself fully inside her. The force shoved her up the bed. He waited a moment, breathing raggedly, holding himself back. Despite her encouragement, he was still waiting, letting her get accustomed to his throbbing member lodged full inside her.

They were both panting as though they had run a

long distance, their chests rising and falling together. Then he began again, moving at a steady pace, his hand tight on her hip, anchoring her for his thrusts.

It didn't take long for that pressure to build back up inside her. He had her back where she had been moments ago, so close to climax. She angled her hips and lifted her thighs, wrapping them around his hips. He groaned and dropped his head into her neck, hammering faster, harder, beating her into the mattress with his big body as her sex clenched and flexed around him.

She curled a hand around his nape and held him there, reveling in his warm breath on her neck as he pumped deep and fast and wild. She came in a blinding flash, arching under him.

He kept going, riding straight through the shudders of her orgasm until she was rising up on another wave, edging closer and closer to another climax. His free hand swept over her breasts, squeezing and fondling the ice-cream sticky mounds. She felt a rush of new moisture between her thighs as he pinched down hard on one of her nipples.

"Oh, Knox," she pleaded. "I can't . . . what are you doing to me . . ."

"Again," he commanded. "Come for me again."

Her body obeyed. Her sex pulsed and clenched around him, the tug in her belly almost too tight, too painful. Too much. Everything was too much. Too sensitive. When he dropped a hand between them and found that hidden spot in her folds, she screamed and came again. She went limp beneath him, certain she might have just died.

He drove into her one more time and stopped, stilling, his chest lifting high as he came hard, pulsing inside her, a strangled gasp leaving his lips.

He lowered down slightly, his hands braced on the mattress on either side of her. He bowed his head, still buried inside her, breathing quick, shallow breaths. She lifted a hand, tempted to touch him, but an overwhelming sense of uncertainty swamped her.

What now?

It seemed she had her answer when he slid out from her body and got up from the bed. Without a word, without a look, he disappeared inside her bathroom. She heard him remove the condom and drop it into her small wastebasket. The sound of running water followed. She bit her lip and curled onto her side, waiting for him to return and imagining a million things to say as he dressed and took himself away, leaving her on the bed. Leaving her apartment.

She commanded herself to be an adult. No matter what, to not look as crushed as she felt. It was just sex. She should be grateful that it had been so good. Fabulous even. He'd given her unbelievable pleasure and he wasn't going to make it complicated with talk or speeches or promises that he would never keep.

He returned then and stood looking down at her for a moment. She could hardly breathe as they stared at one another, not speaking. Suddenly she wished she had pulled the covers down to cover herself. With every inch of her exposed to his perusal, she felt self-conscious. Already this wasn't going as predicted. Why was he still here? Why didn't he say good-bye and go?

Knox reached to the top of the bed and tugged the comforter. She scooted to the opposite side of the bed, bewildered but giving him the access he wanted—which was to apparently pull down the covers. That accomplished, he reached for her and placed her in the middle of the bed on her cool sheets. Her mind was reeling. She blamed her sluggish thoughts on the multiple orgasms. When he slid in beside her and turned her so that she was spooning him, she was still slow to process what was happening.

He was staying. Spending the night.

Every alarm bell in her head should be going off, but she could do nothing but hold herself still against him, her heart beating like a drum in her too tight chest as he wrapped one hard arm around her waist and pulled her back until she fit snug against his chest.

Briar finally found her voice. "What are you doing?"

"Going to sleep."

She moistened her lips, somehow doubting she

would ever be able to fall asleep like this. She had never slept with a man before. She and Beau had always gone to their separate beds. This was alien and strange. *And it was Knox Callaghan.* At the moment that struck her as the weirdest thing of all. He had been an inmate a short time ago, as off limits as a guy could get, and now they were spooning in her bed.

But it didn't seem to affect him. She listened as his breathing slowed and evened. He was actually going to sleep. She squeezed her eyes shut in a hard, punishing blink, telling herself she would never be able to do the same. Not with his big, delicious body wrapped around hers. It wouldn't be possible. Her hand came up to cover his forearm, enjoying the tight ropes of sinew beneath his skin that made her feel so safe. So protected. That was her last thought before she drifted to sleep.

FOURTEEN

KNOX WOKE WITH a start in the dark, disorientated . . . feeling like he was back in the prison again. In the hole where everything was darkness and cold. He whimpered, feeling lost, alone. Except there was warmth. Another body beside him. Wrapped up around him. Soft with sweet-smelling hair and a rounded ass that was rubbing against his dick. *Pears.*

His body knew her. Wanted her. He curled a hand around her hip and dipped down her navel to her beckoning pussy. Thighs parted sweetly at the first foray of his fingers. She was wet. Ready for him.

Briar sighed, moaned his name and rubbed back against his cock. He didn't even hesitate. He removed his hand and positioned himself, sliding inside her, pushing deep. Tight heat surrounded him and he ground down against her, pumping faster, sliding through her slick warmth. Nothing had ever felt this good. So perfect.

Soft cries filled his ears, and his hands found her breasts, molding the plump mounds as he rolled over, pinning her under him and working in and out of her body.

"Knox, yes, yes, yes . . ."

The sound of his name drove him into a frenzy. She grew tighter around him, closing and squeezing him like a fist as he pumped in and out of her, slamming into her hard. He pushed and pulled and came with a groan, spilling himself deep inside all that sweet, milking heat.

He collapsed on the pliant body under him, feeling as warm and satiated as he had ever felt.

"Uh," a voice said from under him, "you're a little heavy."

He stiffened and jackknifed into a sitting position.

He fixed wide eyes on Briar as she lifted to a sitting position beside him.

He dragged a hand over his skull, chafing the back of his head where the hair was the shortest. "Oh, God." He'd just fucked Briar. Half asleep. Without a condom. "A-Are you okay?"

He inhaled a thin breath, wondering if this was what he had become. It was one of his worst fears. That the Rock had made him into a monster that destroyed those softer than him.

She released a breathy little laugh that didn't exactly scream you-animal-get-the-hell-away-from-me.

"Well, that was one way to wake up, that's for sure."

"Oh, shit, Briar." He reached out a hand to touch her and then dropped it at his side. "I'm sorry. I didn't mean—"

"Why are you apologizing? I wanted it, too. I didn't tell you to stop. I didn't say no."

I didn't say no.

He tried to take comfort in that. He did, but he wondered . . . would he have heard her if she had? Bile rose in his throat because he wasn't sure. He hated himself right then. How could he be . . . *this*? It became painstakingly clear to him that he needed to get as far as possible from Briar Davis. Before he fucked up her life as much as he had his own. He dragged both hands over his skull.

She sighed then, looking so calm when he was losing his shit. "I guess the whole no condom thing was reckless," she admitted, and that's when he heard the shakiness in her voice. She wasn't as composed as he thought.

"I'm clean, Briar," he sought to reassure her—of at least that one thing he could reassure her. "I don't use drugs . . . I haven't been with anyone in a very long time." It felt like forever. Because the last time he was with a girl, he had been that other person. A boy. The Knox Callaghan of another life. Another world and time. That Knox Callaghan might have been good enough for the likes of Briar Davis. He could have asked her out and taken her on an actual date. The kind of thing that good people did. Guys that didn't kill. Guys that didn't spend the better part of a decade penned up like an animal.

She hesitated. "Really?"

He sucked in a breath and admitted what she needed to hear. What she deserved to hear. "I haven't been with anyone since I went in. When I was twenty. And I didn't have sex while I was in there either." It was necessary to state. Plenty of guys did. Both willingly and unwillingly.

"Wait . . . so you've been out for almost two months now?"

"Yeah."

"And you haven't . . ." She couldn't hide the incredulity from her voice or the widening of her eyes in the gloom of her room.

"Why is that such a surprise? I didn't sleep with anyone for eight years. What's another two months?" He detected her shock in the long pause of silence. He reached out and pushed the hair back off her shoulder. "I went a long time without. Figured I might as well wait for something good." Something other than a quickie with someone he just met. "And you were very good . . . Nurse Davis."

A dark shadow crept over her cheeks and he knew she was blushing.

His levity slipped, remembering that it had been so good that he didn't even use a condom just now. "But I shouldn't have done that. Not like that."

"According to my menstruation app, this isn't even the time of the month when I'm most fertile," she said quickly, like speaking the words fast made it somehow less embarrassing. She reached for the comforter as though recalling her nakedness. He watched hungrily as she pulled the covers over her, hiding her body from his eyes. That would be his last glimpse of all those curves, and that knowledge filled him with an ache. A longing that shot straight to his cock. He felt himself harden all over again and knew he had to get the hell away from her. Fast. Before he lost control again and she was too sweet and obliging to deny him.

"It's not likely . . ." she hedged.

Not likely. He supposed she would know about that better than anyone. She was a nurse and it was her body, but he still wasn't proud of himself, and he *still* wasn't okay with what happened. No matter how much he'd reveled in her . . . bare-skinned. No matter how much he wanted to lose himself in her again, he couldn't.

She was as bad for him as he was for her. Around her, he lost control. And he needed to be in control. Losing control was what got him in prison. And he had vowed to never make that mistake again.

He stood up from the bed and reached for his clothes. He dressed in the dark, watching her watch him. Emotion flickered over her gaze. She was so transparent. Wore her emotions like a badge on her face. It made her all the more enticing. She wasn't hard to read. He didn't have to wonder what she felt or thought. Unlike everyone else he had been around in the last eight years. Always distrusting them. Always second-guessing.

She looked wounded. And that only made him feel like a bigger bastard. He pulled his shirt back on and then stood there, his hands hanging at his sides, empty, bereft.

"You're going." Not a question. Just a simple statement. She lifted her chin as though his leaving her in the middle of the night didn't bother her in the least. As though he hadn't just screwed her and was now running for the door. No, it wasn't a huge fuck-you at all.

"I should go."

She nodded stiffly in lieu of a reply.

"You'll let me know," he added, his words hanging with implication, his gaze sharp on her. *You'll let me know if I messed up your life and knocked you up.*

"Of course," Briar said quickly. Too quickly. And he knew she was lying. She wouldn't let him know. The good, responsible, respectable girl in her wasn't going to reach out to a felon she had a one-night stand

with for anything. For her, this was where it would
end. If the possibility of fatherhood wasn't hanging
over him, he could let her do that. But she *would* be
hearing from him again.

Fatherhood.

A bolt of panic shot down his spine. Knox never
thought he would be a father. Never wanted to be.
It was enough for him to take care of Uncle Mac,
run Roscoe's, and convince his parole officer that
he was walking the straight and narrow. Eventually,
North would get out and together they would take
care of Uncle Mac and Roscoe's. The bar had been in
his family for over seventy years. It was their legacy.
Roscoe's had been standing when Sweet Hill was
nothing but tumbleweeds. For now it was on him to
make sure it kept standing. Fatherhood wasn't supposed to happen. Not to him.

North wasn't like him. He still smiled. Still found
things to laugh at—even in prison. North could be
a father someday. Married with a couple of kids.
Not him. He had ruined enough lives. He wouldn't
ruin some innocent kid's life, too. And he sure as hell
wasn't going to ruin Briar Davis.

If it wasn't already too late for that. That fate might
already be decided. In that case, he would make the
best of it. It was the only thing he could do.

"Briar . . ." He hesitated, hating to make any de-
mands on her. Knowing he didn't have that right, but

she had to understand. She had to believe she wasn't alone in this. "I want to know."

"Okay. Fine." An edge entered her tone. "I'll let you know."

He pulled his phone from his pocket and opened it to his contacts. "What's your number?"

She paused for a moment, and he arched an eyebrow, waiting until she rattled off her number. He punched it in, saving her to his contacts and then sliding his phone into his back jeans pocket. "I'll text you so you have my number."

"Okay." Another one word reply. He didn't like it. Her cold acceptance. He wanted her to talk. To say something. To not sit bundled under her covers looking so wounded. But then he would have to be someone else. A guy that would spend the night with her. Take her to breakfast. To church. To dinner at his parents'. Not him.

"All right." He moved to the door, feeling like a grade A bastard. He hovered in the threshold of her room. Nothing about this was right. Leaving. Staying. "You'll be hearing from me."

Turning, he walked out of her apartment. And tried to forget the sight of her sitting alone in that bed.

FIFTEEN

THURSDAY NIGHTS WEREN'T the busiest at Roscoe's but they still saw a hefty crowd. Bud was closing up tonight, so Knox left just shy of midnight. The crowd had already started to thin by then. Some people actually had to get up early for work. Aunt Alice had off tonight and she promised to take dinner to Uncle Mac. Knowing her, she had probably stocked the fridge with fresh groceries, too. At least the old man had a good meal tonight. Knox would get up early and make him some eggs and bacon before he took his run.

He rarely missed a morning run. After eight years locked up he couldn't get enough of jogging in the wide-open spaces and dragging all that clean fresh air into his lungs. He wasn't in a ten-by-eight cell. He wasn't in the yard either. He didn't have to worry about where he could and could not go. There was none of the constant tension. Just freedom.

The back parking lot was empty as he made his way to his pickup. He pulled his phone out of his back pocket, checking for messages. He didn't have many contacts. Only a few people even bothered to text him. His aunt and uncle. Couple of guys from work so they could verify work schedules. His cousin Becky texted him occasionally.

But he wasn't checking for them. He was checking to see if Briar had texted. He knew it was probably too soon for her to know one way or another if she was pregnant, but it had been almost a week since he saw her, and he couldn't get her out of his head. He told himself it was because he'd screwed up and neglected to use a condom, but he knew that wasn't it. That wasn't the only reason. He couldn't stop thinking about *her*. How she felt against him. How she tasted. One night together hadn't purged her from his system. It only made him want her again.

Loose gravel skidded beneath his boots as he came to a hard stop at the sight of his truck. It was the same truck he owned before he went in. He'd saved up a lot of summers for it. It wasn't in the best shape, but it ran smooth, and it definitely looked better before he went in to work tonight. A couple of the windows were crashed in and it looked like someone took a baseball bat to the body of the truck.

They'd also written in red spray paint across his door. *KILLER*.

"Shit." He exhaled a heavy breath. His aunt had mentioned that a couple of guys stopped by Roscoe's asking for him. She suggested that they might be old friends, but he knew better. He didn't have any friends left. He hadn't kept in touch with anyone while he was inside.

They were probably friends of Mason Leary. The guy he killed. He'd had friends. Family. People who refused to believe that Mason was a brutal rapist. They would care if Knox was out. They would take exception to the fact that he was free to walk the streets. They'd do this to his truck. And maybe it was their right. He'd taken someone from them, after all. Leary might have destroyed Katie and deserved a cold grave . . . but that didn't mean other people weren't hurt over losing him. Knox was responsible for that.

Opening the door, he brushed the glass off his seat and climbed in. Starting the engine, he pulled out of Roscoe's parking lot and headed down the street, the word *KILLER* emblazoned across his door.

He clenched his hands around the steering wheel and tried not to let it bother him, tried not to let the sour taste suffusing his mouth spread and sink its teeth into him. Every muscle in his body tightened, squeezing hard, rejecting this even if he knew it to be the truth. It had never mattered in prison if he was a killer. Everyone was guilty of something there.

But out here it did matter. It mattered that he wasn't decent or respectable. No one would ever look at him and see anyone worth a damn. As far as the world was concerned, he was better off in prison. Out here he was just a fucking waste of space.

KNOX DIDN'T CALL HER. Well, other than his initial text giving her his contact information. Briar couldn't bring herself to call him even though he was all she thought about. She had no reason to call him. It had only been six days since they were together. He'd asked her to let him know whether she was pregnant or not, but she wouldn't know for certain this soon. She could have bought a home pregnancy kit—or even tested herself at work—but it just seemed too soon to yield accurate results. Not to mention she didn't want to attract anyone's attention at the clinic. The last thing she wanted was to start tongues wagging around the water cooler.

Plus, she refused to believe it was possible. The odds were slim. She clung to that.

She stepped out of the shower and didn't even bother with a towel, simply folded herself into her terry-cloth robe. The sound of the TV carried from the living room, a low rumble on the air. A side effect of living alone. Even when she wasn't watching TV it was always on, so that the silence never got to be too much.

She stood in front of her bathroom mirror and spritzed her hair with the necessary detangler. Breathing in the familiar aroma of pears, she set about brushing out the wet snarls. She almost didn't hear the knock—at first thinking it was just the TV. She paused mid-stroke and stuck her head out of the bathroom.

The rap came again and she moved forward, her bare feet padding over the carpet. She peered out of the door's peephole and gasped. The sight of Knox on the other side hit her like a punch to the chest. He propped one arm against the door frame and seemed to be staring right back at her.

She stepped back with a gasp. Running a hand over her wet hair, she gulped down a nervous breath and unlocked the door.

"Hi," she said, gratified that she managed an even voice.

His gaze traveled over her, not missing the fact that she stood in front of him in a bathrobe. Maybe she should have taken a minute to get dressed. *Maybe she shouldn't have answered the door.* Unease dripped through her. This couldn't be healthy. A guy like him wasn't going to give her the things she needed. *Well, aside from orgasms. She needed those. She loved those.*

She gave herself a swift mental kick. A relationship was out of the question. He might have proven that he possessed a code . . . that he possessed honor enough to save her life, but he was still a dangerous man. Briar didn't need a doctorate in psychology to know he had his demons. Eight years in prison, who wouldn't? He was unpredictable, damaged, and she needed to steer clear of him. She should just end it now and close the door.

She shifted her weight.

"Hey," he returned. "Can I come in?"

There was something in his voice that she hadn't heard before, and she thought she had seen him in every incarnation. Scary inmate. Fierce protector. Hungry lover. Apparently there were more layers to him.

Several moments passed and she blinked, realizing she hadn't replied yet. She just stood in her doorway, uncertain what to do, staring at him like she didn't know him. And she didn't.

With a shaky breath, she stepped aside. He strode past her.

She shut the door and locked it. Tightening the belt at her waist, satisfied that it was still in place, she turned, determined to keep her head. Determined to tell him that he couldn't just drop in unannounced. That despite what happened the last time she saw him, she wasn't just going to drop everything and roll over for him like some kind of—

She didn't get a word out. He grasped the lapels of her robe and hauled her against him. She managed a squeak before his mouth claimed hers. And just like that she was on fire. She stood on her tiptoes, trying to keep up as he devoured her, forcing her lips open. His tongue slicked over hers as his hands slid inside her robe, rough palms gliding over her flesh to splay over her back.

He broke away and spoke against her mouth, his forehead pressed to hers as he inhaled a ragged breath. "I don't even know why I'm here. One minute I was headed home and the next thing I know I'm at your door." His hot gaze roamed over her features and he shook his head with a sound of disgust. "Fuck. Yeah, I do know." His hand slid from her back and dove between her legs. She gasped as he touched her there. Mortification burned through her. She was already wet for him. He pushed a finger up inside her and she gasped, grabbing onto his shoulders for leverage. "I'm here for this. You okay with that?"

Her chest squeezed, all the air trapped inside at his declaration. He was asking her if this was okay. Sex. Fucking with no promises. In his rough way, that's what he was doing.

She opened her mouth, ready to tell him to stop. Ready to explain that she wasn't the kind of girl who did this sort of thing. Not with a guy like him. Her brain shouted at her to be careful, to use her head and stop letting her body rule her.

He pushed even deeper inside her, his finger curling and massaging that spot she had never known existed before him and she saw spots. The elusive G-spot. Not so elusive anymore.

She gave a strangled sound of assent and nodded wildly, her legs starting to shake and buckle as an orgasm welled up on her. Just like that. He knew what to do, how to play her.

"God, yes," she sobbed.

"Good," he growled. Then his mouth was on hers again. He wrapped an arm around her and lifted her off her feet, hugging her to him. He broke off kissing her to bury his face in her hair. For a moment he held her like that, his body locked tightly against her own, his face buried in her neck, in all her damp free-flowing hair, as his hand still worked between her legs. Rubbing. Stroking, Pushing and pulling until she shattered, came apart, shuddering and boneless.

He pressed a kiss into her hair as his fingers slipped out from her. Tenderness washed through her. She smoothed a hand over his dark cropped hair. "Knox," she whispered, her voice cracking a little, unsure at this side to him.

He lifted his head, and she recognized the stark look in his gaze. The hunger. Still holding her, he started walking, and she nodded as though convincing herself that this was okay just one more time. She still felt shaky inside. Shaky but certain that she wanted him, too.

He carried her into her bedroom and set her down on the bed, pushing her robe off her shoulders so it spread wide beneath her.

Using her elbows, Briar crawled back on the bed. He came over her, his gaze hungry as he examined her like he was committing her to memory. He made her feel beautiful. She'd never had that with another guy. Beau had suggested on more than one occasion that she needed to lose a few pounds.

Knox touched her, skimming a palm down her body, between the valley of her breasts and down the center of her stomach. He palmed her sex like he owned it—owned her—and she arched up with a gasp.

He crouched between her thighs, using his big shoulders to push her legs wide apart for him.

"Knox," she cried out, clutching his skull as his head dipped. His mouth latched onto her and she bucked at the pressure of his lips, the swipe of his tongue along her wet seam. No one had gone down on her before. It wasn't Beau's thing. He had been interested in only receiving.

Knox made a low, satisfied sound, animal-like, and settled in deeper, one hand splayed wide on the inside of each thigh as he lapped at her like she was a feast to be savored. His mouth found her clit and pulled it between his lips, flaying it with his tongue. Each stroke made her buck and cry out.

He pressed a hand on her abdomen and pushed

her down on to the mattress, stopping her from rearing up on the bed. She moaned, all kinds of embarrassing sounds escaping her lips, but she didn't care. In that moment there was only feeling, sensation, Knox's mouth on her sex, his finger plunging inside and hitting that spot until she screamed her release a second time.

Suddenly he was over her, hands braced flat on either side of her head, drinking those sounds of her orgasm from her lips. He kissed her hard and wild and that only got her hotter. She needed him inside her.

She held his face, her palms rasping against his bristly cheeks. "You have entirely too many clothes on," she panted.

He flashed her a grin that made her belly somersault, and then he was reaching behind his head and pulling his shirt off with one move, tossing it aside and revealing that beautiful chest that looked like it was honed on a battlefield. She sat up, running her hand over his smooth skin, tracing the fierce-looking dragon.

"When did you get this?"

"Right before I went to prison. My brother and I both got one the night before we went in. We might have been drinking." A corner of his mouth kicked up. "We picked a dragon since it could fly." He glanced down, watching her fingers trace one of the dark sharp lines that sat on a hard ridge of flesh. "Like it would be a part of us that was always free."

"You're free now," she whispered.

A cloud passed over his face. "Yeah, only sometimes it doesn't feel like it. Sometimes it feels like I'm still in there . . . stuck behind bars."

She frowned. "What do you mean?"

He shook his head and undid the snap of his jeans, clearly not in the mood to say any more. Shoving them down, he distracted her with his nudity. His manhood sprang free, large and hard, curving toward her as though seeking home. He pulled a condom from his discarded jeans and climbed back between her thighs. "Nothing," he muttered, his mouth claiming hers again.

He kissed her until she forgot the question. Until she was hot and aching and arching under him again.

"Knox," she pleaded.

"Say it," he ordered, his eyes gleaming darkly, like a beast emerging from the woods. He rubbed himself against her folds, teasing her, taunting her as his big body hummed, all coiling tension and checked brutality hovering over hers.

She twisted under him, her head tossing on the bed. She thrust her hips up to take him but he still continued to torment her. Fisting his cock, he rubbed harder against her without penetrating.

She was practically sobbing. "I need . . ."

"What?" he demanded, his features harsh but no less beautiful.

"You—"

"What do you want me to do to you, Briar?" Now he was nudging against her opening, giving her just a little of his engorged head.

"Fuck me," she begged in a strangled voice.

The words hardly made it out before he was slamming into her, so big inside her that she gasped, nails scoring deep in his back. He pulled out nearly all the way and shoved in again, harder, pushing her up the bed from the force of his movement. She squeaked and clung to him. He paused for a moment, clearly letting her catch her breath.

He took longer than she liked and she wiggled under him, swallowing her breath and working her hips, a plaintive little mewl escaping her. She leaned up and bit his chest lightly, pumping her hips under him.

"That's it, Briar," he encouraged. "*You* fuck me."

In a move that stole her breath, he flipped over so that she was astride him. Without ever dislodging himself from inside her, he anchored her atop him, his big hands fastened on her hips.

It was a new position. She floundered for a moment, feeling awkward and not quite knowing what to do.

"I—I don't . . ." she stammered, her hands coming down to flatten on his chest.

"Just ride me," he instructed. "Fuck me however you want. I want to watch you . . . touch you." His hands came up to claim her breasts, his strong fingers playing over her sensitive nipples.

"Ohh." It was like his hands had a direct link to the magic happening between her legs. She threw back her head as her sex throbbed and squeezed around him, buried inside her.

He groaned. "That's it. See. Your body is milking me tight . . . it knows what it likes. Now ride my cock." Her face burned at his blunt speech even as another part of her thrilled. She pressed down on his chest and lifted herself up, then came down once, grinding on him in the down stroke. Sparks of sensation shot through her, all springing from her core.

She moaned, repeating the move, leaning her hips forward and finding her angle, crying out as her clit ground down against him. She started to shake, her movements becoming wild and frenzied.

"That's it, baby," he panted, clenching handfuls of her ass as she worked over him. "Come apart for me. I want to feel you come." He aided her rhythm, his fingers digging into her and slamming her down harder every time she dropped down on his cock.

She shook her head, her hair tangling at her mouth. She clawed the strands away. "I—I can't—"

He reached between them and found her swollen clit. He pinched and rolled it while sitting up under her. Her legs wrapped around him as he looped an arm around her waist and surged up inside her in a single stroke that made her bounce deep on him. Everything inside her released then, bursting apart and erupting into a million tiny pieces. She flew apart at the seams, bits of herself she felt certain would never come together in quite the same way again.

His bright eyes clashed with her. With him sitting up and her astride him, they were at eye level. The position might have been the most intimate they had shared yet. "Don't ever say you can't come." His eyes drilled into her. "You'll come every time with me."

She nodded mutely, her body practically limp as he continued to thrust inside her. He wasn't done with her. His hands locked squarely on her waist and he lifted her like she weighed nothing at all, forcing her to finish out riding him. His pulsing length stroked against her newly sensitized and quivering walls. She was soon gasping again, her fingers clawing into his shoulders. "Oh, oh, oh . . . God . . ."

"Again," he commanded, his face stark and beautiful as his own orgasm came over him. He pushed up into her and she shattered, coming in waves as he growled his own release in her ear.

She collapsed against him, her arms draped over his shoulders. They both breathed raggedly against each other for a few moments before he disengaged from her body and rose to dispose of the condom.

When he returned, she almost expected him to say good-bye. After last time, she knew he felt guilty for waking up in the middle of the night and taking her without using a condom. She doubted he would fall asleep beside her again.

But he didn't leave. He turned out the lights, slid into bed beside her and pulled her into his arms. She sighed against the warm solidness of his body, thinking she could get accustomed to this. Which was a scary thought. He wasn't exactly the kind of guy a girl attached herself to. He wasn't the settling down type. Just the idea of introducing him to her sister made her feel slightly ill.

She mentally shook herself. No one was talking forever here. Certainly not him. He hadn't even reached out to her since the last time they hooked up. No call. No text. And that's all this was. Knox showing up at her doorstep for a hook-up. Sex.

She fell asleep in his arms, only to have him wake her up twice more with deep-mouthed kisses. Once to her lips and another time she woke to find him tonguing her sex, bringing her to hair-clutching, shuddering release before he pushed himself deep inside her, wedging his thickness inside the aching walls of her channel, working her into such a state that one of the neighbors below pounded the ceiling for them to shut up. Briar Davis, sex goddess. Who knew she had it in her?

Knox was never so overcome that he forgot to put on a condom again. He was controlled yet driven, relentless as he took her with such rawness, such need. She was sore by the third time he made love to her just before dawn, but she couldn't deny herself or him.

Every time they came together, something unraveled inside her. Each time with him was better than the one before and it scared her shitless. A real problem, considering she had long ago promised herself to never live a life of fear again.

All those reasons why they couldn't be together, why it was wrong for her to take a man like him into her body . . . into her life . . . faded to murky shadow. Something to be examined later. Reality was for later.

By the time she woke, sunlight was pouring through her blinds. She was definitely going to be late for work. But she didn't care. The only thing that mattered to her in that moment was that he had left her. Again, without a word. He was gone.

SIXTEEN

"**So you're still** holding down your job?" Polansky asked as he pushed his glasses up his nose and walked down the porch steps into the sun-baked yard. He glanced back at Knox with an arched eyebrow, almost like he expected him to admit that he'd quit. Or been fired.

Knox held back his snort. It was his family's business. Did Polansky think his family was going to fire him? Instead, he nodded and murmured assent. He never volunteered more than asked to his parole officer. This was Polanksy's second visit to the house. Such visits were routine, to check out his living conditions and make sure Knox wasn't running a meth lab. He didn't have a history of drug-related offenses, but Polansky always surveyed his house as though he expected to find a cook pot. He insisted on checking the basement, too. Maybe he thought Knox might have a few people chained down there.

He paused at the door of his nondescript sedan and nodded at Knox's motorcycle. "New hobby?"

The shiny chrome beast was parked on a tarp with several tools littering the area around it. He'd been working on it when Polansky made his unannounced visit. Knox had saved up and bought it his last year of high school. He'd been in the process of restoring it when everything had happened with Katie. It felt good to get his hands back on it. It felt familiar and right.

Knox shrugged. "I enjoy working on it."

"Hope you're not considering joining an MC gang . . . that could have consequences on your parole."

A bitter sigh welled up in him. "I'm not joining any gang." He'd done what he had to do while in the box, but he wasn't looking to connect with any local gangs. Just because he was friendly with a few of their members didn't mean he was one of them.

Polansky crossed his arms in front of him. "Several gangs frequent Roscoe's . . . I had my reservations about you working there but set them aside because it's a family business and your family has always been law-abiding citizens despite owning such an unsavory establishment."

Knox stared coldly at the man, wiping his hands on a rag. It didn't matter. The grease didn't seem to want to come off. "I haven't broken any laws since I got out and I don't intend to."

"Yes, well, we'll see. Won't we, Mr. Callaghan?

One misstep, one infraction of your parole . . ." He thumbed the air behind him for emphasis. ". . . and you're headed right back to Devil's Rock."

Knox nodded once, not trusting himself to speak. This guy with his unsubtle threats pissed him off. It reminded him that he wasn't really free. Not fully. Maybe he never would be. Not as long as this asshole kept popping in to criticize him anyway. He couldn't even work on his fucking bike in peace. Polansky ducked inside his car.

Fuming, Knox fixed his expression into an impassive mask as his parole officer drove away. Turning, he started toward his bike to continue where he'd left off, but stopped with a glance down at his dirty hands. They were shaking. With a curse, he stormed up the steps. The contentment he had found working on his bike was gone.

A restless anger prowled loose inside him. He felt close to exploding.

Uncle Mac called out to him from his chair, where he was watching *Wheel of Fortune*, "Everything go okay with the visit?"

"Everything's great," he lied.

His mood was dangerous. He wasn't fit company. He should go for a run and work off some energy. Except he didn't feel like running. He had another activity in mind. Activity that involved losing himself in soft eyes and wild caramel hair.

He'd left Briar's apartment two mornings ago and hadn't seen her since. He knew he'd hear from her eventually. She'd have to let him know if she was pregnant. She would do that. She wouldn't keep him in the dark. She was too honest, too good, not to let him know one way or another.

In the meantime, until the matter was resolved he could see her. Be with her. As long as she was willing, he wasn't going to deny himself.

Oh, he knew she had her doubts. When she had opened the door for him last time, he read the wariness in her eyes, but he'd sent those reservations running. Kissing her and sinking his fingers into her heat, giving her the orgasm she so badly needed.

And that was the truth of it. She needed what he could give her just as much as he needed to give it. And he planned on giving it to her until he had his fill.

AFTER WORK, BRIAR parked her car and stared at her building in the early evening sunlight. She could see her balcony from where she sat. The aloe vera plant on the balcony looked a little wilted. She made a mental note to give it water. Tapping the steering wheel anxiously, she debated whether to go inside or keep driving. She didn't have a destination in mine, but she could come up with something else to do.

Going inside, where she would only have silent

walls for company, didn't appeal to her. Even with the
TV on that was a lot of time alone with her thoughts.

Knox hadn't come over since two nights ago, and
she told herself she didn't want him to. She stopped
herself from texting him or calling him. That would
send out the wrong message. The only time she in-
tended to text him was when she knew for a fact that
she wasn't pregnant. She'd be strong until then. She'd
start listening to the alarm bells in her head and not
give in to the urge to reach out to him.

Deciding she couldn't hide from her own home—
she wasn't that pathetic—she stepped out of her car,
slamming the door after her. She winced at the sight
of her dirt-coated hood. It needed a good washing.

Seized with sudden inspiration, she hurried inside
and changed out of her scrubs into a pair of wind
shorts and a T-shirt. She collected a sponge, soap,
and some old towels and headed back outside.

Hopping back inside her car, she drove past the
gas station where she had run into Knox. She shook
off the memory of him and Cherry Garcia ice cream.
She'd never be able to eat it again without thinking
of him. Unfortunate. She'd have to find a new flavor.

A few blocks past the gas station she pulled into
an old outdoor do-it-yourself car wash. Growing
up, Dad had bought both her and Laurel cars when
they turned sixteen. It was part of his image. Giving
so generously to his family. His daughters were an

extension of himself, and they had to appear better than the average teenage girl rolling into the parking lot of Polk High School.

In reality, the cars were just one more thing he would shout at them about. They didn't drive them properly. Didn't park in the driveway correctly. He insisted, of course, that she and Laurel keep their cars spotless. God forbid if the inside was a mess. She knew how to wash a car so that it passed her father's eagle-eyed inspection.

She fished out enough spare change for ten minutes of water—just for starters. Water was a precious commodity out here in the badlands. She tried to preserve when she could.

Once the car was soaked, she began soaping it with the sponge, humming under her breath. She didn't mind getting wet. It kept her cool. Even at five o'clock it was still warm.

She paused and tried to shove several strands that had fallen loose back into the bun on the top of her head. Then she bent back over her car, standing on her tiptoes in her flip-flops so she could reach as much of the roof as possible.

A car honked driving past, the guys inside catcalling her. She sent a glance over her shoulder, satisfying herself that they weren't stopping.

"What the hell are you doing?"

She yelped and whirled around, her back slamming into her wet car as she gawked at a very pissed-looking Knox in front of her. She forgot that she held the hose in her hand. Water sprayed down the front of his big body. His hands came up to ward off the water.

She lowered the hose. "What are you doing here?"

He looked down at himself, his dark eyebrows drawing tight. "Getting soaked, apparently."

Her gaze followed his stare to his soaking wet shirt. It was plastered to his chest. She swallowed a suddenly dry throat, tracking the outline of every delicious muscled ridge and indentation.

"You startled me," she accused just as her water slowed to a weak drizzle and shut off, her ten minutes at an end.

"I was driving by and spotted you. Hard not to when you're sticking your ass out for every passing car to ogle." His gaze dropped to her chest and his eyes darkened to slate.

Her gaze dipped and heat scalded her face at the sight of her breasts. Her nipples poked through her bra and T-shirt. She hunched her shoulders self-consciously. Pointless, she supposed. He'd seen, tasted, and touched all of her.

"I—I'm washing my car." She glanced out at the road. "Were you just driving by or . . ." She couldn't finish the question. *Was he coming to see her?* presumed too much.

"Something like that," he murmured, dragging a hand down his dripping face. He turned and dug into his pocket. Pulling out more change, he turned and fed it to the ancient machine, adding more time.

He faced her. A muscle worked in his cheek, feathering his bristly skin there. "The sooner we finish, the sooner every jackhole that drives past won't drool over you like some piece of meat." He picked up the soapy sponge and easily reached the roof of the car, covering all the areas that she could not reach. She watched, frozen for a moment as he washed her car. *He cared that jackholes drooled over her?* Even though she thought that an exaggeration, pleasure suffused her chest.

He glanced back at her. "Come on. Water is running. Wash off the soap."

She blinked out of her daze and proceeded to rinse the soap off the gleaming hood. She followed in his wake, spraying off all the suds, her gaze repeatedly straying to him. She couldn't help herself. She tracked the way his muscled body stretched and worked, walking purposefully around her car. The water finally stopped and she hooked the hose back into place. Opening her car door, she reached inside and tossed him one of the towels she'd brought. Grabbing the other one, she started rubbing her car dry.

"You know there are car washes where people do this for you?" he asked.

She grinned at him over the hood of the car. "I didn't think you were the kind of guy to pay someone else to wash your car."

"I'm not. But I thought you were."

Briar worked her towel in fierce circles, fighting a grin. "You don't know everything about me."

"So I'm learning."

Something warm unfurled in her chest at his deep voice. Did that mean he wanted to? *No, no, no, no.* She killed that thought and her budding smile. She couldn't get her hopes up about this guy. Not him. He wasn't anyone she could bring to Thanksgiving dinner. She couldn't forget that fact.

"For example," he added, "are you a pepperoni kind of girl? Or do you like the works?"

She paused and blinked at him over the car. He didn't even look up as he worked to dry the rear window. "What do you mean?"

"Pizza," he elaborated, flicking her a glance that was faintly amused.

"Oh." Was he leading up to asking her out to dinner? "Who said I like pizza at all?" she hedged, her mind working feverishly. Did she want to go out with him? When she was so desperately fighting for distance?

"It's un-American not to like pizza. Of course you do." He crouched to dry her front fender without even looking up at her. Her breath caught as she watched the way the back of his T-shirt hugged his flexing shoulders and back.

"I like everything on my pizza," she admitted. "The works."

He straightened. "Good. Me, too." He stepped back and surveyed the car, making sure it was dry before looking at her again. "Think it's all dry now."

She spared a cursory glance for the car, nodding. "Yeah. Thanks for the help."

"So how about that pizza?" Knox scanned her, his eyes stopping on her breasts. Her nipples reacted, hardening beneath his perusal. She pulled at her damp shirt self-consciously and pressed her legs together against the sudden clenching ache. "Maybe we should order in," he suggested.

As in order pizza at her place? Where they would be alone? This had BAD IDEA written all over it. Would they actually eat? They only ever seemed to do one thing when they were alone together, and for the life of her she couldn't think very clearly on why that wasn't what she wanted.

She cleared her throat. "Uh—"

"Have you eaten yet?" he asked.

"No."

"Well, you gotta eat. Let's go." Decision made, he turned and strode to a motorcycle parked a few yards away that she hadn't noticed before. He straddled the big machine. His big body on top of that beast of shiny chrome and metal made her girl parts melt and quiver. She watched him for a moment, her resistance dissolving to dust.

Nodding dumbly, she climbed into the driver's seat of her car. Her gaze flicked several times to the rearview mirror, watching as he followed her to her condo and doing her best to ignore the fluttering in her stomach. She sucked in a calming breath, convincing herself that this was just pizza. If that's all she wanted, then that's all it would be. It didn't have to be like last time. No one had to get naked.

She parked and got out as he pulled in beside her, shutting off the bike's loud engine and swinging off his bike. They walked up the steps to her condo, his steps a heavy thud that matched her pulse. *This was just dinner. This was just dinner.* Maybe she should establish that once they got inside.

Unlocking the door to her apartment, she stepped into the welcoming blast of air-conditioning and dropped her keys on the counter. She moved into the kitchen, plucked her favorite pizza place menu off the refrigerator and called in, staring conveniently at the menu in her hand, not looking up at the man who seemed to make everything inside the apartment smaller. The air felt thicker as she ordered. When she hung up, she turned and gasped to find him right in front of her. She inhaled and smelled the damp heat of his skin. "They said thirty minutes."

He nodded, still staring at her in that devouring way of his. She swallowed and stepped around him, escaping the narrow space of her kitchen. Walking backward, he still followed, looking all at once leisurely and predatory.

She gestured toward her bedroom. "I—I'm going to take a quick shower before the food gets here."

She'd backed away as much as she could, finally stopping when she came in contact with the wall and could go no farther. He stopped a few inches in front of her and her hand shot out, flattening against his chest. She resisted the instinct to curl her fingers against the shirt perfectly molded to him. To feel his skin. The thud of his heart.

He glanced down at her hand and back up to her face, one dark eyebrow arched.

"We can't," she breathed.

"We already have," he countered, his tone even and reasonable and so deeply tempting it sent a shiver down her spine. "Several times."

"It doesn't mean we should. Again." Was that strangled voice her own? It sounded pathetic even to her ears. Hardly convincing.

He angled his head, something glinting in his eyes. He stepped forward until his chest pushed against her breasts and all the air left her in a rush.

"And why shouldn't we? Again?"

His question rattled around in her mind like a marble flying through a pinball machine. Why? *Why?* She was having trouble coming up with a coherent answer. She'd possessed reasons enough earlier, but she just couldn't think of a single one anymore. And that's pretty much how it was around him. Briar ceased to think.

"It just complicates things, blurs l-lines . . . boundaries." *Sweet Jesus.* She was rambling.

A dark shutter fell over the blue of his eyes. "Suddenly so concerned with slumming it? No one has to know, Nurse Davis. I promise I'll keep your dirty little secret between us."

"It's not like that at all," she hotly denied.

"Isn't it?" He shrugged. "I'm okay with that. It's actually not complicated. It's called fucking. That's what we're doing here."

She gasped and she didn't know why. She should expect bold language from him by now. She knew he was all rough edges. Nothing soft or malleable to him.

His mouth grazed her ear. "So I say let's get this out of our systems." The back of his hand trailed down her front, brushing over her aching breast. She whimpered as his hand continued its descent.

His voice continued, too, languid and deep as warm honey rolling through her. "We can keep scratching that itch of yours." His blunt-tipped fingers slid under the elastic waistband of her wind shorts, under the thin fabric of her panties and straight between her legs.

Knox palmed her, flexing his hand over her sex like he owned it. And she supposed he did. One touch and she was putty, completely at his mercy.

He bit down on her ear, and her knees threatened to buckle. They would have if not for his grip between her legs. "You know the itch I'm talking about. Back at the Rock, you wanted it from me then, too." He stroked the wet seam between her legs, back and forth, back and forth, exerting a little more pressure with each sweeping pass of his fingers. "Every time you opened your mouth, every time you looked at me, *this* was between us. It was only a matter of time."

Embarrassing little sounds escaped her. Noisy pants and choked gasps. She sealed her lips into a tight line and brought her hands up to his shoulders.

"Even though you couldn't admit it, not even to yourself, you wanted me to give you this then." He brushed her clit with the pad of his thumb and she cried out like someone lit fire to her flesh. "And you want it now."

He followed the statement by easing his finger deep inside her. He curled inward, hitting that happy spot that she had thought nonexistent before him. She came apart, shaking all around him as a keening hum built in the back of her throat.

She bit her lip until she tasted the copper of blood. The slight pain didn't even bother her. She welcomed it. Just another layer to the sensations overrunning her, waking her up all over again.

Her head fell back against the wall, lolling from side to side. She blinked, trying to clear the cloudy haze from her eyes. A swift breeze slid over her legs and she was vaguely aware that her shorts and underwear were at her ankles. A faint crinkle of a condom wrapper followed and then her feet lifted off the floor, her back sliding against the wall.

She looked down, met his dark-rimmed blue eyes just as he shoved up inside her, his hardness filling her so completely her lips broke apart on a moan.

He held himself still inside her, hands cupping her ass. Pinned between his big body and the wall, she inhaled deeply, her chest lifting as she tried to catch her breath. An impossibility. She felt swallowed up. Surrounded and invaded by every part of him. There was no separating her from him. Him from her. His gaze fixed on her, holding her hostage.

She swallowed, searching for her voice, desperate for him to move, to sweep her back to that place where she flew out of her body. Left her flesh and skin and bones behind. He pulsed inside her, his cock buried deep. She gulped for air, swallowing hard, fighting against the impulse to pant and make more embarrassing sounds.

She stretched high against him, her hands clutching the taut curve of his shoulders as she tried to move her hips, but it was useless. He had her trapped between him and the wall.

"Still say we can't do this?" he challenged, holding himself agonizingly motionless.

She writhed, desperate to move. To fuck. And the glint in his eyes told her he knew that. He was playing with her, using her desire against her.

She whimpered, hating how easily her body turned on her. Hating herself for being so weak. Her face flushed hot. She nodded drunkenly. "Yes! We can, okay!"

"Can what?" His voice flayed like a whip. The laser focus of his eyes cut deep into her, striking bone. "Say it, Briar."

"We can . . . we can fuck."

He cocked his head to the side as if to say *not good enough*. He gave the barest pump of his hips, but that drag of their skin together shot sensation to every nerve in her body. "You sure?"

"Damn it, yes," she hissed, her nails digging into him as she strained to lift up and ride him.

It was what he had been waiting for. Her unflinching consent. Her total surrender.

"Remember that," he growled, his fingers flexing on her ass. "Then we won't have to have this conversation again."

She nodded, even knowing some of her should bristle at the command in his voice, at his total domination of her, but in that moment she didn't care. She wanted to be dominated by him.

He pulled out and thrust back inside her, finally unleashing himself, giving her what she wanted. What she needed. And he didn't stop. Filling her, pushing and pulling, rocking against her. She slid up and down the wall from the force of his thrusts.

"OhGodOhGodOhGod," she sobbed, wrapping her arms around his shoulders, clutching him tightly and burying her face in his neck.

His breathing grew shallow against her ear. The harsh rasp turned her skin to goose flesh. He slowed and she moaned her frustration, turning her face and biting into the side of his neck. "Don't stop," she choked against his heated skin.

"Oh, I'm not stopping, baby. Not yet. Remember what I told you." He increased his pace then like he was determined to get her off. "You'll come for me. Every time." Her orgasm hit hard as the deep rumble of his words sank into her. Her thighs squeezed tight around him as she rode out her orgasm. He moved inside her several more times, harder, faster against her oversensitized flesh.

He grunted and sighed, reaching his own release. She ducked her head, breathing in his skin, reveling in the sensation of him twitching inside her. She smoothed her hands down his biceps as her heavy breaths evened out.

A knock sounded at her door.

She lifted her head. Her stare collided with his waiting gaze. "Pizza," she murmured.

"Yeah." He stepped back, withdrawing from her. "I'll get it."

She slid down to her feet, her legs wobbly. Knox turned and got rid of the condom in the kitchen before stepping back out, zipping his jeans back up.

Averting her gaze, she snatched up her shorts and underwear. "Let me just get some cash—"

"I got it," he said, a slight edge to his voice, which stopped her from reaching for her purse. "A pizza's not going to break me."

Heat crawled up her face. She'd offended him. His face flushed as he dug out his wallet from his back pocket. Nodding, she dove into her room. Closeted in her bathroom, she stripped off her clothes and stepped into the shower. Standing under the showerhead, she let the water beat down on her.

She filled her palms with shower gel and lathered her body, but it didn't matter. No amount of soap could ever erase the memory of him from her body. She would still feel him. She would always feel him. She didn't want to stop feeling him.

So much for thinking she could resist him. She couldn't deny it anymore. She wouldn't even try.

SEVENTEEN

THE NEXT FEW days passed in a blur of mind-numbing sex. Knox showed up at her place every day. Depending on his work schedule, sometimes he was waiting for her when she got off work. Other times he showed up late. Either way, it didn't matter. She always opened her door to him and they always ended up in bed. Well, if they made it that far. Sometimes they got as far as her living room couch. Once they didn't even make it past her small foyer area. She only managed to close the door before they went at it.

She never had this before. To be sure, she was no experienced lover. Her ex had told her that when it came to sex she was lacking. At least that was Beau's excuse when she caught him with another girl their sophomore year of college. She didn't have what it took to please a guy but apparently Kylie-Marie three rooms down the hall did. With Knox, though, she forgot all about that. Her insecurities flew out the window. He made her feel skilled. Powerful. Irresistible. It was going to be hard to let this all go.

Even though a voice continued to whisper in the back of her mind that this was a bad idea, she couldn't put a stop to any of it.

"What were you like? Before?" she asked, sprawled on top of Knox after round two of the night, her ear pressed directly over his heart where it beat a strong rhythm in his chest.

His hand stilled on her back, where he had idly been tracing small patterns. "Doesn't matter. That's in the past."

She bit her lip and darted a glance up at his face. He stared stoically through the gloom to the ceiling as though something of great interest was etched into the plaster.

"I'll tell you something about me," she coaxed. Only in that second did she realize he probably didn't care to know anything personal about her. Past or present. He might not care about her at all. Not beyond this. Not beyond their physical relationship. Fucking, he said. That's what this was.

"You don't have to do that." Translation? Don't share.

That only seemed to confirm her suspicion. An awkward silence fell between them. She held still, sprawled stiffly over him, and tried not to feel all kinds of awkward.

His chest lifted with a sigh under her. "I played football in high school. I was pretty good."

She absorbed that for a moment, a smile creasing her face at the small admission. *Pretty good.* She bet he was better than good. He was amazingly fit at twenty-eight years old. What had he been like in high school?

"I played in college—"

"You went to college?" she asked abruptly.

"Is that such a surprise? I had a full ride at A&M. Went for my first year. I was home for the summer when I got arrested."

"I guess I never saw you as someone . . ." Her voice faded and she felt him tense under her.

"Someone with a brain?" he finished. "Someone with ambition?" Briar cringed. God, she had sounded like that. She opened her mouth to apologize, but he continued. "It's a shock, I know. I didn't grow up with dreams of going to prison. I actually wanted to be someone once." He moved then, sliding out from under her and leaving the bed.

"Knox, I'm sorry—"

"No need," he said, but his tone was hard, biting. He was gone from her already. "I gotta go."

"You could still finish. Get your degree," she hurriedly suggested, clutching the sheet to her chest and watching as he dressed in the near dark of her room.

He stopped and stared at her with his hands frozen

on his fly. "Would that make you feel better?" He motioned to the bed. "About this?"

"No!" She shook her head. "I'm just thinking of you."

"Well, don't. Things can't be undone. And I can't go back." He pulled his shirt over his head and nodded at her on the bed. "And don't feel bad about this. It's just sex. Nothing to feel ashamed about."

"I'm not ashamed—" she denied, but he was already walking out of her room.

She heard the door click behind him. With a strangled cry, she fell back on the bed, staring helplessly into the dark. Could she have done a better job of inserting her foot in her mouth?

She tried to go back to sleep, but it was useless. After a few hours of tossing and turning, she got up to take a shower and get ready for work. Reaching inside her shower, she turned on the water, waiting for it to reach the desired warmth. While waiting, she used the restroom . . . where she faced the irrefutable fact that there was no possible way she was pregnant with Knox's baby.

SHE WASN'T PREGNANT.

Elation should have been her reaction—the *proper* reaction. She wanted children one day, but in the natural order. With a man who wanted children with *her.* Preferably after love and wedding vows and a mortgage.

Yes, elation would have been natural, welcomed even. Except that she hadn't heard from or seen Knox in two days. Not since she stuck her foot in her mouth and he stormed from her apartment. Maybe he didn't care.

Every time she thought about that possibility, she felt a pang in her chest followed by a swift wash of nausea. She had started to count on seeing him again. *Being* with him. As though crazy-hot sex with Knox would now be a thing—a regular occurrence in her life. He'd lit something deep inside her when he looked at her in that stark way of his and said that he needed her. Even if he was just talking about sex, it had started to mean more to her.

No man, no past boyfriend, had ever claimed that he needed her before. He was in her blood now. She didn't think she could ever go back to being that girl who viewed sex as an obligatory thing you had to do when you were in a relationship . . . a thing that she was *bad* at, according to Beau.

Then she felt awful, ashamed of herself for even thinking that she needed a baby to keep Knox around. As though that was the only way she could keep him.

She had to tell him. Rip off the Band-Aid and get it over with. She had waited two days already, hoping he would show up at her place again. She'd debated exactly how to do it. Call him? Text him?

And what was the protocol on that text message exactly? *No worries! You're free!* Or maybe something along the lines of: *Hey there! Turns out I'm not going to be your Baby Mama.*

By the time she got around to doing it, she simply went with: *I'm not pregnant.*

And then she waited. Although not very long. Instead of a text, he actually called her.

She stared at her ringing phone for a moment in astonishment before answering it.

"Hi," she greeted, hating that she sounded out of breath even though she wasn't doing anything more strenuous than folding towels.

"Hi," he returned, and then a pause fell. She heard muffled music in the background and guessed he was at work. She felt a little better knowing he had made the effort to go to a back room to call her. "You all right?"

She hesitated, not sure how to answer that. Did he expect her to be upset because she wasn't pregnant? It's not like they were hoping for a child. "Of course. I told you there wasn't anything to worry about."

"Yeah. You said that."

Another awkward silence fell. "So how've you been?" She winced. God, she sounded lame. She might as well announce that she missed him. That she hated the way he'd stormed from her apartment like he couldn't stand the sight of her. Her voice rang with neediness even to her ears.

"I've been busy. Working at night and patching things up around my uncle's place. Been gone a long time. Lots of things need fixing."

"Oh. Busy is good." Lame response, take two. "I've been busy, too," she flung out almost desperately. "Flu season is kicking into gear." She'd made more kids cry today than she could count.

He hardly let her finish her last comment before cutting in. "Look, Briar, I better go. People are getting off work and the place is starting to get busy."

She flexed her fingers around her phone. "Yeah. Sure." Other words hovered on her lips, but she bit them back. She didn't want to come across as clingy.

" 'Bye, Briar." His words rang with a finality that she heard clearly over the line. What she heard was *good-bye forever*. "You have a good life. You deserve that."

She sucked in a breath. No mistake about it. This was it. He was dumping her. "Yeah," she said tightly. "You, too."

The phone went dead in her ear. She lowered it in her hand and stared at it for a long moment, wondering at the sudden sting in her eyes.

It wasn't like a real breakup. They'd never declared themselves a *thing*. Besides, maybe she was wrong.

Maybe she would see him again. Maybe he would show up again at her door for another midnight booty call. Yeah, and how long would that satisfy her? Better it ended now. Before she really got hurt. She already felt pretty terrible. She didn't need to feel any worse.

A text beeped on her phone. Her heart jumped, thinking it might be Knox. She flipped her phone over. Nope. Her sister. *BBQ for Caleb this Sunday. You in?*

She typed back. *Yes.*

Good. Boss's son will be here.

Briar blew out a breath, remembering that her sister wanted to set her up with Caleb's boss's son. An accountant, if she remembered correctly. Great. The BBQ was going to be a blind date.

Her fingers flew over the keys. *Please no. Don't make it weird.*

She waited as Laurel texted back. *Can't promise that. That's what big sisters do.*

She snorted. At least she was honest. *Luv you. Night.*

Her sister texted back. *Luv you too.*

Sighing, she carried the towels to her linen closet and put them away, cringing when she thought about her sister's reaction if she knew the main reason she wasn't interested in meeting anyone right now was because she was getting over an infatuation with a hardened felon.

Laurel wouldn't just get weird then. She'd lose her shit.

Fortunately, she would never have to find out. Briar would never tell her about Knox. Because there was no longer anything to tell.

KNOX SLIPPED HIS phone in his back pocket and leaned his head against the outside wall of Roscoe's. He needed to get back inside, but he couldn't imagine facing a room full of carousing drunks just yet. Not after ending that call with Briar.

The phone call had been a shit move on his part. When her text came through, he'd debated whether he should see her in person and explain why they shouldn't continue doing whatever it was they were doing, but then he doubted he would have kept his hands to himself. And he wasn't dick enough to fuck her and then end it with her in the same breath. So he'd called. And he'd ended it. *Them.* Whatever they were, they were done.

He should have fucked her out of his system by now—God knew that's what he had been trying to do—but he wasn't tired of her, and a stab of alarm told him he might never be.

A couple of guys walked up from the parking lot. One locked eyes on Knox and stopped hard before catching back up with his friend. He elbowed him and nodded toward Knox, whispering something indiscreetly. They paused again, eyeing him like he might be something contagious.

Knox tensed, watching from hooded eyes as they resumed walking again, approaching the long stretch of porch where he lurked. He'd gotten enough stares and whispers since he was paroled to know they recognized him. Knew him. *Killer Callaghan*. He'd heard it whispered around Roscoe's ever since he got out. Luckily, most of their clientele wasn't too discerning.

Up on the porch, the two guys shot him several more glances. "Hey," the first guy said, stopping in front of him before going inside. "You, uh . . . are you Knox Callaghan?"

"Who wants to know?" He braced himself, wondering if they were going to give him shit. There were plenty of people in this town that definitely wanted to see him with his face in the dirt. In his current mood, he would gladly take them on.

"Went to school with your brother North. I'm Wayne. Played second string when you were a senior."

Knox considered him for a moment. He vaguely remembered him. The guy had been a sophomore and warmed the bench. Unlike North and Knox, who were starting linemen.

"Yeah. I remember you."

Wayne's chest seemed to deflate a little, as though he wasn't so nervous anymore. As though that admission meant they were suddenly friends. "How's North?"

Knox narrowed his eyes on him. "He's in fucking prison. How do you think he is?"

The guy flinched. Even in the dim light, Knox detected the rush of color in his cheeks. "S-Sorry," he stammered, taking a step back.

"C'mon, Wayne." His friend pulled on his arm, looking at Knox warily, as though he was an animal that might pounce. They hurried back inside and left Knox alone, sulking in the shadows.

Not a minute passed before engines roared on the air. A few bikes pulled into the parking lot, spitting gravel up into the night. He stayed in the shadows as the group of bikers headed for the doors. A big bearded man marched at the center of the group, and Knox felt a jolt of recognition. He knew the man. The biker must have had a similar thought, for his eyes widened beneath the bandanna covering his forehead as his heavy boots stepped up on the wood porch.

"Callaghan, you bastard! That you? When did you get out?"

Knox couldn't help but grin and push off the building. He hadn't seen Blue McClintock in two years. He was part of Reid's crew. He'd been there when he and North arrived at Devil's Rock.

"Got out a few months ago," he said as the two embraced in a quick hug.

"No shit? North out, too?'

His smile slipped and the usual twisting weight returned to his chest whenever he thought about his brother still behind those bars. "No. Not yet."

"Ah, man, that's too bad. Sure he'll be out soon." Blue clapped his shoulder encouragingly. "What are you doing with yourself?"

"Working here now."

Blue nodded. "Well, you look good. Strong as an ox." He clapped his back. "We spend a lot of good money at Roscoe's. Glad to know some of it's going to your pockets." He smiled and nodded to his buddies. "These are some of my boys. They're your friends now, too." His expression turned solemn. "We're still a crew, Callaghan. You need anything, I'm here."

"Appreciate that, Blue."

The biker turned, keeping a hold on Knox and bringing him with him toward the entrance. "Come on now. You can get me a drink on the house. Had a shit day and could use one."

"Yeah, me, too," Knox sighed before he could think about it, but Blue heard.

"You, too, huh?" he proclaimed as they stepped inside Roscoe's. "Don't tell me." Rubbing his chin, he examined Knox. "Women troubles?"

Knox winced and shook his head, but it was too late.

"Of course it's women," Blue blustered. "You're a good-looking sonuvabitch. You've probably had more ass than you can handle since you've been out."

Knox shook his head as he stepped behind the bar. Blue and his friends took up the space in front of him, ordering their beer.

He pulled the bottles from the ice behind him, shaking his head. "Not like that, man."

"Ohhh, shit," Blue said knowingly. "It's worse than that. It's one woman."

He started to deny it but closed his mouth with a snap. Blue wouldn't believe him anyway. Hell, he didn't know if he even believed that himself.

He shook his head. He and Briar were over. Done. A clean break. She wasn't pregnant. He had no reason to continue seeing her. No more showing up in the middle of the night at her place, using her to fill the aching bleakness inside him and then slinking away before morning. She deserved better than that. Better than him.

She and he were worlds apart, and that's how it would always be.

EIGHTEEN

"So HAVE YOU told your sister?" Shelley asked as she carried over the sweating pitcher of homemade margaritas and poured more into Briar's half-full glass.

Briar snorted and brought the frothy concoction to her lips. "The only thing Laurel knows is that I worked one day a week at the state prison and now that's over." That alone displeased her sister. She didn't need to know more. She didn't need to know about the lockdown. She didn't need to know about Knox.

Shelley's dark eyes boggled. "Seriously? You didn't ever tell her about the attack?"

"No."

Shelley plopped down on the couch, tucking her legs under her. Margarita sloshed over the rim of her glass and she licked the green froth from her fingers as she continued to stare wide-eyed at Briar. "So the whole being taken hostage and nearly getting raped by convicts . . ." She fluttered her fingers in the air as she took another sip. "Rescued by a hot-ass convict and then running into the same convict out on parole at the local corner store . . . bringing him back to your place for some hot monkey sex? None of that was worth mentioning?"

Briar lowered her glass from her lips. "God, no. You've met Laurel. Can you imagine? I would never hear the end of it."

Shelly shrugged. "I'm sure if you really drove home how hot he is . . . and that he saved your life, she would have been down with you bringing him back to your place and fucking his brains out."

"Uh. No." Briar tossed a pillow at her friend. "He's a dangerous felon. That's all my sister would see."

"He's a hero," Shelley countered, and Briar frowned, wondering why they were even talking about it. She hadn't talked to Knox since that awkward phone call last week. A phone call that had felt a lot like a breakup. *Worse.* It actually felt worse than the time she walked in on Beau with Kylie-Marie. Except it shouldn't have hurt that much. She and Knox hadn't been in a relationship. It was only sex. He'd made that clear.

She told herself it was for the best. Butterflies in her stomach every time she got within five feet of a dangerous criminal wasn't healthy. No matter how shattering the sex was . . . no matter how, sometimes, his eyes seemed to smile when he looked at her.

"Hmm." Shelley traced the rim of her glass in slow circles. "Imagine all that *sex* he's got stored up inside him from being locked up all these years."

Briar's fingers tightened around the stem of her margarita glass and she took another gulp, those butterflies back, rioting in her belly. Yes, she could imagine because she knew. She hadn't told Shelley that she'd been with him multiple times. She'd only divulged that first time. She wasn't sure why except that it had started to feel too personal. She certainly hadn't shared with her neighbor that there had been a pregnancy risk either.

"Too bad you're not going to see him again," Shelley continued. "He's going to need someone to release all that energy on."

"I know where he works," Briar murmured automatically . . . unthinkingly. "Place called Roscoe's—"

"The bar off Highway 51?"

Briar did a half-nod, half-shrug sort of thing. "Yeah, but I don't really—"

Shelley hopped up from the couch, her legging-clad legs doing a wild little jig. "We have to go! Tonight!"

"Uh . . ." Briar motioned to the back bedroom where they had just tucked in Shelley's children not half an hour ago.

Shelley nodded. "I can get a sitter. Seriously. We have to do this. Before you lose your nerve. I've been there a couple times. The place is wild on the week-ends."

"*Lose* my nerve?" she squeaked. "Shelley, I didn't say we were going." Nerve was for someone who had made a dramatic decision. A decision as dramatic as showing up at the workplace of the panty-dropping-hot felon she'd had a fling with. Had. As in *over*. And she had most definitely *not* made that decision. "I haven't even got any nerve."

"Briaaaaar," Shelley cajoled.

"This is crazy," she muttered. "He'll know I'm there because—"

"You want to fuck his brains out," Shelley finished with an emphatic nod, her voice matter-of-fact.

"Shelley," she snapped. "You know I don't—"

"I know that, but God, Briar, don't you just want to ever go after what you want? And I know you want him." Her dark eyes peered at Briar closely, like she was trying to see under her skin. Heat flamed Briar's face because, yeah, she did want him again. It had been a week, but she'd been on edge without him the entire time, craving him like an addict needed her fix.

"I know in the two years that you've been living across from me there hasn't been anyone. God, I'd die without sex for that long. Then you meet him. Are you really okay with just letting him go? Going back to an existence void of sex? I don't know if you can handle another drought. You know what they say if you don't use it." She paused, staring at Briar meaningfully, her perfectly groomed eyebrows arching. "You lose it."

"My vagina falls off?" Briar asked incredulously. "It's not a penis, you know."

"Oh, you can lose a vagina." Nodding fiercely, Shelley moved to the counter and snatched up her phone. "I'm calling the sitter." She pointed at the door. "Get yourself home and in the shower. Hurry! And be sure to shave." Her sparking eyes traveled up and down Briar, stopping to rest on her hair. "And no ponytails. Use that conditioner I gave you to tame that nest. Use like half the bottle if you need to."

"Fine," Briar grumbled, clambering off her friend's couch.

Stepping outside, she crossed the walkway and slipped inside her town house. Her stomach fluttered with excitement as she headed into her bedroom. She started sliding hangers, looking for something sexy to wear. There was no denying it. She was looking forward to seeing Knox again. Despite any promises she had made to herself to let it end . . . despite the ring of finality she had heard in his voice on the phone last week, she wanted to see him again.

ROSCOE'S WAS A broad wood building sitting back off the highway. The wood looked weathered and so stressed it might collapse in the next big storm. Antique signs and rusty license plates decorated the outside of the building. There were several motorcycles parked out front, along with an assortment of trucks. Shelley's neon coupe looked decidedly out of place in the gravel lot.

"You've been here before?" Briar questioned as they made their way up the wood ramp to the door.

"Not in a few years."

Briar nodded. Shelley's life was busy. She had her hands full with her children and only minimal relief from her ex-husband. When she did go out it was usually on a date with some guy through an online dating site. She was naturally picky about those dates. She wanted a professional man, and Sweet Hill was full of blue-collar types. Which was ironic since she was pushing Briar to hook up with a convict. *Ex*-convict, a voice inside her reminded. It was the same voice that reminded her that he had saved her life.

When they entered the room it was to the sound of a small, three-man band playing classic rock at the far end of the room. Shelley was right. The place was packed. And it seemed predominantly full of men. An assortment of leather-clad bikers, good ol' boys, and redneck types still wearing the wrinkled clothes they went to work in.

She followed Shelley across the wood plank floor.

"Was it like this when you were last here?" Briar asked as they made their way to a high table with three stools surrounding it.

"Yeah, it was a little rough then, too, but I didn't know any better in those days."

"Uh, but you do now?"

"Yeah, I'm older now. I don't do the dumb shit I used to."

Briar fought a smile. She sounded so ancient. At twenty-seven, Shelley was only two years older.

Hopping up on the high stool, Briar was suddenly grateful that she had decided to wear jeans. Shelley approved because she deemed them snug enough. *You need a pair of jeans painted on so tight that nothing is left to the imagination.*

Briar smoothed her hands over her thighs and glanced down at the skintight denim. Mission accomplished. She just had to pretend her ass didn't look huge in them.

She glanced around the bar, searching.

"Do you see him?"

"No." Her heart sank like it probably shouldn't. Knox was the only reason she was here. *And* the reason for the hair and the jeans and the makeup. Not to mention the slinky camisole-style top that showed off her shoulders and cleavage in a way that made her feel naked.

Several men and women danced on the sawdust floor on one side of the building.

"Want to dance?" Shelley asked.

Briar shook her head. "I haven't had enough alcohol for that yet."

Shelley signaled the waitress. "Well, let's rectify that."

A platinum-blond waitress walking past detoured for their table. "Hey, there, girls, what can I get you?"

"Two Shiners." Shelley winked at Briar and her stomach sank again, sensing what her friend was going to ask next. "Is Knox working?"

The waitress froze and looked Shelley over speculatively. "Who's asking?" The woman was pushing fifty and still looked good. She was plump with a fresh face. The only makeup her bright red lipstick.

Shelley nodded at Briar. "My friend here knows him."

The waitress glanced at her. "That so?"

Briar lifted one shoulder in a half shrug. It was as far as she could go to admitting that they were friends—or *something*.

"Yeah, he's working," she admitted. "I'll let him know his 'friend' is here. You got a name, honey?"

Briar started to shake her head, but Shelley went ahead and answered for her. "Tell him Briar is here."

"All right." She nodded slowly, as though she

wasn't too sure about either one of them. "I'll be back in a moment with your beers."

As soon as she slipped away, Briar turned on Shelley. "What did you do that for?"

"Just to speed things along."

"God, Shelley, now he'll know that I'm here because—"

"Because of him," she finished. "Yes. You are here because of him. You don't think he'll figure that out the moment he sees you? Men appreciate directness, Briar."

Still annoyed, Briar turned to stare straight ahead at the dance floor, crossing her arms in front of her.

"Oh, come on. Don't pout. Look, our waitress is getting our beer at the bar . . . and holy hell, who is *that*? Please tell me that's not him. If that's your guy I think I'm going to face-punch you, Briar. You have been holding out on me, girl."

Briar swung her gaze to the long stretch of bar that backed against the wall. It was Knox, all right. In the flesh. Looking better than ever in a pair of faded jeans and black T-shirt with Roscoe's logo stamped on the pocket.

She blinked, finding the sight of him here, in his element, a little strange. This was his world. Not the prison. Not her apartment. She glanced around, noticing that she wasn't the only one looking at him. A few others slid him sidelong glances. Women checking him out. Men looking at him almost warily. She guessed he got that a lot. His reputation preceding him.

She shook the hair back behind her shoulders and drew a ragged breath. He hadn't spotted her yet. He was standing behind the bar, leaning over to hear what the waitress was telling him. *Their* waitress. Oh. God. She knew what she was telling him. Her stomach plummeted to the soles of her boots. Any moment he would know she was here. He would look up and—

His head shot up at whatever and his eyes scanned the room until finding her.

"Oh, shit," she breathed, the crazy urge to dive under the table seizing her.

"Oh shit is right," Shelley echoed as he came around the bar, carrying the two Shiners he was about to give to the waitress. "He's coming this way and it looks like he wants to devour you."

"Or strangle me," she muttered.

He didn't look happy to see her. Her chest tightened as she recalled that phone call last week. He hadn't said the words directly but she'd understood his meaning. *Have a good life.* She'd heard it in his voice. In his good-bye. He was done with her. And now she had shown up here.

He was treating her to that same intense, unsmiling stare he had treated her to all those times he visited the HSU.

"Oh my. That body. He's ripped. I can actually see the definition of his six-pack through his shirt. Girl, you better get all over that," she hissed, her words ending right before he stopped at their table.

"Hey," Briar greeted, her voice weak.

"Your beer." He set a bottle in front of each of them, but his gaze trained on Briar with laserlike focus. It was almost like he didn't quite recognize her. Or perhaps he simply couldn't reconcile her presence here. In his world.

She had been in his world, on his turf, before. In the prison. Why was this so different? Even as she wondered that, she knew.

The balance of power had shifted. They weren't in the prison any longer, where he lacked power. The beast was out of its cage and there was no telling what he would do. He could do anything. This was Knox unleashed.

"Hey," Shelley announced, stretching out her hands to shake his. "I'm Shelley, Briar's neighbor."

He managed a polite nod as they shook hands. "Knox." Then he was looking at Briar again.

"So this is where you work," she said lamely, fingering her sweating bottle nervously.

The band suddenly started playing an old ACDC song, and it was even harder to hear. But that didn't stop him from asking what was so clearly weighing on his mind. He leaned in to demand, "What are you doing here?"

What was she supposed to say? *I came here to see you?* That only smacked of desperation.

She shrugged. "Just felt like going out." She nodded toward the stage. "Great band."

He stared at her dubiously and she waited for him to call bullshit. He didn't. Instead, he gestured to the bottles, all businesslike. "Let me know if I can get you anything else."

She nodded dumbly.

"How about you have a drink with us?" Shelley cajoled. Trust her to cut right to the flirting. It was as natural as breathing to her.

"Can't. I'm working."

Shelley pouted, jutting out her bottom lip prettily and Briar felt a stab of jealousy as Knox studied her neighbor. Did Knox like what he saw? What wasn't to like? Shelley was sultry and sexy. Two kids hadn't altered her tiny size-two figure.

Shelley cocked her head, coyly twirling her hair. "Aw, you don't get a break?"

Briar sucked in a breath, stifling the urge to face punch *her.*

"It's pretty busy tonight and we're short-staffed."

Shelley brought her beer to her lips, talking against the bottle's mouth as she pouted, "Oh, fine. But we're going to need more beer soon, Knox. I hope you'll bring them to us."

"Sure. Just signal me." Without a glance for Briar, he turned and headed back to his spot behind the bar.

"Hmm, now that's a view." Shelley cocked her head, admiring his ass as he walked away.

"Did you have to do that?"

"Do what?"

"Flirt like that!"

"He was about to leave. I was trying to keep him here longer. "

"Yeah, by hitting on him."

She shrugged. "Well, you weren't doing anything. Besides. You've been insisting that you don't want to fuck him again . . ."

"That doesn't mean it's okay for you to," she shot back.

"Fine. Don't be mad at me. You know I love you. I just got carried away. He's so yummy."

"Fine." Briar supposed she could forgive her. She better than anyone understood Knox's impact on the female's senses, after all.

Shelley hopped down off the stool. "Let's go dance."

"What? I don't dance—"

"You need to loosen up. C'mon. We're here. Why not?"

They were here. And she had just told Knox they

were here to have fun and listen to the band. *Not* stalk his ass. What was the harm in dancing with her friend?

"Okay." Hopping down from her stool, she tipped her beer and finished it in a long gulp, taking it as fortification. Slamming the bottle down on the table, she met Shelley's gaze. "Let's do this."

NINETEEN

*B*RIAR—*HIS* BRIAR—WAS WORKING it on the dance floor like it was something she did every Saturday night at Roscoe's. *Shit.* Not his. Not *his* Briar.

She wasn't one of the bar trolls who skulked in here night after night, seeking validation through booze and strange men pawing at her. She was the type who preferred a book or television to a wild night out. Knox liked that about her. He liked that every time he touched her, every time he kissed her, she looked faintly surprised. And he fucking loved the sounds she made as she pulled him closer, urging him to do things to her he was positive no man had ever done before.

He wanted to be the only man to touch her. It was total caveman of him, but that's what he was. A fucking caveman that reveled in rocking her staid little world and making her fly apart. She made him want to pound his chest. *Christ.* Thinking about her that way was making him rock hard. Thankfully he was standing behind the bar where no one would notice.

His gaze tracked her. For being not much of a party girl, she was doing a good job faking it. He glared across the distance, straining and twisting his body as he worked the bar, determined to keep her in his sights. She held her hands up in the air and swayed those hips he remembered holding in his hands, anchoring her as he slid home inside.

He lifted on the balls of his feet slightly, following her stripper moves between bodies and over the tops of people's heads. *Where the hell did she learn to dance like that?*

Her hair was wild and free, shining as bright as a copper penny in the dim light as she danced. He suspected she was already halfway drunk. She hadn't imbibed much since she got here, but from the glassiness in her eyes, he would stake money that she'd had a few drinks before showing up here. Maybe she had needed the liquid courage to face him again.

Over the past week he'd felt an odd mixture of relief and disappointment that she wasn't pregnant, and that was just all kinds of messed up. He didn't wish her pregnant. That wasn't right. Although as wrong as it was, he understood the disappointment. If she was pregnant, he would be a part of her life. He'd still be seeing her. What was to keep them from sleeping together more? All the time even? He could keep showing up at her apartment. Kissing her, having her, waking up tangled in her hair.

Unhealthy thinking all around and great motivation to give her a wide berth. Which he had been doing successfully. Until tonight. Until she showed up here.

He couldn't take his eyes off her. She never wore her hair down like that. The only time was when he pulled it loose so he could fist his hands in it as he fucked her. It felt like she was showing off his secret to the world. *His*. There was that word again.

He poured Blue a fifth of whiskey, still keeping a careful eye on her as a pair of losers closed in on Briar and her friend like fresh meat thrown to the wolves.

Annoyance burned hot though him. *Annoyance?* Hell, he was pissed. Just like that first time he saw her at the prison and he thought she didn't belong. It was the same sensation but only worse. Now he *knew* her. He felt proprietary. Caveman and all that shit. She didn't belong at the prison and she sure as hell didn't belong here. She was as clueless now as she had been then. His chest tightened with a rumbling growl.

"Hey, you're spilling good whiskey," Blue complained, and Knox quickly pulled back the bottle.

"Sorry," he mumbled.

Blue followed his gaze to Briar and Shelley on the dance floor. "Which one?"

Knox frowned. "Which one what?"

"Which one you fucking?"

"Neither," he snapped, not even bothering to feel offended by the biker's crudeness. The guy had served time with him. He'd heard worse out of him.

His aunt pushed up to the bar with more drink orders. "She's the one with all that curly hair." Apparently she had overhead Blue.

He glared at her. As much as he loved the woman, she was a busybody that needed to mind her own business.

"Ah. You've got no stake in her, then?" Blue winked knowingly at his aunt.

"That's right." Knox nodded and wiped down the bar where he'd spilled the whiskey.

"Then you don't mind that guy all over her?"

His gaze swung back to the dance floor to watch a long-haired guy in a Metallica T-shirt bump and grind behind Briar.

Hell. No.

"Aunt Alice?" he said, not looking away from the dance floor.

"Yes?"

"Tell Jack I'm taking a break."

"Sure thing, Knox."

He walked around the bar, ignoring Blue's and Aunt Alice's snickers. He didn't care if he looked like a jackass. He wasn't going to let any man put his hands on Briar. Not in front of him. It was one thing to let her go so that she could continue her life without him. A life that would naturally include her seeing other men. Touching them. Letting them touch her. Knox had just never counted on watching that unfold in front of him. And he didn't have to watch it. Not in his bar.

He cut a hard line across the room, stopping in front of her with a thud of his boots. She appeared to be enjoying herself. Dancing as the greasy-haired bastard grabbed onto her hips and pushed himself against her ass.

"Briar." She looked up at his hard bite of her name. "I think it's time for you to leave."

The color bled from her cheeks as she took in his face. She stopped dancing.

Shelley crowded close, glaring at him. "You're kicking us out? Why?"

The guy that had been grinding behind Briar stepped forward, his chest puffing out belligerently. He threw an arm around Briar's shoulders. "Yeah, why do they have to go? We're not causing any trouble."

Knox stared at him coldly. "Trouble is about to happen to you if you don't get your arm off her."

Greasy Hair looked down at Briar. "This your man?"

Color flooded her face and she paused a moment before shaking her head swiftly.

For some reason this only made him angrier. His hands curled into fists at his sides.

"All right, then." Greasy Hair met his gaze again. "Then fuck off."

Briar gasped. Even her friend inched back, smart enough to know that shit was about to get real and she needed to get out of the way.

Briar shook her head, her expression twisting with embarrassment. She stepped out from under the guy's arm. "It's fine. I'll just go."

"No," her would-be savior declared, grabbing her arm and tugging her back, farther from Knox. And that was his mistake. Pulling her away from Knox when the only thought pounding through his head was: *mine*.

Knox reached for her. "Let's go, Briar."

The bastard shoved him in the chest. Hard. "I don't know who the fuck you think you are, chief, but you can't come in here and—"

Knox cut him off, grabbing his hand and twisting it hard, yanking it in an unnatural angle until a sharp snap cracked the air. The guy screamed. Several of his friends stormed the dance floor, surging toward them. Only when they spotted Knox, they stopped. Unlike Greasy Hair, they recognized him and weren't about to make a move.

"What are you looking at?" he snarled. Knox jerked his chin, ready for them, almost wanting them to come at him. Then he could unleash some of the aggression pumping through him. Somewhere in the far back of his mind he heard his parole officer citing his numerous warnings, one of which was to avoid all altercations. *No fighting, whatsoever.*

Only he didn't give a fuck. He wanted to keep twisting the asshole's arm until it broke. He'd break all their arms if he could right now. The punks exchanged glances with one another and backed down. "Knox! Knox! Stop." Briar was there then, her hands on his chest, her eyes pleading with him.

"I think all you fuckers need to consider what happens next here." It was Blue's voice snarling over the air. Several of Blue's friends flanked him as he stared down Greasy Hair's punk-ass crew.

Knox tightened his grip and twisted a little tighter on the guy's wrist. Greasy Hair whimpered. "Shit! You're breaking my arm."

Knox released the asshole and grabbed Briar's hand. Holding her cool fingers in his grasp, he led her past gawking onlookers.

A voice, a single whisper, wove through the crowd, reaching his ears. "*Yeah, Knox Callaghan . . . murderer . . .*"

Grim futility flashed through him, sinking past muscle and tissue, settling deep into his bones. That's right. He was that. He would always be that.

Maybe it was time Briar understood as much. If

she hadn't figured it out, he'd make sure she knew now. And then he wouldn't stop her as she walked out the door.

HE LED HER through the swinging door with a sign above it that read EMPLOYEES ONLY. His warm, big hand enveloped hers, helping her stay upright. She practically tripped in her ridiculous heels as he dragged her after him, and she wished she had worn flats instead of letting Shelley convince her to go with these boots.

They passed through a small kitchen with a harried-looking man washing glasses and into another back room lined with boxes and walls of shelved liquor.

Knox pushed her back against a wall and then dropped his hands from her. He tucked those hands behind him then, sliding them into his back jeans pockets as if he needed to do that to keep from touching her. Or maybe that was just wishful thinking.

Her blood pumped from what had just happened out on the dance floor. Her skin felt feverish. She told herself it was the alcohol and all the dancing, but she couldn't fool herself. It brought to mind that day in the HSU when he had reacted so quickly, with such lethal skill. A viper striking with deadly precision. *God*. She was turned on. She could barely stop her body from leaning in toward him.

"Are you okay?" His gaze scanned her face, searching.

Heat crawled over her cheeks, burning all the way to her ears, and she fell back against the wall with a gulp of a breath.

"I'm fine," she said, trying to regain her composure . . . and some restraint.

He angled his head, his eyes sharp and glinting in the near dark. "Maybe you've had a little too much to drink."

"Maybe I have," she agreed, holding his gaze. "But no worries. I have a designated driver."

He snorted. "Your designated driver doesn't appear in much better condition than you."

"Is that why you dragged me back here?" she challenged. "Because you're worried I've been drinking too much?"

He glanced away then, staring somewhere into the darkness before looking back down at her. "What are you doing here, Briar?" He sounded tired, and she was the reason for that. "Why are you . . ." His voice faded, but she understood. She knew what he was asking.

Why was she coming around him?

It was a good question and she didn't know the answer. She couldn't explain why she lost all sense of pride when it came to him. There was only need.

"I can't stop thinking about you," she whispered,

her voice sounding as anguished as she felt over that fact.

His eyes gleamed almost black in the poorly lit room, and then whatever light she saw there suddenly banked itself. A fire snuffed out. He was Callaghan again. Prison inmate. "We can't do this, Briar."

She nodded jerkily, a stupid lump forming in her throat . . . emotion . . . hurt that she didn't want to feel. "Yeah. Okay."

She started to move past him, but he stopped her, clasping her shoulder and putting her back against the wall. He locked his jaw, tension feathering along the tight skin, just beneath the scruff that she wanted to stroke.

She shook her head, staring at him helplessly. "You haven't come by my place. Not since—" She stopped, but he knew what she meant to say. Not since she told him she wasn't pregnant.

His voice cut hard through the stillness of the room. "Is this what you want from me?" He seized her hand and pressed it against his cock. She gasped, feeling him swell against her fingers. She tried to pull free, but he held fast. "Because this is all I've got. All I can give, Briar. Sex. Meaningless fucks." He pushed her hand harder against him, moving her up and down his erection. "Now tell me to go to hell. Tell me to fuck off." He paused, his gaze flicking over her face. "Say it."

She stared at him, her heart pounding in her too tight chest.

His head dipped, lips a hairbreadth from her mouth. "Say it," he whispered harshly. "Say you don't want me."

She sucked in a deep breath. "No."

TWENTY

On THE NEAR dark, Briar's eyes glowed amber fire. *No.* She had said no. The single word rocked him. He dropped her hand like it scalded him. Only she didn't remove her hand from his cock right away. No, she kept it there, palming him before dropping away. Knox bit back a groan.

Heat crept over her face, shadowing the apples of her cheeks, and that made his stomach clench. He'd been inside her but she still blushed like a girl on her first date. She was still so sweet and untainted. Even after him.

She was a contrast to everything he was . . . everything he had lived through, and he wanted to pull her in and have her. Again and again until he killed that need. Until he stopped wanting her so much.

He cleared his throat. "It's better if you go." Better for her. Better for him, too.

God knows the impulse to keep her, take her, was

there, pounding through him. She had become a craving, an addiction. A compulsion as necessary as food. He thought once would have been enough to break the habit. Then he could move on. But here she was and he still felt it.

"So we're done, then?" She looked so purposeful as she asked this. Like it took everything in her to school her features and voice into total blandness.

He glanced away and then back to her again—like he needed a break from looking at her with her face all made-up and her hair wild and flowing. Like a woman ready to party. And there were a lot of men out there that would be more than willing to party with her once he set her free from this room.

Something swift and visceral rose up in him at that possibility. He knew she hadn't been into the greasy-haired punk, but it wouldn't be long before she was into someone else. Before she was *with* someone else. He curled his hands into fists at his sides to stop from reaching for her, to stop himself from burying his fingers in that wild hair and dragging her painted mouth to his.

"Yeah, we're done," he lashed out. "I can't make it any more clear for you."

She flinched before recovering. "So that's it." Her jaw locked and something glinted in her eyes that should have warned him. Should have told him she wasn't done. Her hand came between them and cupped his dick again. "This has had enough of me, then?"

A hissed breath escaped him.

The corners of her mouth tipped up in satisfaction. "Still hard," she mused. Her other hand popped open the button at his fly. The zipper sang down and God help him he couldn't stop her. She delved inside and circled him with her warm, slim fingers. "You don't feel done."

"What are you doing, Briar?" he growled.

She worked her hand between them, pumping his cock in a few hard strokes.

She didn't say anything, just continued to glare at him, and he knew. He knew she wanted to prove him wrong. She wanted him to eat his words.

She tugged his jeans down his hips and dropped to her knees.

Fuck. His hands clenched at his sides. She looked up at him from beneath heavy eyelids. Her look was all cold fury. She wanted to punish him. Her tongue darted out to lick the head of him and he was lost.

His head fell back against the wall of liquor bottles with a rattle. He moaned as she closed her lips around him, tormenting him with her tongue.

He balled his hands into fists to keep from grabbing her head and forcing her mouth to fuck him harder. Faster.

His hips had a mind of their own, however, thrusting into her mouth, but she still managed to tease him, taking only half his cock past her lips.

He looked down and met her taunting eyes. She was a siren looking up at him.

"What do you want, Knox?" she whispered, her breath fanning his wet dick.

You. He wanted to shove deep into her mouth. Or better yet, he wanted to haul her up and seat her on his aching dick.

"We're two consenting adults. What's so wrong with this?" she taunted, her tongue sneaking out to swirl around him again. Her gaze slid sideways, eyeing one of his clenched fists. She reached out and took that fist and brought it to the back of her head . . . inviting. He held his fingers locked against all those soft strands. But he couldn't resist forever.

His fingers unfurled, relaxing into her hair as her mouth worked over him furiously. He was so close, the small of his back tightening . . . he didn't even register the sudden burst of music from the bar signaling the door had opened. Or the footsteps.

He only heard the voice. "Nice, Knox."

His head snapped up and he looked over at Dean, one of the busboys.

Briar squeaked and let go of him, tipping sideways and falling on her hip. Her hair was wild around her, her deep amber eyes bulging. The classic red lips were gone, lipstick smeared onto her chin. In the near dark, color stained her cheeks like someone had just slapped her.

He looked back at Dean. The way he leered at Briar made Knox feel like breaking his nose.

"Get the fuck out of here!" he snarled.

The guy held up a hand. "I'm going! I'm going!" He picked up a case of beer and hurried back out into the bar.

Knox stuffed himself back into his jeans, turning his back on Briar. He was still aching for her. Longing for relief so much that he physically hurt.

She made him forget about the world, and he couldn't do that. If she wasn't smart enough to see that, then he would have to be smart enough for both of them.

He spun around, putting several paces between them, staying clear of her touch, but he didn't have to say anything. Her expression stopped him.

She looked stricken, her eyes liquid-dark like some wounded animal as she rose to her feet. "You're right. This is crazy. What am I doing? Someone saw us . . ." Her voice faded and she shook her head, searching his face.

Now was the time. If he wanted her to stay, if he wanted to make things right, he needed to say something now.

He held silent.

"I'm out of here," she whispered, and rushed from

the room. A brief punch of Creedence Clearwater hit his ears as she passed through the swinging door.

Well, he'd handled that like shit. But at least she was gone. It needed to be done. He reached down and adjusted himself, still aching. He sucked in a deep breath and waited for his erection to subside. A hissed breath passed through his teeth. He counted to twenty before following.

Ignoring the hollowness in his chest, he stepped back into the bar. It was even more crowded than half an hour ago.

He scanned the crowd, looking for her, still wanting to assure himself that she was all right after what just went down.

He couldn't spot her, but he found her friend parked at a table. Shelley wasn't alone anymore. She was laughing with two other men, a row of shots in front of them. Suddenly, Briar was there, stopping before her. He watched, his stomach knotting as the laughter faded from Shelley's face. He knew Briar was telling her that she wanted to leave. Because of him. Whether she said that last part or not, her friend could figure it out.

Shelley patted her shoulder and nodded sympathetically. Without another word, Briar turned and wove through bodies until she was out of the bar. As though she couldn't stand to be even in the same vicinity with him.

Which was just as well.

He watched Shelley follow after Briar, ignoring the sinking sensation in his chest and shoving away the deep ache that whispered he was making a mistake. Shaking his head, he told himself that it was the right thing to do. He might be a free man, but he wasn't free enough. Not free to be with her. He was trying to get his life together and he didn't need a complication like Briar Davis. She made him feel like he was unraveling at the seams.

The next hour passed in a blur.

Aunt Alice appeared before him with a huff. "Okay, that's the third drink order you messed up. At this rate I won't have any tips tonight. Clearly your head's somewhere else." When he opened his mouth to protest, she held up a hand, cutting him off. "Nope. Not gonna hear it. Ever since that pretty thing showed up and you disappeared with her in the back, you've been distracted. Why don't you take off early? Jimmy and I will lock up." She waggled her eyebrows at him, clearly indicating she thought he should go after Briar.

"Aunt Alice, I got this—"

She pointed in the direction of the door. "Go on now. You been here almost every day this week. Don't come back tomorrow. I'll see you Monday."

With a sigh, he nodded and stepped around the bar, exiting through the back. He could at least check in on Uncle Mac. Hopefully, he'd eaten something besides Hostess cakes for dinner. Knox had made spaghetti yesterday so he wouldn't have to resort to his usual junk food dinner.

Aunt Alice had done her best to take care of him over the years, but she had her own family to look after, in addition to working at Roscoe's. Now that Knox was out, he was hoping to ease some of the burden for both his uncle and aunt. He had a lot to make up for.

He sat in his truck for a moment before starting the engine. He stared vacantly into the back parking lot. Some of the perimeter lights were out and he made a mental note to take care of that this week.

The old farmhouse where he grew up was only ten minutes from Roscoe's. He drove past the fallow fields that Uncle Mac, North, and he had planted and harvested growing up. The sight of it in the moonlight, darkly barren with only patches of wilted grass, settled like rocks in the chest.

The porch light was still burning brightly as he drove up. Sandy hopped down the steps and barked at him as he pulled next to his uncle's pickup. Uncle Mac didn't use it much these days—the stiffness in his left leg getting to be too much even for a simple drive into town. He added getting his uncle's truck inspected to the to-do list growing in his head.

It wasn't even midnight yet, but Mac kept odd

hours. His various medications kept him up at night. Unsurprisingly, his uncle was camped out in the living room in front of the television watching a rerun of *Mash*.

"Uncle Mac," he greeted. "How's it going?"

He waved from his recliner. "Good. Not closing tonight?"

"Alice offered to."

His uncle nodded and glanced at the clock. "Eleven-thirty on a Saturday. In my day, the night would have just been getting started."

His uncle wanted him to have a life outside of work and looking after him, and he didn't bother disguising that fact.

"Alice mentioned that you've got a few admirers at Roscoe's."

Knox laughed once, shaking his head. Of course they were talking about him and his nonexistent life, as they deemed it. Those admirers were regulars and had more mileage on them than his uncle's old Dodge. He wasn't interested in any of them. Briar flashed across his mind. Fresh-faced and smelling of pears. Shit.

He patted his uncle on the shoulder. "Can I get you anything?"

"No, I'm fine."

Knox made a move toward his bedroom down the hall, but his uncle's beefy hand shot out to grab his arm. His grip was still surprisingly strong. Even after the stroke, after losing Katie . . . after Knox and North went to prison and Aunt Sissy died, his hands were still strong. So capable.

They were the same hands that had picked up Knox and his brother when they'd fallen off their bikes as boys. He was the only father they had ever known. Knox wouldn't fail him. He couldn't. Not again.

He met his uncle's rheumy gaze. "You can't run from life," his uncle said. "From living. I don't want that. Neither would Katie or your aunt."

Knox sucked in a breath and blinked suddenly burning eyes. It was the first time his uncle had mentioned Katie or Aunt Sissy in years. Certainly the first time since Knox had gotten out of prison. It frightened him a little . . . in addition to making him want to blubber like a baby. It was one thing knowing they were gone, but another thing to talk about them being gone, lost forever, so openly. He didn't talk about it with anyone. He never had. It tore him up too much.

He blinked fiercely, feeling so damned weak and small. He had a flash of himself when he was seven years old and his mom had driven them all the way from Plano to drop him off at her brother's place. *Uncle Mac's gonna take care of you and your brother now. Don't cry. Be brave.*

And Uncle Mac had taken care of them. He took Knox and North in when their mom went to live with some deadbeat that didn't want kids. He and Aunt Sissy fed them casseroles, got them haircuts, and drove them to little league. A year later his mom had died of an overdose.

"You need to make a life for yourself," Uncle Max said gruffly. "A little happiness. Believe it or not, you deserve that. Find someone to spend your life with . . . to love. A woman. Kids."

He shook his head, "Uncle Mac—"

"Nothing's worth anything unless you have that." His voice dipped deeper. Rougher. Like he was battling emotion, maybe holding in tears. Knox hadn't seen him cry since the night they found Katie in the bathroom, an empty bottle of pills next to her. He hadn't cried at her funeral.

Knox hadn't been there when Aunt Sissy died four years ago, but when Uncle Mac called to tell Knox and North the news, there had been no tears in his voice. Only weariness. A weariness that Knox took deep inside himself. Because it was all his fault.

If he had kept his shit together all those years ago, maybe Katie would still be here. Maybe Aunt Sissy would never have been so weak that winter and she could have beaten the pneumonia. Maybe, the following year, his uncle wouldn't have had that stroke. It was a horrible chain of events. A domino effect that Knox blamed himself for starting. He had been the first one to drop, after all.

"You've never disappointed me," Uncle Mac said gruffly. "But if you quit on building a real life for yourself, you will have."

Knox nodded, not knowing what to say. Or think. He settled for, "Okay, Uncle Mac."

His uncle released his arm with a satisfied nod as if the matter were resolved. Knox went to his room. It was exactly the same as when he graduated from high school. Same trophies and plaid quilt comforter. Even his old baseball mitt sat on the dresser. When he entered this room, he felt like he was stuck in a time warp. A teenager again and not a man that had lived through all he had.

Suddenly, the air felt too tight in his lungs. He had to get out of here. Turning, he headed back down the hall.

"Hey, I'll be back later, Uncle Mac. Don't wait up."

Uncle Mac waved from his chair, his eyes gleaming with satisfaction. He probably thought his talk did some good and Knox was going out to live it up.

Knox didn't know where he was going. He only knew that he couldn't sit in that room tonight, reflecting on his lost boyhood. Before everything went to hell. Especially with his uncle's words echoing all around him: *Find someone to spend your life with . . .*

He made it sound so simple. Like he could go pick

out a woman, decide to be happy, and all would be well. Nothing was that simple.

He drove down the county road until he hit the highway. Then he passed Roscoe's and kept going, heading into Sweet Hill. He drove almost blindly, some other force, a deep-buried instinct, guiding him. The way Briar had looked before she turned and left him in the back of Roscoe's. That nagged at him, tangling with all the other bullshit weighing on him. He was a Grade A asshole who treated nice girls like shit. And his uncle thought he deserved happiness.

His uncle didn't get it. Knox had tossed out any chance for a life like that when he was twenty. Sometimes you fucked up so badly, you didn't get a chance for normal. You definitely didn't get a chance for happiness. His uncle didn't realize that.

But he did.

TWENTY-ONE

*W*ITH HER FACE scrubbed free of makeup and her hair pulled back into its usual ponytail, Briar felt more like her old self. She certainly didn't feel like the strange creature that got down on her knees in the back of Roscoe's. Where anyone could see her. Where someone *had* seen her. That wasn't her. She didn't do those things. Really.

With a miserable groan, she fell sideways face-first into one of the couch pillows.

She didn't know what she had been thinking. That this fling could keep going? That it could be something real? That it could last? She had been listening to Shelley too much when she should have asked herself what Laurel would do.

She reached for the pack of M&Ms on the table and tore into it. Pouring several into her hand, she tossed them into her mouth. Once she let him know she wasn't pregnant, he had cut ties. She wouldn't embarrass herself and chase after him anymore.

When the couple on her television screen started kissing, she punched the remote control with more force than necessary and raced through channels, images blurring until she stopped on a rerun of *The Walking Dead*.

Perfect. Nothing sappy. Just what she needed. A little pulse-pounding action and horror.

Her phone buzzed on the coffee table and she hesitated before answering it. It was probably Shelley sending a well-meaning text, calling Knox a jerk and telling her she could do better. Like she had the entire drive home. Only it didn't make her feel *better*. It made her feel worse.

Her phone gave a reminder ding and she sighed, snatching it off the table. The last thing she wanted was Shelley knocking on her door. A very real possibility if she ignored her text.

When she spotted Knox's name at the top of the text she choked on an M&M. Lurching up from the couch, she held the phone in both hands as though it might suddenly fly away.

A single word stared at her from her phone. *Sorry*.

Why was he sorry? She waited, staring at her phone and wondering if he would elaborate. Her fingers flew over the keys, not bothering to wait to see. *Why??*

She waited as he typed back. When his words burst to life on the screen of her phone, she sucked in a breath. *Open the door.*

She bounded off the couch and stared at the door as if it were an animal that might spring to life and bite her.

Knox was on the other side of that door. Why? *What did he want?* After tonight, she was certain he wouldn't be dropping by anymore.

She quickly typed back. *Don't think that's a good idea.*

Instantly, he replied. *Please.*

Her chest clenched. It was tempting, but a recipe for disaster. Her fingers flew over the keys. *We have nothing left to say.*

"Briar, open the door." His commanding voice carried through the door. "Please," he added.

Her phone slipped through her fingers and thudded to the floor. The "Please" was her undoing.

She moved toward the door, unbolting the top lock.

Her chin shot up. This wouldn't be another booty call. She wouldn't be used . . . or use him. Not anymore.

Before she could reconsider, she yanked the door open. Knox stood there in the same black T-shirt and jeans from earlier, still looking bigger than life and sexy as hell in the frame of her doorway. A plastic grocery bag dangled from his hand.

"What are you doing here?" she demanded, refusing to let the sight of him wreak havoc on her senses and undermine her determination to resist him.

He surveyed her, looking her up and down, making her acutely conscious that she was braless under her T-shirt. Her face burned and she blinked, hoping she didn't bear the evidence of the chocolate she had been inhaling like oxygen.

"I came to say I was sorry for the way I was with you earlier and . . . to see if you're okay."

She crossed her arms over her chest. "You wanted me to leave. I left." Only after she had flung herself at him. Heat crept up her face and her composure threatened to crumble. "No big deal," she added with a shrug.

"Yeah. Well. I could have been less . . . harsh."

A short laugh escaped her. "Do you know how to be any other way?"

"I can be . . . not harsh," he responded without the faintest smile.

"*Not* harsh? You can't even bring yourself to say *nice*."

He nodded slowly, scrubbing a hand over his dark cropped hair. Her belly contracted as she watched him. She knew the shape of his skull. The velvet texture of his hair against her palm and fingers.

"Well, I'm not nice. I know that, but I'm trying to make this right with us."

"You can't, Knox. It's done. We're done." She moved to shut the door in his face but he stopped her, wedging his boot in the way and preventing her.

With a growl, she yanked the door back open. "What are you doing here?"

He lifted his hand and dangled the bag between them. "Dammit, Briar. I brought you this."

She stared at the bag, able to make out the Ben and Jerry's logo through the thin plastic.

She shook her head, at a loss. "You brought me ice cream?"

He lifted one shoulder. "Yeah. I'm sorry I was a dick. I didn't mean to hurt you tonight. I wasn't trying to do that."

She opened her mouth, ready to ask him what it was he had been trying to do. Or maybe, more importantly, what he was trying to do *now*. But then something made her snap her mouth shut.

He held the bag up higher between them. "This ice cream is melting."

She hesitated only a moment before stepping aside. "It'd be a shame to let it melt. We should eat it. I guess."

He stepped inside, and she shut the door after him.

"I guess so," he agreed, his expression unreadable.

An eruption of screams exploded on her wide

screen. She glanced over her shoulder to catch Rick busting zombie ass.

Facing Knox again, she caught him looking in that direction.

"You like scary movies?" he asked.

"The Walking Dead," she replied unthinkingly, glancing at that bag in his hand, feeling some of her anger slip away as she struggled to wrap her head around the fact that he had brought her ice cream. All her girl parts heated and quivered as she remembered what he did with ice cream last time.

"Never heard of it."

She blinked, shaking off her erotic memories. "You've never heard of *The Walking Dead*? Where've you been? Under a rock?"

"Just prison."

"Oh." Her face burned. "There are TVs in prison," she reminded him.

"I never spent much time in the rec room watching TV."

No, from the looks of him he had spent all his time working out, honing his body into a weapon that could protect him while he was in there. *And me.* The reminder of what he had done for her, how he had saved her, was never far, but right now it went a long way in softening her toward him.

He moved ahead of her, sinking down on her

couch. He seemed to dominate everything, making the space of her living room somehow tighter, but not in a bad way. It just seemed cozier. It felt more like a home with him in it. Dangerous thinking.

She fetched two spoons from the kitchen and returned, sinking down on the couch beside him, careful to leave space between them. "Well, c'mon. It's a marathon. We're halfway through season two but I'll catch you up."

She pulled the carton out of the bag, pausing when she looked at it. Her face warmed. "Cherry Garcia," she murmured, easing off the lid. "My favorite."

"Yeah. I remember." His voice had gone all gravelly. Her gaze cut to him. His bright blue eyes went dark as they stared at her face, then lowered, dropping to her chest. Her breasts grew aching, straining against her T-shirt, nipples hardening as she remembered his fingers rubbing cold ice cream on her, followed by the hot swipe of his tongue. The nip of his teeth. The squeeze of his fingers. *Oh. God.*

She dug her spoon into the semisoft ice cream and shoved it into her mouth, hoping that would cool off the sudden heat of arousal swamping her.

She handed him a spoon and he dug in, taking a big bite. She pointed her spoon at the TV. "That's Rick and that's Shane. They used to be best friends . . . but at this point Shane has gone kind of bonkers."

They watched the drama unfolding on the screen

for several more moments. She inserted explanations when necessary. Even though she'd seen it before, she gasped when Rick stabbed Shane.

"Well, that was coming," Knox declared.

She snorted. "Oh, like you absolutely knew that was going to happen."

"He wanted Rick's wife for himself."

"So?"

"Rick was gonna kill him," he answered, as if it were the most simple explanation in the world.

"How do you know that? You've just started watching—"

"It's a zombie world, right? Normal rules of society don't exactly apply."

She looked at Knox, studying the hard set to his features and realizing that he had lived in a place where the normal rules of society didn't apply. When he'd come to her rescue in the HSU, he had been primitive. An animal uncaged.

He had lived in a place void of civilization. Maybe, in his mind, he still lived there. That's what set him apart. He had an edge to him even out here. He always would.

They were still staring at each other when he calmly added, "A man has to defend what's his."

Had he seen her as his then? Even in that prison? It was crazy. He certainly didn't view her like that now. He might be here, but it was just because he felt sorry for the way things went down between them at Roscoe's and wanted to make amends.

She looked back at the TV, just in time to watch as a full-scale zombie herd started attacking everyone.

"Wow," he announced at the end of the episode. "That was pretty intense."

"Good, right? Want to watch the next one?"

He nodded, and she settled back down on the couch, not minding anymore that their shoulders touched. It actually felt . . . companionable. For a fleeting moment she wondered if this could be the start of a friendship between them. Was that even possible? Could they be friends after everything?

She focused on the TV screen. Of course, it didn't escape her notice that they were starting the season where the group took refuge from the zombies in a prison. Apparently Knox noticed that plot point, too.

"You'd never see me back in a prison," he said after a while.

"But it's fortified. It has walls and fences. Makes sense that they can keep the zombies out of there," she argued. "Otherwise they're risking themselves out in the woods—"

"I wouldn't care." He shrugged and she let the matter drop. Obviously he would feel that way, but then she couldn't help the next question from slipping out of her mouth.

"Do you regret it?" She felt his stare on the side of

her face, and forged on, fixing her gaze on the screen as she asked what had always been in the back of her mind, lurking, a shadow that wouldn't fade. "What you did . . . do you regret it?'

"Do you know what I did?'

She shook her head.

"I served out my sentence," he responded, his tone revealing nothing.

"That's not an answer."

"I'll never do it again, if that's what you're asking me. I won't go back there."

Not exactly an admission of regret, and she wanted to know. As frightened as she was to hear it, she wanted to know what he had done. She wanted to know his crime. She *needed* to know. As though it would complete her picture of what manner of man he truly was. As though hearing him admit it all would once and for all relegate him to a category marked DO NOT TOUCH.

"What did you do?" she whispered.

He said nothing for a while. The air crackled between them. The sounds of the television echoed within the space of her condo. She stared at the TV screen as though she wasn't breathlessly waiting for his answer.

The silence ate at her, gnawing at her composure until she had to turn and face him.

His gaze was locked on her, his blue eyes bright

and intense, his body wound tighter than a spring beside her. "You want to know what I did to get locked up?'

She nodded, unblinking.

"You don't think I'm innocent? You don't think it was a mistake?" He smirked, that corner of his mouth kicking up.

She lifted one shoulder in a half shrug. "Was it?"

His lips curled now into a full-fledged smile that set loose dark and wicked things inside her. "No." He inched closer, his big shoulders angling so he faced her more fully on the couch. His fingers brushed her cheek, making her skin pucker to gooseflesh. "You know what I am."

"What's that?"

"I'm guilty."

"Guilty of what?"

"Murder."

She gulped, fighting against the sudden lump in her throat. "Who?"

His gaze flicked over her face, assessing before he answered. "One night my cousin went on a date. She was seventeen. Shy. She hadn't been on many dates. Never had a boyfriend before. This boy took Katie to a party where he raped her." Briar inhaled sharply but said nothing, afraid that a word from her would put an end to the recounting. "Everyone at the party . . . his friends . . . they all backed him up and said she wanted it. That she had been all over him. It was her word against theirs. My brother and I paid the boy a visit to get him to admit what he had done to her. We wanted the truth out of him. We wanted him to stop lying." He nodded, his gaze faraway, as if he was there now. "We went there to get him to admit what happened. We wanted justice for Katie. Yeah, we wanted to hurt him. I don't deny it, but we didn't set out to do that. When he started mouthing off and calling her dirty words and saying things about her—" He stopped hard, his throat working as he swallowed.

"You killed him," she finished.

He nodded tightly. "I just saw red. I lost control. I was young. Stupid. I caused my family so much pain." He inhaled deeply. "Katie killed herself during the trial. It was all too much. It broke her." Something sharpened in his eyes, a brightness that spoke of suffering. His family wasn't the only one he hurt. He hurt himself. He *still* hurt. That much was clear. "I did that. I broke her. And I dragged my brother to prison with me. He was only eighteen, just following my lead." His voice grew tight. Bitter emotion twisted his features. "And he's still in there. While I'm out here. How messed up is that?" He laughed roughly. "I'm not in prison anymore, but I'm still paying for my crime. I'll pay every day for the rest of my life."

Before she could think, she was taking his face in both hands, running her thumbs over the planes of his cheeks. "No, it doesn't have to be like that. You weren't stupid, Knox. Just young, like you said. And hurt. You're honorable. You're a protector. There is good in you. The same goodness that saved me in the prison. Not just me, but Dr. Walker and Josiah, too. You could have just sat there and let them do—"

"No," he bit out. "The minute I heard what those guys were going to do, I made sure I got injured in a fight and taken to the HSU."

She stared at him in shock, her stomach bottoming out. "You went in there on purpose?" It wasn't some split-second decision on his part to step in and save them?

He nodded once.

She moistened her lips. "I didn't know . . ."

He stared at her wordlessly, his gaze roaming her face.

Without thinking, she leaned in and kissed him. Softly, tenderly. Holding his face in her hands, she opened her mouth against him, not realizing until that moment that her face was wet, coated in salty tears.

His hands came up on either side of her head, holding her as she held him. His fingers brushed the tears from her cheeks and pulled her back so he could stare at her. "Why are you crying?"

She gulped back a sob, not understanding it entirely. His story, the truth of what happened to him and his family . . . that he got himself into the HSU deliberately for her. All of it tore loose something inside her and left her raw and bleeding. The only thing she could think to do was kiss him. As though that would somehow patch her up.

Instead of telling him that, she shook her head, sniffing back tears.

"Don't," he whispered, pressing his mouth to her cheeks, kissing away her tears. And then she was crying over this from him. This tenderness from a man that thought he was something broken. "Sssh." His mouth, moist with her tears, came back over her trembling lips.

She whimpered and opened to him. He brought her onto his lap. She straddled him and they kissed like that. Forever and ever. One hand came up to tug at her hair band, snapping it free so that the heavy mass tumbled loose to curtain them.

"God, I love your hair," he muttered against her mouth, running his hands through it and holding it back to keep kissing her.

She was breathless and panting when he suddenly broke off. "Briar, believe it or not, I didn't come here to do this."

She backed away from him, fighting the urge to beg him to keep going. She had already bared herself to him in a way that left her exposed and vulnerable tonight. She wouldn't do it again. She carefully chose her words. "Why did you come here, then?"

He gazed at her, one hand buried in her hair, the other still holding her face as though she were some fragile piece of crystal. His thumb trailed down her tear-moist cheek.

As though his silence was answer enough, she nodded once and started to pull away from him. No more disregarding her dignity. She wasn't chasing him.

His hands tightened around her, hauling her back. "I don't want to hurt you, Briar." He spoke so fiercely that she knew he was saying that as much for himself as her. "I should do the right thing. I tried tonight at Roscoe's. You know what I am. You shouldn't even let me near you. I should let you go. Leave you alone."

"If that's the right thing . . . why doesn't it feel like it?" she asked, unsure whom she was posing the question for. Him? Or herself?

He stared at her for a long moment before giving a single nod. "Okay." Something shifted in that single word. The plank she had been tottering on finally tipped and she fell to the other side.

Somehow he had just agreed to . . . what? Be with her? *Date* her? That word felt so small and weak compared to what she felt as he tucked her against his side and settled back on the couch, his strong arm wrapped fully around her.

TWENTY-TWO

*B*RIAR WOKE TO bright sunlight pouring in the blind slats and the smell of frying bacon. The bed she didn't remember climbing into was warm and cozy, the space beside her empty, but she knew the bacon wasn't frying itself.

Knox was still here.

A stupid smile broke out on her face, which she instantly tried reining in. She didn't want to look too eager. Just because they'd spent a night together that involved talking and cuddling and watching TV on her couch like a couple—*and* he didn't disappear before morning—did not mean they were in a committed relationship. If that's even what she wanted from him. She snorted, internally laughing at herself. Was there really any doubt anymore?

She stretched against her sheets and that stupid smile returned when she thought about the fact that he must have carried her to the bed. Her hand drifted to her mouth. She let her fingers play over her smile, not even caring that she must have weighed a ton. He'd carried her to bed rather than wake her up on the couch . . . or just leave altogether.

Hopping up from the bed, she smoothed a hand over her wild hair, caught a glimpse of herself in the mirror and shrugged. Deciding it was hopeless, she padded barefoot into the kitchen.

Knox stood shirtless in front of her stove. She stared at his broad, sinewy back with the dragon tattoo that wrapped around his side, disappearing around his ribs. Her mouth watered at the sight and she shifted on her feet, commanding her libido to get back down.

"Hey," she greeted, butterflies erupting in her stomach at the full impact of him, in a pair of jeans that sat low on his narrow hips, in her kitchen. Making breakfast.

He had actually stayed.

"Hey." He turned halfway and smiled at her. "Hungry?"

She nodded and plopped down on one of her bar stools, pressing her legs together as if that would stop their sudden shaking. She could probably count on one hand the number of times Knox smiled, and most of those times had been last night. She liked that they were continuing into today.

"Good. It's just about ready." Two pieces of toast

popped up and he did this little bounce step to pluck them from the toaster that ended with him swearing and tossing the hot bread around until they landed on the waiting plates.

She clapped. "Impressive." And she was impressed. Not just with his toast-saving expertise but with the play of cut muscles along his ribs and torso.

He winked. "I have mad toast-making skills."

He dished up the rest of their breakfast. So much food she wondered if this was meant to be her last meal. Ever. "Who is going to eat all this?"

"We are." He surprised her by pressing a lingering kiss to her mouth before settling back down on the stool beside her.

"I usually skip breakfast," she confessed.

"Terrible. Hasn't anyone told you it's the most important meal of the day?"

"Yes. I've heard that. I just would rather sleep the extra ten to twenty minutes."

At the mention of time, she glanced at the clock and gasped. "Is it really eleven?"

"Yeah. Guess this is technically brunch." He gestured to their plates of scrambled eggs, bacon, and toast.

"I can't remember the last time I slept this late."

"You had a late night." He stared at her in his devouring way, swiping back the heavy fall of hair off her shoulder.

She looked at him steadily. "It could have been a longer night . . ." If they had sex . . .

His gaze moved over her face, the searing blue darkening and heating her skin. "Your food is getting cold."

She dropped her attention to her breakfast. "Mmm," she murmured in appreciation as she scooped the first bite of buttery eggs into her mouth. "This is really good."

"Not much of a cook, but I can make some mean eggs and spaghetti."

"It's great. Thanks."

He winked at her and her stomach gave another flip at this lighter side of Knox. She could get used to him like this.

A text dinged on her phone. She could glimpse the screen from where she sat.

Don't forget to bring a dessert for the BBQ!!

"Dammit," she cursed at the sight of her sister's text.

"What is it?"

She nodded at the phone. "My sister. I forgot I promised to go to her barbecue today."

"Oh." He turned his stare back to his eggs, stabbing a fluffy bit with his fork. He dropped it into his mouth and followed it with a big bite of bacon.

She stared at his profile for a moment before she

heard herself blurting, "Would you like to go with me?"

She wasn't sure why she asked. Her sister would freak out, but she wasn't thinking about her sister right then. She was thinking about him. About right now. Sitting here having breakfast with him and how she could get used to that. Maybe it was a test, too.

Maybe she needed to see if he made up some excuse and scurried away. She might as well find out now if this was maybe something real. If there was that chance.

It was some time before he answered, and by then she was calling herself an idiot and fully expecting him to decline. They were still in unchartered territory and she had just invited him to a family barbecue?

"Yeah." He finally said. "I would."

KNOX WAS GOING to meet her family.

He wasn't certain what had inspired him to agree. He could claim it was the soft hope gleaming in her eyes when she invited him. That was definitely a part of it. He wanted to make her happy, and for some reason taking him to this barbecue and bringing him around her people would do that.

He didn't know why—he was certainly no prize for any woman—but she wanted him there. And he just wanted her. He knew that now. He accepted it. He felt lighter owning that fact. He wanted her around him. He wanted her under him, and he wasn't going to pretend differently anymore.

There were several cars parked in front of the two-story suburban home. It was a nice house even if it did resemble every other one on the street. Better than the old run-down farmhouse he grew up in with peeling linoleum floors. Except it never bothered him much as boy. He and North had run over those floors in their football cleats. They'd explored every acre surrounding the house, hunting for arrowheads. He preferred the wide-open space of the country to living in one of these boxes. It reminded him of his cell block back in the prison. Relentless uniformity.

At least at his house he could walk out his front door and see trees.

As they made their way to her sister's front porch, he took her hand in his. She sent him a startled look that was replaced with a smile he felt like a punch to his stomach. It was soft and tender and gave him all kinds of ideas. He suddenly regretted that he hadn't touched her last night because all he wanted to do now was haul her off somewhere and taste all those parts of her that were soft and tender. The places that made her melt and sigh for him.

They were almost to the door when he tugged her back a step. "Hey," he murmured.

She looked up at him curiously, stopping in front of him. "Hey." She angled her head, still wearing that smile.

He reached up and dragged a thumb down her cheek, staring into her eyes and thinking that he'd never seen softer eyes.

He kissed her, taking his time, parting her lips and sweeping inside her mouth, tasting her until he felt her hands crawl up his chest and wrap around his neck.

He pulled back with a ragged breath. "Okay. Let's go in."

She made a small sound of disappointment, staring up at him with a cloudy gaze. "I say we forget the barbecue."

He chuckled, readjusting his grip on the supermarket bag that held cookies. "Can't do that. You promised your sister."

"She won't even notice if I'm not there."

Still holding her hand, he stepped forward and pushed the doorbell. "Something tells me she will." And if he was going to be in Briar's life, then he needed to meet this sister and try to win her over.

"Fine," she grumbled and started to say something else but the door suddenly opened.

"Briar!" The woman he had noticed in pictures at Briar's place leaned forward to hug her. She sent him a suspicious look as she pulled back. "Who's this?"

"This is my . . . friend. Knox. Knox, this is Laurel."

They shook hands. "You didn't mention you were bringing a friend." Laurel shot a pointed look at Briar that told him all he needed to know. She wasn't happy he was here. She glanced down at their clasped hands and frowned. Yeah, she definitely wasn't happy. There'd be no winning her over today.

"Well, come in. Everyone's out back." She plucked the bag of cookies from Knox and tugged her sister inside, effectively breaking their linked hands.

Briar shot him an apologetic look over her shoulder as her sister dragged her ahead of him into the house.

He shut the front door and followed at a sedate pace.

Yeah. This was going to be fun.

TWENTY-THREE

LAUREL WASTED NO time hauling Briar into her bedroom and shutting the door, cutting them off from the rest of the party so she could get to the bottom of Briar bringing a guy to the barbecue. "Who is he?"

Briar shrugged and glanced around Laurel's bedroom. She ran a hand over the bed, pretending to admire her sister's new comforter. "Is this Pottery Barn?"

"Don't try to change the subject on me. Who is that guy? He looks a little . . ." Briar's eyes snapped to her sister, something tight and defensive brewing inside her. ". . . rough," Laurel finished, arching both eyebrows, daring Briar to deny that description.

"Knox and I are friends."

"He was holding your hand."

"We're good friends," she amended.

Laurel's eyes widened and she shot a quick glance at the door before hissing, "Oh my God! You're sleeping with him!"

A flush crept up Briar's face. Was she that transparent?

"This is serious and you haven't even mentioned him to me," Laurel accused. "You haven't slept with anyone since Beau."

Briar rolled her eyes. "Yeah, I'm kind of aware of my sexual history." Limited as it was.

Laurel cocked her head to the side and propped a hand to her hip. "Are you also 'aware,' or did it slip your mind, that I have a *date* for you here today?"

"What?" She dropped her hands to her hips, dread pooling in her stomach. "I didn't ask you to set me up—"

"I told you Martin Ford was going to be here weeks ago. He's been asking when you're going to get here. I invited him for you! What am I supposed to do now that you've shown up with a date?"

"Tell the truth. I started seeing someone and you didn't know." She shrugged. "Sorry," she added, even though she wasn't. Laurel had created this situation. Briar refused to let it be her problem.

"Who is he?" Laurel crossed her arms over her chest and leveled Briar with one of her parent death-stares. "Where did you meet? What does he do?'

Briar sucked in a deep breath. She knew these questions were coming, but that didn't mean she was ready to answer any of them. She edged toward the door. "Shouldn't we get back to your guests?"

"Briar . . ." her sister said in that warning voice she used when dealing with her children.

"He doesn't know anyone here. It's rude to just leave him alone out there."

"He's a big boy. Now answer me, damn it."

She closed her eyes in a tight blink and then focused on her sister's face. "I met him at Devil's Rock prison."

Her sister paused, processing this. "He works there?" she asked with a slight flare of her nostrils, and Briar remembered that this Martin guy was an accountant. That was the type of man her sister wanted her to go out with. "What is he? One of the corrections officers?" Her top lip curled faintly, clearly thinking Briar could do better than that.

"No."

Her sister stared at her. "Did he work in the clinic with—"

"He was an inmate, Laurel."

Laurel staggered back a step, her arms dropping to her sides. Revulsion rippled over her face. "No."

Briar nodded. "He served his time and he's out now—"

"Oh my God." She clutched her chest. "You're just like Mom—"

"No," Briar bit out. "He's a good man who made a mistake and served out his sentence for his crime."

"Are you even listening to yourself?" She nodded

her head doggedly. "He went to prison! What did he do?" Laurel's eyes burned laser-hot into her.

Briar shook her head once and looked down at her feet, unwilling to say it, knowing how it sounded. She'd thought that way at first, before she knew Knox. Before he'd saved her life and Dr. Walker and Josiah.

"Un-fucking believable." Briar flinched. Her sister never cursed. "Whatever he did, you can't even say it. Was it murder? Did he kill someone?"

She looked up at her sister. "You don't understand. He never meant to kill anyone . . . and the guy he attacked did a horrib—"

"Stop! Stop it! You're making excuses for him. You sound just like Mom. I can't believe you even brought this man into my house, Briar." Her eyes widened and shot to the door as though it dawned on her that this *dangerous* man was out there with all her friends . . . with her children.

"I really need you to have an open mind about this, Laurel, and trust my judgment," Briar whispered. "You're all I have for a family." Her relationship with her parents was nonexistent. Her mom lived to serve her father, taking his abuses, weathering his temper, bowing to all his whims, even at the loss of her daughters. That would never change. It would always be that way. Her sister was all she had left.

Laurel smoothed her hands over her silky smooth

Keratin-treated hair. "I'm going to go back out there and act like there isn't some dangerous criminal in my home—"

"He's not—"

"And then *you*!"—Laurel's gaze cut her like a knife—"are going to promise me that you will never bring him around me or my family again. Go ahead. Ruin your life, Briar. I can't stop you from being with him, but I don't have to watch it or be around it."

Briar nodded stiffly, frustration an aching mass in her chest. It hurt because she loved her sister and wanted her support. "I understand," she said.

With a single stiff nod, Laurel swept out of the bedroom. Briar lingered a moment longer, blinking stinging eyes and telling herself that she wasn't wrong in this. Last night . . . this morning, she knew what she was doing. She knew who Knox really was. Or at least she knew enough to know that he was no threat to her. No more than Beau or any other seemingly *good* man. He wasn't her father and she wasn't her mother.

Who they could be together . . . no matter what her sister thought, she wanted to find out.

SHE HAD TOLD her sister about Knox. He knew the minute Laurel emerged from the house and leveled bitter-cold eyes on him as he stood nursing the beer Briar's brother-in-law foisted on him. That look said it all. She knew he'd done time and she thought he was scum for it.

He didn't feel much like drinking, but he clasped his sweating bottle as he waited for Briar to return.

Laurel's reaction didn't surprise him, but he was surprised it still stung. He'd lived with the world's low opinion of him for over eight years, and the only reason it didn't destroy him was because he didn't give a flying fuck what others thought of him. Hell, he'd been driving a vandalized truck around with the word "killer" emblazoned on the side.

He only cared what his family and the few friends he had thought of him. And Briar. He cared what she thought. Hell, he wouldn't be here feeling so out of place if he didn't care what she thought. Admittedly, it would be nice if her sister didn't hate the sight of him. It would make things harder for Briar.

Kids ran around the adults, screaming and hitting each other with foam balls. The men were discussing their jobs, while the wives were talking about the sports their kids played. Like these kids were headed for the Olympics or some shit. Caleb was a friendly enough guy and talked to him as he flipped burgers on the grill.

After delivering him that cutting glare, Laurel made a beeline for some guy grazing at the spread of food. He held a beer in one hand and his phone in the other, as if he couldn't be apart from the device.

Laurel beamed at him. No flinty-eyed stare for him. She talked with her hands, her gaze flickering in Knox's direction. The smile slipped off Phone Man's face, and Knox guessed that she was explaining that Briar had showed up with a *friend*.

Briar arrived then, stepping out onto the crowded patio. She scanned the people milling around. Her amber gaze lit up when she spotted him and his chest loosened like he could breathe again.

And that's why he was here. It was the only reminder he needed.

"How long you been dating Briar?" Caleb moved some burgers, lifting them to the upper rack, and then reached for the waiting package of cheese slices.

"We met a few months back." Not a lie precisely.

Caleb began arranging cheese on top of the burgers. "She hasn't mentioned you."

It was said innocently enough but it felt like an accusation. Knox looked back, only to see that Laurel had snagged Briar and was tugging her toward the food table and Phone Man.

He watched with narrowed eyes as Briar's sister introduced them to each other with great flourish. Phone Guy shook Briar's hand, holding on longer than necessary.

"Who's that?" he heard himself asking Caleb.

Caleb glanced up from the grill. "That would be my boss's son, Martin Ford. He's a CPA. Laurel's been trying to set them up for a while." He took a pull from his beer and considered Knox. "Guess that's not happening today." He shrugged and leaned in conspiratorially to add, "Fine by me. The guy's a prick."

Knox nodded noncommittally, not voicing agreement but already disliking the guy just from the way he looked Briar up and down, openly assessing her in her floral print sundress like she was some buffet spread out before him. It wasn't a flashy dress. It ended just at her knees, but Phone Man looked at her like she wasn't wearing anything at all.

"Everyone knows it," Caleb grumbled. "Except for my wife." He shrugged and shot Knox a grin. "Whad'ya going to do, though?"

He nodded, fighting the urge to stay where he was and not act like a guy straight out of prison—even if he was. This was a family barbecue. Briar's family. He didn't need to lose his shit and embarrass her.

"You like cheese on your burger?"

He dragged his attention away from Martin Ford, who stood with his hand on Briar's shoulder, keeping it there longer than necessary. A CPA. He was wearing khaki slacks and an immaculately pressed plaid button-down. He looked like the kind of guy that would date a nice girl like Briar.

"Yeah, thanks," he replied.

Caleb looked toward Briar and Martin and shook his head. "How about another beer, man?"

Knox exhaled, wondering how long he could stand by like it didn't bother him that Briar was across the patio getting pawed by some guy handpicked by her sister. "Sounds good."

Briar looked across the distance at him, her eyes full of apology. He nodded at her like none of it was a problem—being here among these people who lived their gingerbread lives in their gingerbread houses . . . her sister hating the sight of him. He tried to look like everything was going to be okay even though he was starting to wonder if that was true.

"I'VE BEEN HEARING about you for months," Martin said as he swirled a carrot stick in some dip. Crunching down on it, his gaze drifted back to her face almost expectantly. Briar stared at him, unsure how to respond.

Laurel had disappeared after whispering in tight warning, "Talk to him. Don't be rude."

"We finally meet." He rocked back on his heels, showing off crunchy bits of orange carrots coated in white dip in his mouth.

"Yes." She nodded awkwardly, glancing over to where Knox stood chatting with Caleb. At least her brother-in-law was being a good guy and talking to him. Unlike her sister. Laurel was probably hiding all their valuables right now.

Martin nodded, bobbing his entire head and eyeing

her. "So we should go out. You know, on a date. I know this place that makes the best enchiladas."

"Uh—"

"Oh, you're serious about this guy you brought? Your sister said it wasn't anything serious."

She winced. Of course her sister would have told him that. "I'm not really interested in seeing anyone—"

"What's he do?"

"Excuse me?"

"What's he do?"

"For a living?" she asked.

"Yeah. Last year I cleared six figures. Bought a BMW. What's he do?"

Oh, he was a definite prize. "I'm going to go now." She started to turn away, but he grabbed her arm.

"Hey, I'm just kidding with you, don't get your panties in a knot," he cajoled. "Where's your sense of humor? It's called a joke."

"Oh." She laughed weakly.

He chuckled, still holding onto her arm.

"Hey, there." Knox sidled up to her, slipping an arm around her waist. She practically sagged against him in her relief.

Martin looked him up and down. "Ah, is this him? The devil himself? Hi, there. I'm Martin. Looks like you beat me to the goal. I was supposed to go out with Brianna here."

Knox reached out to shake his hand. "Her name is Briar."

"Yeah. I said that." He nodded, unfazed. "What's your name, man?"

"Knox Callaghan."

Martin held a hand up to his ear like he was imitating an old man with failing hearing. "Knox? What's that? A nickname of some kind?"

Knox stared at him a moment before answering. "No. That's my real name."

"Huh." Martin nodded as if that made sense. "Well, we were just talking about you."

"Were you?" He glanced at Briar and then back to Martin.

"Yes, she was about to tell me what you do for a living . . . Knox."

"I work at Roscoe's."

"Roscoe's? That shithole outside town?" Martin took a deep swig of his beer.

Knox clenched his jaw, not answering.

"Yeah," he continued. "I've driven by the place. Never went in, though. Figured I'd have to get my tetanus up-to-date first." Chuckling, Martin dove a hand into a bowl of chips on the table.

"Asshole," Briar bit out, not even caring that she had just called the guy her sister invited for *her* an asshole.

Laughing, Martin tossed some chips back into his

mouth. "Hey, just kidding. You need to lighten up
. . . You're not offended, right?" He clapped Knox
on the shoulder and jabbed a thumb at Briar. "A real
firecracker, this one, huh? But you know what they
say about girls with potty mouths . . ."

Briar looked around, wondering if other people
were aware of the total assholery this guy was radiating.

"And what's that?" Knox asked, his hand exerting
more pressure at her waist.

"You know." Martin brought his fist to the side of
his mouth and made the motion for a blow job.

Briar gaped. Her sister actually thought she should
go out with this guy? She started to leave, and she
didn't care if he insisted he was "kidding" again. She
was out of here. Martin clucked his tongue. "Didn't
expect you to be so sensitive, Brianna. You're hook-
ing up with a guy that works at Roscoe's. You'd have
to be a little adventurous for that."

If he was going to say anything else, the words
were cut off. Knox grabbed him by the back of the
neck and brought his face crashing down into the
table with such savagery that chips flew up in the air
and scattered out of their bowls.

"Knox!" she cried out, horrified, her hands flying
to her face.

Knox ignored her and bowed close to Martin's
ear, whispering as he mashed his face into the table,

"Now in what life do you think it's okay to talk like that?" Knox turned him slightly, still gripping his neck and forcing him to glance up at her. "You don't get to say things like that to her. Understand?"

Martin's eyes were dazed. Faint blood dribbled from his nostril. He didn't look coherent enough to even process what Knox was saying. Briar doubted anyone in his entire privileged life had ever laid hands to him in such a brutal manner.

A quick look around her sister's patio revealed everyone was as horrified as she was. Even the kids had stopped running and were watching in wonder.

"Knox," she breathed, reaching out to grip his tightly coiled arm. He was in the prison again. Barely checked violence, ready to snap. "No, Knox, no!"

Everyone had gone silent and her words sounded almost obscenely loud. A little girl sitting at the picnic table closest to them started crying. Her mother snatched her up and hurried inside the house.

Briar tightened her grip on Knox's arm. "C'mon. Let's go."

Knox released him and Martin staggered back, trying to gain his feet and failing. He fell against the table before dropping to the ground.

No one else moved. Everyone stared, looking at Knox like he might suddenly turn his fists on them.

In the sudden silence, the only thing she could hear was the hiss of the grill and the rasp of her breath.

She glanced at Knox to see that he was looking, too. Watching everyone watch him with a blank expression.

With a curse so soft she barely heard it, he shoved past her and wove through everyone until he disappeared inside the house.

Briar hurried after him, her heart still hammering.

Her sister called her name right before she was about to enter the house. She sent Laurel a sharp look followed by a swift shake of her head. Laurel was the last person she wanted to talk to right now.

She caught up with Knox outside. He was waiting beside her car. One look at his face and she decided to let him cool off before they talked. And maybe she needed time to digest what just happened, too. She couldn't get his enraged face when he'd unleashed on Martin out of her head. There was murder in his eyes.

He held out his hand and she dropped her keys into his palm.

They drove back to her place in silence. Tapping her fingers along the edge of the door, she stole several glances at him. His jaw was locked in tension, his hard eyes focused straight ahead on the road. She opened her mouth at one point to tell him it was okay, but it didn't feel right. Nothing felt okay in this moment.

As angry as she was with him for exploding like that, she felt him slipping away from her, becoming his old self. The inmate that hardly spared her a word, and when he did it was fierce and brutal.

By the time they reached her condo, she was ready to talk. He unlocked her door for her and handed her back her keys.

"Thanks," she murmured.

She stepped inside and he followed her, closing the door behind them.

She dropped her keys on the counter and spun to face him. "What the hell was that back there? I mean I know he was an asshole but was it really necessary to—"

He kissed her. Circled her neck with his hand and hauled her against him. There was nothing soft or tender about it. He claimed her, his teeth tugging hard on her bottom lip, and she opened for him with a moan. He picked her up, his hands guiding her legs around his waist as if she weighed nothing at all.

A few short strides and they were in her bedroom. On her bed. He fell over her and yanked her dress up to her hips with a single rough move. Everything was happening so fast. Her heart was pounding. Her blood roaring.

His mouth fused hotly to hers, not even coming up for air as she felt his hand between them, working his zipper down. He grabbed her hand and shoved it inside his jeans to close around him. "Touch me," he ordered.

Her fingers circled his hardness, her thumb dragging over the swollen tip of him.

"Christ," he muttered.

He fumbled in a pocket. She heard the crinkle and tear of a foil condom wrapper. He broke away long enough to shove his jeans all the way down his hips.

Propping up on her elbows, she watched him slide latex over his erection, so turned on at the sight that she couldn't breathe. He spread her thighs wide and reached down to jerk her panties to the side with an impatient twist.

And then he was in her, pushing deep. She surged against the fullness of him, her head dropping back as he yanked her hips closer. He sank all the way in and didn't wait for her to catch her breath at the sudden invasion.

He pumped inside her, his expression savage as he worked to his own release. She clutched his biceps, needing something to hang onto as he pounded out his need.

Abruptly, he paused and flipped her over on all fours. He ripped her underwear fully off and splayed a hand under her stomach, lifting her higher, positioning her how he wanted her on her hands and knees.

He slid into her from behind, his hands gripping her ass. She moaned, a rush of wetness meeting the thrust of his cock. He'd never been like this before.

This was an unfiltered Knox. He took her fast and rough. For himself. And that only made it hotter. Made her sex clench and burn around the slide of him. She backed up into him, meeting his thrusts in her own frenzied need. Their bodies crashed together with loud slaps.

The sensation of his hands gripping her bottom, and the delicious friction of him sliding in and out of her, exhilarated her. She glanced over her shoulder at him, and the sight of that brutally handsome face, like something carved from stone, so feral and stripped bare with wild hunger for her, made her knees shake and threaten to buckle.

He leaned over her, his hard chest curving over her back. One of his hands slid around her hip and arrowed straight to the core of her, finding her clit and rolling it deftly. She came apart, her world splintering into shards of light and then descending to darkness, where, for a moment, she couldn't see anything at all. But she felt. She felt him still going, hammering into her almost desperately, her breath coming in rapid gasps as he barreled toward his own release.

She felt the scrape of his jaw against the side of her face and then the sink of his teeth into her earlobe. And just like that she shuddered all over again, her body vibrating and humming as her sex squeezed around him.

"Oh," he groaned. "That's it. Milk my dick." She

felt him come inside her as he held himself deep, spasming almost in rhythm to her own contracting body.

His voice breathed into her ear, "Mine."

She felt the word echo through her, felt it sink deep and root inside her in the most hidden crevices of her heart. Her chest expanded on a silent *yes*. She was his. And he was hers. She felt that, too, even if she couldn't say it out loud.

She collapsed on the bed, not even minding his weight over her, pressing her into the mattress.

She turned her face to the side, still gasping. He braced his arms on either side of her, keeping his weight from fully squashing her. His harsh breath fluttered the hairs at her neck. She rubbed the tickle away with her fingers.

He lifted himself off her, and she felt an ache at the sudden loss. As he went into the bathroom to dispose of the condom, she sat up, smoothing her wrinkled sundress down her thighs. She was standing by the time he returned, ready to have the conversation she had tried to start with him before he kissed her.

He stepped out of the bathroom wearing a familiarly distant expression on his face. The sight of it stabbed her in the chest, and suddenly he felt out of her reach. Already gone. She ignored the feeling and told herself she was overreacting.

She took a breath and started. "Knox, about what hap—"

"I'm going to head out."

She blinked and shook her head, sure he did not just cut her off to announce he was leaving. "We need to talk," she said, nodding at him as though encouraging those words to sink in. For him to understand.

He rubbed his fingers over the center of his forehead like he suddenly had a headache. Like *she* was his headache. Which stung. "I don't think we should do this, Briar."

She flinched. "What is 'this' exactly? Let's be clear on that point since you don't want to do it again. Fucking?" She managed to not even shock herself at uttering the profane word. "Is that what you mean? You don't want to fuck anymore?" She motioned savagely to the bed. "You could have fooled me."

He looked almost bored as he gazed at her, tilting his head to one side. "Let's not do this, Briar."

"Oh, let's do it. I want to. Really." She crossed her arms. "I thought you coming here last night established you were interested in me."

"There's fucking and there's having a relationship. I'm not the relationship type. You are."

"And you're just now deciding this? You seemed to have a different attitude last night . . . and this morning."

"There's never been a chance for us. Don't you see that?" He waved his arms, some of his austere facade cracking as his frustration bled out. "We were just fooling ourselves, Briar."

She shook her head. "I—I was willing to try—"

"Consider it tried," he said, taking another step away from where she stood in front of the bed, like he couldn't wait to escape. "You're not the kind of girl who gets involved with a man like me."

Her chin went up. She fought against the wave of pain rolling through her. "Maybe you're right."

He hesitated, looking at her oddly, and she gave herself a pat on the back for catching him off guard. Did he want her to plead and beg? No. She would reach him a different way. With the truth.

"Today my sister told me I was just like my mother." At his silent stare, she continued, "She said that because my mother married my father. And she never left him even though he beat her and humiliated her and made her every day a misery. Even though she lived in fear of his voice, she stayed. She stayed and made us stay, too. She still stays with him even though we've offered her a place to live. A home with either one of us. She stays with him. This danger-ous, abusive man." Emotion bubbled up in her chest, threatening to overtake her, but she held on.

He finally spoke, "You never told me—"

"About my father? Why would I? He's not part of my life anymore. He doesn't deserve to be remem-bered but I'm telling you now. Maybe I didn't go to prison, but I know what it's like to live every day waiting to be free, waiting to escape a shitty existence. I know about abusive men."

He closed the space separating them and cupped her cheek. "Your sister is wrong. I would never hurt you, Briar."

"You're right. I'm not my mother. But you're leaving me now because you think you're the same as him . . . this *thing* I've been careful to stay away from."

"Briar . . . you're smart enough to see—"

"Smart enough to know you," she quickly cut in, triumph flashing through her at making her point. "I'm not my mother and you're not my father."

His hand dropped from her face. "I never worried that I would hurt you. It's the rest of the world I worry about. I never planned to kill that boy all those years ago. I just wanted the truth out of him. Justice for Katie. It could happen again. I could lose control. Around you, I feel that way. If anyone ever hurt you—" He stopped and shook his head. "That's why this ends here."

"Nothing is going to happen to me," she insisted, even though she knew as she uttered the words that they would have little impact. His mind was made up.

"You're not hearing me," he growled, his eyes growing more distant. Cold, shuttered blue. He was already gone from her. She was talking to air. "I've got to be in control now . . . I can't be that kid I was

all those years ago. With you, I feel like him again."
He motioned between the two of them. "This . . . us
. . . is me out of control."

She sucked in a deep breath and angled her head,
truly hearing what he was saying even if he did not.
"So what you're saying is that *I* am no good for *you*."

Her words hung between them, a truth that felt
as awful as teeth sinking in, latching onto muscle
and sinew, striking bone and sending pain vibrating
through her. This wasn't about him being so fucking noble and letting her go because he wasn't good
enough for her.

He thought *she* was bad for him.

He looked angry and a little bewildered. "I didn't
say that—"

"*Yes.* You did." Essentially *that* was it. The truth.

She backed away, sipping air into lungs that felt
raw. "I get it now. It doesn't matter what I think or
feel. It doesn't matter that I might be a little in love
with you."

As soon as the words escaped, she knew they were
a lie. There was no *might*. She was a *lot* in love with
him, and she stood before him exposed, her heart
bared and bleeding.

"Briar." He said her name gently, pitiably. As
though she were a dumb girl who went and fell in
love with him when he didn't want that. When there
was no chance in hell he would stick around and love

her back. God. She *was* that dumb girl. "You don't feel that way. This was sex. Good sex. Sometimes that gets confusing—"

"No," she snapped. "Don't talk to me like I'm an idiot who doesn't know the difference between sex and love. I know what I feel."

For a moment he looked like he might touch her again. If he touched her, she would fall apart.

But he didn't.

"And," she added hoarsely, the words sliding from a throat that felt raw with burning tears, ready to fall, "I know what someone looks like when he's running away. Because he's scared."

"I am scared," he admitted, his jaw locked tight. "Scared of making the same mistakes and going back in that box again."

So she would be a mistake.

"Understood," she said, with far more composure than she felt. "So go," she commanded. When he still stood there staring at her, she blurted out, "Get the fuck out." The sooner he was gone, the sooner she could fall apart.

He didn't even flinch at her language. He nodded once, looking so damned stoic. The same impenetrable mask he wore the first day she met him at Devil's Rock.

Without another word, he slipped out of her bedroom and out the front door.

HE CURSED AS he slammed into his truck and pulled out of Briar's parking lot. Regret welled up bitter as blood in his mouth, but not for walking away from Briar. That had to happen. She thought she loved him, but she didn't. She was wrong about that. She couldn't love him.

He was getting out just in time. Hell, he probably should have gotten out sooner. When he initially tried. Before she showed up at Roscoe's and threw his world off kilter.

He wouldn't lose control again, and Briar made him do that. He felt too much around her. He wanted her too much. Cared about her too much. His mind shied from thinking about love in relation to her. It wasn't love. He came from a world where you staked a claim. Prison taught him about taking, having. Marking what was his. That was his instinct when it came to Briar. Not love.

She was risk, and he had vowed to leave risk behind when he stepped out of that prison.

He regretted ever starting this between them in the first place. He regretted that he hurt her. He should have fucked his way through half of Roscoe's instead of having something clean and sweet like Briar.

His phone started ringing in his pocket. A quick glance down revealed his aunt's name. He felt a flash of worry. He hoped everything was okay with Uncle Mac.

He answered, "Hey, Aunt Alice, everything okay?"

"Knox, have you seen the news?"

"No, what's wrong?"

"There was a riot at the prison."

His stomach heaved. "North?"

"We just got a call. They took him to Memorial Hospital."

"What's his status? Will they let us see him?" He knew the only way they let family visit inmates in the hospital was when the prognosis was grim. As in deathbed grim.

"Not yet. The social worker said he'd call back with an update."

"I'm on my way. Be there in ten minutes."

He hung up and stared straight ahead into the setting dusk, his gaze burning. The guilt he felt for leaving North behind twisted and swirled like an angry hive of bees in his stomach. It was just one more thing. One more weight added to the piles of bricks that already crushed him.

He should have been there. Then maybe North wouldn't be in the hospital now.

He pressed down on the accelerator, eager to get home and be near the phone when they called back.

TWENTY-FOUR

DEEP SHADOWS DRAPED the hospital room. A dim glow radiated from the panel above Reid's hospital bed, saving the space from complete blackness. Someone outside his room laughed as they passed his door. The footsteps faded. Otherwise the hospital was quiet with that humming quality of a building that never shut off. Like him. Reid was wired tight. Tension knotted his shoulders as he reclined in the bed. He never shut down. Never turned off. He couldn't afford to. Not until he was a pile of ashes in a box. Then, he'd rest.

Doctors, nurses, and other personnel worked the six floors of Sweet Hill Memorial with seemingly little thought to the felon in Room 321. Exactly the way he wanted it. He'd been here eight days. Eight days since he was taken from Devil's Rock in an ambulance. In that time, he'd been an exemplary patient. He withstood all the poking and prodding without complaint. He slept and he ate. You could say whatever you wanted about hospital food, but compared to prison food it was five-star cuisine.

He'd used his time to store up energy and plot his next move. He had only one chance and he couldn't fuck it up.

He'd be sent back soon. He wasn't hooked up to any beeping machines anymore. His wounds had pretty much healed, leaving only the black lines of stitches and fresh, itching scabs. No threat of infection or continued bleeding. His arm sling could come off in a few days. According to the doctor, he was lucky to be alive. Half an inch to the left and the shiv would have hit his heart.

He'd said nothing when the doctor told him that, looking at him so expectantly. As though Reid might express relief or gratitude. He might be alive and breathing, but he had died a long time ago. Nothing but a walking ghost now.

A ghost with nothing to lose.

Still, starting that fight had been a gamble. He winced, recalling how quickly everything had escalated and turned into a full-on riot. He'd only meant to get himself injured. Instead inmates had died. Guards were injured. He'd seen North go down in a shower of blood. He felt like shit about that. He'd promised Knox he would look out for the kid. Reid had made inquiries and knew he was in a room somewhere else in this hospital. Thankfully, North would recover, but that face of his wouldn't be so pretty anymore.

And that sucked. More guilt. More sins to heap at his feet. But it was done. He, better than anyone, knew you couldn't change the past. He just had to make sure it meant something. That it wasn't for nothing. Then he could go back to rotting away for the rest of his life.

He took a deep, mostly pain-free breath as a nurse entered his room for a final bed check of the night. He was the last to be told anything concerning himself, but he knew. Even if he hadn't spied the paperwork on the doctor's clipboard authorizing his release, Reid knew. His time here was done. It was now or never. He had to act tonight.

"Are you comfortable? Can I get you anything? Another pillow?" Nadine asked as she adjusted the one beneath his head, bringing her chest close to his face. It was a game she liked to play. Tease the hard-up convict. Lingering touches on his body that didn't feel quite so clinical. It'd been a while but he knew when a woman was into him.

The guard who'd accompanied her into the room snorted. Reid leveled his gaze on Vasquez. The man clearly found her compassion toward a scumbag like him unnecessary.

Reid looked back at the nurse. "I'm fine." He smiled at her. It felt a little rusty. He hadn't done a lot of smiling in the last eleven years, but it seemed to work. She smiled back.

He picked up the remote control with his arm that wasn't in a sling. "I might watch some television." The more noise coming from his room, the better.

He punched the on button and the TV flickered to CNN, the channel Landers, the day guard, preferred. It was a good thing Landers wasn't here tonight. He hung out in the room with Reid a lot. Vasquez, on the other hand, only entered the room to accompany hospital staff. The rest of the time he stood watch outside the door.

"Don't stay up too late," Nadine advised. "You need your rest."

He nodded, training his gaze on the TV as if he cared about what was happening in the rest of the world.

Footage rolled across the screen of a vaguely familiar female dressed in a boring gray suit that hung on her like a sack.

". . . an inside White House source reports that the First Daughter has been missing for over twenty-four hours, ever since Wednesday afternoon following a luncheon with the Ladies Literacy League in Fort Worth, Texas, where she delivered a speech on . . ."

The nurse tsked. "Can you believe it? Someone abducted the president's daughter. What's the world coming to?"

He shook his head as if this was indeed something he gave a fuck about.

"She probably took off for a weekend to Padre Island," Vasquez grumbled. "Meanwhile, every law enforcement agency in the state is on full alert, wasting time and taxpayers' money searching for her."

The timing couldn't have been better as far as Reid was concerned. Deep satisfaction pumped through his veins, mingling with the building adrenaline. That meant they would care less about one escaped convict.

He didn't bother pointing out that the dark-haired female—who looked anywhere between the ages of twenty and forty—was the least likely candidate for a wild weekend at Padre.

"Haven't you been watching the news?" Nadine asked. "They suspect terrorists," she pointed out with an indignant sniff.

"What does the media know?" The guard rolled his eyes. "Watch. She'll show up on Monday."

Nadine shrugged and looked back to Reid. "Good night."

Reid fixed a smile to his face as she slipped from the room, the guard close behind her.

The door clicked softly shut, and he sat there for a long while, letting the minutes tick past, letting the hospital sink further into night, his hand twitching anxiously at his side.

CNN streamed a constant feed of First Daughter Grace Reeves while reporting absolutely nothing new or enlightening. Graduate of some all-girls college with a degree in astronomy. She looked uncomfortable in her own skin. She was dating the White House communications director, with rumors of an engagement imminent. Surprising, since she didn't look the type to be with the slick-looking guy mugging for the camera.

They flashed pictures and footage of Grace Reeves from awkward adolescent to current day still-awkward-looking adult. You would think the President had someone on staff that could coach her not to look so pinch-faced. Maybe they could dress her better, too. Not like a middle-aged bureaucrat.

When the clock on the wall read 12:34, he decided he had waited long enough. He knew when he planned this endeavor they would likely leave him unrestrained. With his level of injuries and a guard standing watch twenty-four/seven, they deemed it unnecessary. The trick would be getting out of the room—and out of the hospital—undetected.

He rose from the bed and slipped the sling over his head. He moved his arm gingerly, experiencing only a slight twinge of discomfort from the deepest laceration in his chest. He'd had worse.

He fashioned a lump under the covers, doing the best he could to make it look like a body. He turned off the light above his bed. It might pass for him if someone took a cursory peek inside the dim room.

Moving quietly, he slipped the surgical scissors out from where he'd stashed them under the mattress and moved a chair beneath the ceiling access panel.

A draft crept through the back slit of his hospital gown as he climbed up on the chair and lifted his arms, working two of the tiny screws loose in the panel. It swung down soundlessly.

Sucking in a breath, he pulled himself up through the panel, grunting at the strain in his still sore muscles. The square space was barely wide enough for his big body, but he managed to heft himself through.

Above his room, the space was dark and crowded with conduit pipes and hot water valves. He ducked his head, walking on pipes, carefully choosing his steps so he didn't crash through the Sheetrock.

Light trickled in from another access panel ahead. He peered down between the slats, identifying the hallway outside his room. He kept going, looking through the metal square panels until he finally came to one that overlooked a break room.

He listened to the rumble of voices below and glimpsed the top of one man's balding head as he changed shirts. "See you tomorrow, Frank." A locker slammed shut. "Tell your wife to make some of those cookies again."

"They're supposed to be for me," Frank complained.

"I'm doing you a favor," the other guy laughed. "You're fat enough." He left the room and it was just Frank for a few more minutes. He was out of his range of vision, but Reid could hear him rustling around. Soon, another locker shut and he left the room.

Reid waited a few seconds and then worked the screws loose until the panel swung open. He lowered himself down, clutching the edges of the opening until his feet landed lightly on cold tile.

He moved swiftly, started with the lockers, hoping there was one where the combination lock hadn't shifted and would lift open for him. He got lucky on his sixth try. Even better, a pair of men's scrubs and a hoodie hung inside. Several dollars and loose change littered the bottom of the locker floor along with a pair of tennis shoes. Reid grabbed it all and shut the locker. Arms full, he disappeared into one of the bathroom stalls to change.

The shoes were a little snug, but the scrubs fit. He tightened the drawstring at his waist and slipped on the hoodie, zipping it halfway up. Snatching up his hospital gown, he stuffed it into a trash can on his way out.

He walked out into the hallway like he belonged there. Squaring his shoulders, he slipped one hand in the pocket of his hoodie and immediately brushed the cold cut of metal. He wrapped his fingers around the clump of keys, thumbing the clicker. Sweet. Lifting a car would be simple enough.

Reid didn't pass anyone as he strolled down the hall. He dove through a corner door that led to a stairwell and hurried down the flights. Vasquez could check on him any time. He needed to be far from here when that happened.

The first floor had a little more life to it. A nurse passed him as he strode toward the front lobby. She barely glanced up from the chart she was studying. He felt the stare of the camera in the corner but kept walking.

Later, they would study the footage and marvel at him walking bold as day down the hall. But by then it wouldn't matter. He would be gone.

He passed through a set of automatic doors and sent a smile to the woman behind the circular counter of the admittance desk. She gave him a distracted nod as she spoke into a phone.

Only two people sat in the waiting area. One dozed. The other stared at the TV in the corner where footage of the First Daughter ran in a constant loop.

His heart stalled and sped up at the sight of the security guard near the door. His attention was focused on the television screen, too. As Reid approached, he looked up and locked eyes on him.

"Evenin'," Reid greeted as he neared the door. Almost there.

The guard glanced him up and down before nodding. "Have a good one."

Reid didn't breathe fully. Not even once he stepped out into the night. Every bit of him pulled tight. He didn't let himself feel free. Not yet. It wasn't time to drop his guard. He still had a long way to go to accomplish what he needed to do and kill the man that needed killing.

Glancing around, he pulled out the keys from his hoodie and pressed the unlock button. A distant beep echoed on the night. He moved in that direction, weaving between cars. He pushed the unlock button again and this time spotted the flash of headlights.

He advanced on an old Ford Explorer and pulled open its door. Ducking inside, he adjusted the seat for his long legs. Turning the ignition, he drove out of the parking lot.

He headed east for thirty minutes, stopping at a gas station to fill up the tank with the money he'd found in the locker. This late, the place was deserted. He kept his head low as he paid the sleepy-eyed clerk, avoided looking directly at the security camera in the corner.

Reid pulled around the back, where a lone car sat parked beside the Dumpster. He swapped license plates with the clerk's car. The guy probably wouldn't even notice anytime soon.

He still had to get rid of the Explorer, but he figured that could be done after he got where he was going.

Satisfied, he hopped back in his vehicle and drove a couple more hours through the night, putting Sweet Hill far behind him. He constantly glanced up at the rearview mirror, half expecting to see the flash of headlights. They never appeared.

The highway was dark, the passing car rare on this isolated stretch of road. He rubbed a hand over his close-cropped hair and settled into his seat. Desert mountains lumbered on either side of him, dark beasts etched against the backdrop of night. He flipped through radio stations. No news of an escaped convict. It had been a long time since he was this alone. He still didn't feel free, though. He doubted he ever would.

Eleven years had passed since he'd been out, but he expected to find Zane in the usual place. His brother was simple like that. Liked his routines.

The cabin sat several miles behind the main house on 530 acres located outside Odessa. The land had been in his family for almost two hundred years, granted to them after the Texas War of Independence.

The authorities didn't know about the cabin . . . or the hidden back road that veered off the county farm road you had to take to get there. The old Explorer bumped along the dirt lane. It was so overgrown with shrubs and cacti that it couldn't rightly be called a road anymore.

After an hour the road suddenly opened up to a clearing. The cabin stood there. Three trucks and a few motorcycles were parked out front, confirming that the cabin was far from forgotten.

The front door opened as he emerged from the Explorer. Several men stepped out onto the porch, wielding guns. He spotted Zane at the center of them. He was stockier, the baby roundness gone from his face. He was shirtless, and Reid marked the dozens of tats covering him that hadn't been there eleven years ago. Most notable was the eagle sitting atop a vicious looking skull. Most of the guys staring Reid down had the same symbol inked on their arms or necks. Once upon a time he would have been the one standing there with that eagle and skull inked somewhere on him. If fate hadn't intervened . . . if his eyes hadn't been opened . . .

He swallowed against the acid rising up in his throat and fixed a smile on his face. "Hey, little brother."

"Holy shit," Zane declared, hopping down from the porch and lowering his rifle. "Son of a bitch! What are you doing here?"

Reid lifted his chin and tried not to stare too hard at the emblems of hate riddling his brother. "Is that any way to welcome me home?"

Zane flung his arms wide. As if the past were forgotten. As if bad shit never went down. As if Reid could still be one of them. "Welcome home, brother."

Zane embraced him, clapping his back hard. Reid pulled back and eyed the other men, meeting their gazes head-on. Several looked at him with distrust. Evidently not everyone had forgotten. His brother's second in command, Rowdy, had a big grin for him, though. Rowdy reached out and clapped hands with him.

"Good to have you back." Rowdy looked him over. "Looking fierce, man. Guessing they didn't release you for good behavior."

"Nah. Thought I'd let myself out."

Zane and Rowdy laughed. "Same ol' Reid."

"You couldn't have come back at a better time." His brother's eyes glinted with excitement, reminding him of the kid he used to be.

"That right?" Reid asked.

Zane nodded eagerly, gesturing to the cabin. "Yeah." He shared a look with Rowdy and the other guys, and Reid got the sense that he was missing out on some joke. "Let's go inside and I'll tell you all about it."

Reid followed him inside and did a quick scan of the living room, noting how run-down the place had become in the eleven years he'd been gone. The place smelled of sweat and stale cigarette smoke. The upholstery on the arms of the couch had worn off. Dirty white threads tufted up as if trying to escape from the piece of furniture.

"We got something big going down, Bubba."

The sound of his little brother using his old nickname elicited a pang in his chest. "Yeah?" Reid looked at the men standing around him, a prickling sensation crawling up the back of his neck.

Zane chuckled lightly and scrubbed at the back of his neck under hair that fell long and greasy. He needed a shower. His brother's eyes were bloodshot from God knew what drug and a patchy beard hugged his cheeks. It was hard to reconcile him to the soft-faced boy Reid had last seen. "Why don't I show you?"

Turning, Zane headed down the dark hall to the back bedrooms. The carpet was flat and matted beneath Reid's shoes as he followed his brother. He felt the other men behind him, crowding close like anxious dogs. Something was definitely in the air. Feral and testosterone-laced. He recognized it from prison. Right when a fight broke out. Blood was in the water and the sharks were hungry.

Zane opened the door to the master bedroom and stepped inside. Reid followed. He sucked in a breath as his gaze landed on the bed and the woman restrained there. His stomach pitched and a fresh wave of acid surged up inside him.

Her hands were bound together with a single cord that extended to the brass headboard. She sat board-straight on the edge of the bed. Her eyes were red-rimmed and puffy. She'd been crying, but her eyes were now bone-dry above the gag. She didn't blink as her wide brown stare flitted over him, assessing him before flicking to the men at his back. Her nostrils flared as if scenting danger. She would be right about that. They were the wolves and she their next meal. Of that he was certain.

She tossed her head and said something against the gag. Her dark hair was loose and tangled around her shoulders, trailing long over her cream-colored blouse. The shiny fabric was dirt-smudged and stained, but still looked expensive. Probably the most expensive thing in this cabin. A bruise marred the flesh of her cheek above the gag where someone had hit her.

Reid still had no problem recognizing her. *Fuck*.

"Surprise!" Zane waved at her.

They'd done it. They'd abducted the president's daughter.

TWENTY-FIVE

*B*RIAR THREW HERSELF into her work. For a long time being a nurse was the only thing that had mattered. It gave her purpose and fed her soul. Then she met Knox and he had filled her mind with other things. Things she had no business thinking or feeling with him. She was determined to forget those things and get back to the way she was before.

When she wasn't at work, she did laundry and watched TV. The media rolled constant coverage about the missing First Daughter. She had watched in fascination initially. Until she realized they only had conjecture and no real information to report.

Then Briar took to cleaning her condo until it was spotless. She went to the store and loaded up on ingredients to cook things like lasagna and pies and cookies from scratch. Things that took concentration and time. When she was done making her pies and lasagna and cookies, she would just sit back and stare at them. And then clean and do more laundry.

But always, Knox was in the back of her mind. His face, his touch, his voice. *I could lose control. Around you, I feel that way.*

She admitted that was maybe his great appeal to her. Why she was so drawn to him. Because she felt *consumed*. She felt needed. As though she was oxygen to him. He had wanted her and there had been something desperate and powerful about it. No one had ever wanted her like that. She wanted him like that, too.

And he had let her go because of it. Even confessing her love for him—or near-love—hadn't mattered. If anything, it made him head to the door faster.

She sighed as she paused amid folding her laundry to take a pie out of the oven. Maybe he was right. Maybe feelings like that were unhealthy.

She set the pie to cool as a knock sounded on her door. Slipping off her oven mitt, she moved to look out her peephole. Her sister stood there alone, and she grimaced.

"I know you're in there," Laurel said, staring back at Briar like she could see her through the peephole. "I saw your car and I can smell pie."

"Fine," she muttered, and pulled the door open.

Her sister stared at her a moment before sweeping inside.

"You haven't answered my calls," Laurel accused.

"I texted you back. I've just been busy."

Laurel sniffed the air. "Blackberry?"

Briar nodded.

Her sister moved into the kitchen to glance at the other two pies already set out to cool. "What are you so busy doing? Opening your own bakery?"

"What are you doing here, Laurel? It's Sunday." She always had family events and activities planned in the afternoon with her family. Briar knew because she was usually there, too.

"We needed to talk, and seeing as you're avoiding my calls, here I am." She spread her arms wide.

"You don't need to say anything about the other day. I'm not seeing Knox anymore."

Her sister dropped her arms. "Oh?"

Briar snorted. "Yeah. He kind of agrees with you, actually. He doesn't think I should date a guy like him either."

Her sister stared at her for a moment. "And what about you? What do you think?"

"Does it matter?" She snorted. "When one person doesn't want to see the other one, things are pretty much over."

Laurel moved into the kitchen and examined the pies for a moment before facing Briar again. "I think you should keep seeing him."

She narrowed her eyes on her sister. "What?"

"Date him . . . be in a relationship with him. Whatever you want to call it." She waved a hand in the air. "The semantics aren't important. Just give this thing with him a try. I think it's worth pursuing." She expelled a breath. "He's worth pursuing."

Briar couldn't believe it. "Who are you and what have you done with my sister?"

"I know, I know. I said all kinds of judgy things, but that was before. You say he's not some dangerous person, and I believe you. I trust you. Look, I'm sorry about Martin. I didn't realize what a jerk he was at first, and even when I started to suspect it, I just let myself be blinded by his good job and bank account."

"But Knox . . . he hit him at your barbecue," Briar reminded. "Caused a big scene . . . freaked out your guests . . ."

"Yeah, because he was defending your honor. He did it for you, Briar. You've never had that before . . . someone willing to protect you. And for God's sake you deserve it. You deserve someone to stand by you. I found that with Caleb, but you've never had that with anyone."

Briar reached out and snagged her sister's hand. "I had it with you."

Laurel smiled tenderly at her and squeezed her hand back. "Yeah, and look what I did for you. Graduated, married Caleb, and never looked back. I left you in that house, Briar." Her voice cracked. "I-left you there for four more years, and I know Dad got worse. I wasn't there for you—"

Briar pulled her into a hug. "Of course you had to go." She patted her back.

Laurel pulled back to look into her eyes. "I was wrong. Knox is what you deserve, Briar."

She smiled sadly and shook her head. "No." He walked away from her when she would have given him everything. She had stood there, offering him her heart, and he turned his back on it. She deserved someone who wasn't afraid to love her. "He's not."

KNOX SAT INSIDE the prison he never thought to visit again. Of course he was in the visiting room, waiting to see if North was actually going to show. He wasn't wearing a white prison uniform. The guards hardly paid him any attention as they stood sentinel in the room.

After a week and a half in the hospital, his brother had returned five days ago. But according to the social worker, he was sent straight to segregation for his role in the riot. Knox hadn't been able to see him until now.

What the hell happened that day? North always tried to keep a low profile. He wouldn't have instigated a riot, but Knox knew well enough that it was war in here and you did what you had to in order to survive.

Inmates filed into the room and moved to the tables

where their visitors sat. Knox tapped his thigh under the table impatiently, desperate to see his brother, to confirm that he was still whole.

Finally, he stepped through the door. Knox shot up straighter in his seat and he felt sick. He hardly recognized the North walking over to him.

He had lost weight. His features were gaunt and ashen. His white shirt hung off his shoulders. He was all leanness. A rangy wolf. He even had that feral look in his brown eyes. Those eyes landed on Knox and narrowed. It wasn't a friendly look. His brother was definitely not happy to see him.

Deep shadows stood out like bruises beneath his eyes, and as he drew closer, Knox saw the wound on his face. A deep angry slash ran down the length of his cheek, the skin held together with butterfly strips. It started near his eye and ran the length of his cheek, ending at his jawline.

North sank down in front of him. "What are you doing here?"

"What the hell happened in here, North?" Up close, he could see that the wound was going to leave a nasty scar. His brother was never going to be that too-pretty boy again.

"Shit happens in here. You know that."

"Never had a riot in the eight years that I—"

"Then we were overdue," he snapped, and Knox fell silent.

The familiar guilt rose up to gnaw at him, and he looked down at his hands.

"Don't do that," North bit out.

Knox's gaze shot back to his brother. "Do what?"

"Look all fucking guilty. That shit gets old. I'm in here because I wanted to go along with you that night. That bastard destroyed our cousin. He killed her."

Knox shook his head. "It was my idea to go after—"

"Yeah. And I threw the first punch. Remember that?" North slumped back in his chair. "Look, I'm going to have a hearing—"

"For what?" Knox demanded.

North stared at him coldly, so unlike the guy he'd left in here just a few months ago. "I'm facing more time. For the riot. They're holding me and a bunch of other guys responsible."

"What?" His world spun and upended. *No. No. No.* North was supposed to get out soon. Maybe a few more months.

"How much time you looking at?" Knox asked numbly.

North shrugged. "Couple of bulls got badly injured. Three inmates dead. There has to be consequences." He paused, his lips twisting. "Reid's gone."

"Gone where? Dead?"

North shook his head. "He went to the hospital

with me. No one's talking about where he is . . . if he's coming back." He looked sideways and leaned forward, lowering his voice. "There's a rumor going round that he broke out. At the hospital."

It all clicked then. The riot had been deliberate so Reid could escape. *God damn him.*

They stared at one another, their suspicion settling on the air between them.

"How long are you facing?" Knox asked, dread pooling in his stomach.

North answered him quietly. "Few more years maybe."

"No." His hands curled into fists on top of the table. "We'll get you a new lawyer. You're not staying in here—"

"Man, cool it. It is what it is. I'll be fine."

He didn't look fine. He didn't even look like his brother anymore. He looked hard. Like a man that didn't expect to ever get out. Like a man who no longer cared. Knox needed to get North out of this place while there was anything of him still left.

North's brown eyes flicked over him. He attempted a smile. "Tell me you've been getting laid a lot for me out there."

Knox snorted.

His brother nodded. "Well, I don't hear any denials. That's good, man. I need to hear that you're out there living and making up for lost time . . . nailing lots of ass. As soon as you leave here, go eat a big burger with a side of onion rings, too. Can you do that for me? And a nice cold beer."

"I can do you the burger and beer, but I wouldn't say I've been banging a lot of girls." There hadn't been anyone since Briar, and he doubted there would be any time soon. Just the thought of being with anyone else left him cold.

"Oh, no?" North arched an eyebrow and considered him for a moment. "Just one girl, then?"

Knox didn't answer, but that seemed answer enough.

North nodded. "Good. Even better. Well, don't wait on me for the wedding. Get on out of here and make me an uncle. By the time I get out, I can take the little guy to a Cowboys game."

That idea shot an image straight to his head—of him and Briar with a little boy. Someone sweet and pure, whose hand would feel tiny and innocent in his own. The thought made him go weak in the knees and played havoc with his heart.

"Fuck. I'm not getting married. I broke up with her." Not that they had been official or anything.

"Why?"

"Look, I don't want to talk about this. Let's talk about your defense for this upcoming hearing. I can talk to—"

"Shit, man. I'm not talking about that. I want

to talk about you and this girl you broke up with. Why'd you dump her?"

"Do I look like a catch to you, North? I'm a fucking felon and this is a nice girl—"

"All the better. Marry her. Take her to the farmhouse. Make it a home again. Uncle Mac and Aunt Alice would love it."

He stared at his brother in shock. "You're serious. You think I deserve—"

"You think I don't?" he countered, raising his voice enough for one of the guards to call out a warning. North glared at the bull and then turned his attention back to Knox. "If you don't deserve it, then neither do I."

An uncomfortable tightness centered in his chest. Of course his brother deserved that. He deserved everything.

North stabbed a finger in the air. "I've always looked up to you, but I won't respect you for shit if you don't grab this opportunity with both hands. Trust me, the moment I get out of here, nothing is going to stop me from living the life I want. Nothing. Now don't be a fucking pussy."

Heat crept up Knox's face. "When did you start telling me what to do?"

"Apparently when you started needing someone to." North's gaze flicked up him and down. "You love this girl?"

He looked down at his hands again, seeing Briar's face. Seeing her that first day in the HSU and every moment in between. Seeing her when she said she might be a little in love with him. Right before he walked out on here. "Yeah. Yeah, I do."

"Then get the fuck out of here and go get her. Don't come back again unless it's with her. Understand? I want to meet her."

Knox wiped at his suddenly burning eyes. He'd never spent one day of his eight years in this prison crying. Not even when the pain had been so great and he thought his body was broken forever. And now here he was, blubbering like a baby in the very place where he had never shown weakness. "Yeah. All right."

TWENTY-SIX

*B*RIAR JUST FINISHED putting the last dish in the dishwasher when a knock sounded on her door. She closed the dishwasher and pushed the start button before padding barefoot to her door. A peek through the peephole had her gasping and lurching back.

Knox stood on the other side. What was he doing here?

He knocked again. Her hand moved to unlock the door and then she snatched it back. No. She wasn't doing this again. No more. She'd offered him everything and he walked away. Because she was *bad* for him.

If she opened the door she would let him in, and then she'd probably let him in her bed. Because she was that weak. Because she was putty in his hands. She wouldn't do that. She wouldn't succumb. She had been working so hard to get over him. She'd even told Shelley that she would go out with her ex-brother-in-law. True, Shelley's ex-husband was a douche but apparently he had a nice brother.

He knocked again. "Briar, please open the door. I know you're in there."

Her skin shivered at the sound of his voice. She'd missed him. It would be so easy to let him in. In her home. In her still raw and bleeding heart. She wouldn't survive him leaving her the next time. This time had been hard enough.

He continued, "Look, I just came from seeing my brother at the prison . . . and hell, I know that doesn't mean anything to you, but it got me thinking and . . . shit, I fucked up. Can you just open the door so I can see you? So we can talk face-to-face?"

She started to open her mouth several times but didn't trust herself to speak.

She felt a soft thud and risked another peek out the door. She could still see his shoulders. It looked like he had bowed his head against the door. He said something so softly, she couldn't quite understand him. She pressed her ear to the door, trying to hear, and when she finally did hear his whisper, her chest squeezed tightly.

I need you . . .

She closed her eyes, reaching deep inside herself for strength. She had to be strong. Nothing had changed. He was still that guy that didn't trust himself, that felt out of control around her. And it didn't matter what he needed. She had to consider herself and what she needed or she would, in fact, be just like her mother.

"I'll be back, Briar." His voice rang loud and clear again. "I'm not giving up."

Then she heard his retreating footsteps.

She turned and slid down the length of the door, hardening her heart. She would not give in to him. He'd eventually give up. She just had to resist him until he did.

HE WAITED OUTSIDE Briar's apartment, telling himself this wasn't stalkerish. She still loved him. He knew she did. And he loved her. She couldn't have forgotten all her feelings for him in so short a time. He hadn't screwed everything up that badly.

It was barely light out. Dawn streaked the West Texas sky, but he knew she left for work this early. Sure enough, at 6:55 he spotted her coming down her stairs in her scrubs. Her hair was still damp and pulled back into a tight braid that his fingers itched to unravel.

He was out of his truck and across the parking lot, planting himself in front of her car door before she could reach her vehicle.

She came to a hard stop when she saw him there. "What are you doing?"

"I said I wasn't giving up."

"I don't want to see you."

"Then close your eyes. Just listen to me."

She shook her head, her gaze skittering around like she was looking for an escape. "I'm going to be late for work. Please move."

So polite. And scared. She looked terrified, but not the kind of terror that worried him. No, this was wariness. As though she didn't trust herself. Clearly, she didn't want him to persuade her to do anything she didn't want to do. It gave him hope. It meant at least a part of her still wanted to be with him.

"Briar," he breathed, stepping away from the car and closing in on her. "I love you."

Her eyes flared. "No! Don't say that. Don't you *dare* say that!"

"It's true."

"I'm bad for you, remember?" she flung out, anger and hurt ripe in her voice. Again, it gave him hope.

He closed his eyes in a tight blink. "I said that and a lot of other stupid shit, yeah. But loving you will make me stronger. I know it now. I can love you like you deserve if you'll just let me."

She snorted and stepped around him. "I don't have time for this." She hit her unlock button and started to open her door.

He came behind her and shut it with the palm of his hand. "Give us a chance." He spoke into the nape of her neck, sending tiny hairs fluttering, tickling his lips. "You said you loved me—"

"Don't twist my words. I said I *might* love you a *little*. I was wrong."

He turned her around, pressing his body against hers, trapping her between him and the car, concentrating on his words and struggling to ignore the distracting softness of her body. No easy task. He'd been too long from her. "Liar. You haven't stopped loving me. You're angry. I get that . . . and trying to protect yourself. I get that, too—"

"That's right. I'm trying to protect myself from you. Now let me go."

He leaned in, holding her gaze. "I love you," he whispered . . . pleaded.

Something flashed in her eyes before disappearing. "I don't love *you*," she said resolutely, so firmly. For the first time dread gnawed at the edges of his heart. Could it be too late?

"No," he growled.

Then he kissed her.

He slanted his lips over hers and poured all his heart, all his longing, into this kiss, coaxing her to respond, to soften. "Please," he whispered over her quivering lips. "Kiss me back, Briar. Kiss me."

With a whimper she caved, her lips yielding to him. A shudder racked him. He slid his arms around her and lifted her up off the ground and against his arousal. He let her feel what she did to him. Her hands looped around his neck and she clung to him, still kissing him back as hot and feverishly as he kissed her.

"There," he growled, lust and satisfaction pumping through him. "You do love me."

She stiffened and then fought to free herself from his embrace. *Damn it*. He let her go, barely having time to look down at her flushed face before she slapped him so hard he felt the force all the way to his teeth.

He fingered his stinging cheek, gazing down at her. Her chest heaved with emotion, eyes blazing up at him. "Stay away from me and stop manipulating me. Nothing has changed. You're still the out-of-control animal you don't want to be. And I do *not* love you."

Her words gouged him as effectively as a swiping claw. Like she knew they would, but he had the taste of her still on his lips. Alongside the sight of her spitting rage, it was all the confirmation he needed. She still wanted him. *Loved* him. "Yes. You do."

She stomped her foot and let out a muffled groan. "You're crazy!"

"Just about you," he returned, then in a more serious tone, he added, "I know I blew it, but I'll wait until you realize I'm sincere. I can be patient. I spent years in prison waiting to be free. *Waiting*, even though I didn't know it then . . . for you."

An alarmed look crossed her face as she stubbornly shook her head. "You don't mean that . . ."

"I do. And time will prove it." He leaned in slowly, his mouth brushing her ear as he spoke, "And once you're convinced, we're going to hole up in your bedroom for a day at least . . . where I will convince you again and again and again . . . until neither one of us can walk."

She jerked her head away from him, her eyes bright and heated. She shook her head again, this time almost sad. Yanking open her door, she slid into her car. He stepped away before she backed out and nearly ran her tire over his foot. He watched her go, telling himself she would relent and give them another chance.

She didn't once glance back at him as she drove away.

KNOX DECIDED TO give her a little more space before coming around again. Two more days. He thought that would be enough time for her to start to wonder if he gave up . . . maybe enough time for her to worry that he had. Maybe enough time for her to miss him.

At her apartment complex, he noticed her car was parked in its usual spot, so he took the stairs to her condo.

He knocked. "Briar?"

Nothing.

"I know you're in there. Baby, please . . ."

"She's not home." He spun around to face Shelley. She was leaning in her open door, a couple of kids crowded around her, watching him with big curious eyes that looked a lot like their mother's eyes.

"Where is she?"

She considered him a long moment before answering, "Now I don't know if I should be telling you that."

He nodded. "All right. That's fair. You're looking out for your friend. I get that."

"Yeah, you haven't been precisely stellar boyfriend material."

He nodded. "I know that. I'd like to make it up to her." He paused for a breath. "I love her."

"She mentioned you said that. She doesn't believe you, of course."

"I'm trying to prove it to her."

"Hmm." Shelley eyed him. "Briar doesn't have a lot of experience with men. Not like me. She doesn't understand that men don't usually profess love. Not after they've gotten what they want, if you know what I mean." She shot a quick glance to her children and then looked back at him, lifting her eyebrows meaningfully.

"Yeah. I know what you mean."

"They don't chase you down and say those three little words over and over unless they mean it."

"I mean it."

She nodded slowly. "I think you do." Placing a hand on top of her little girl's head, she guided her back into the apartment.

He turned to go, assuming she was finished talking. "She's on a date with my ex-brother-in-law at the Bean House. You know the place? It's a fancy little coffee shop on Peek Avenue."

He stopped and looked back at her. "Your ex-brother-in-law?"

"Yep. I set them up. My ex has a decent brother. Thought she should see what else is out there."

He glared at her.

She winked at him. "Maybe you should pop in. Order a latte and scone."

He'd never eaten a scone in his life. Much less a latte. "Yeah. I'll do that."

SHELLEY WAS RIGHT. Daniel was nice and down-to-earth and he smelled good. Like fresh laundry sheets. He owned a hardware store in town. They shared a plate of assorted pastries and sipped their coffees, going through all the usual first date getting-to-know-you banter.

"My mother was a nurse. Worked long hours," Daniel shared as he lifted the lid off his cup to cool the coffee.

"I work in a practice," Briar explained. "Regular

hours. Seven-thirty to four P.M. I get every third Friday off, too. It's nice. A good place to work. Good people."

"Well, that makes all the difference," he said, smiling kindly. "Loving what you do."

She smiled back at him. He really was nice. Nice looking. Steady job. So why could she only think of Knox? Why must she compare Daniel's every feature, his every expression, to Knox? Was she always going to do this? Because there was no comparison. She would never meet another man to hold up to him in the looks department. And why did sitting here with this guy feel like she was betraying him? Knox and she weren't together. She owed him nothing.

"Hello, there." And suddenly Knox was there, pulling up a chair and sitting beside her and Daniel. She blinked for a moment, wondering if her thoughts had conjured him. Was she totally losing it?

But Daniel gaped, too. So this was happening. This was real. Knox was here and crashing her date.

It took her a moment to find her voice. "Knox! What are you doing here?"

"Joining you and . . ." He extended his hand to Daniel. "Hello. Knox Callaghan."

Daniel returned the handshake. "Daniel Ortega."

"Joining you and Daniel," he finished with an easy smile that was so unlike his usual austere self.

"Leave now, Knox!"

"Excuse me, what's happening here?" Daniel gestured at the three of them.

"You see, Daniel," Knox began, leaning back in his chair and draping an arm over the back of her chair. "I only think it's fair to let you know up front that I'm in love with Briar. I messed things up, and she's not ready to forgive me yet, but I'm going to do everything in my power to win her back."

"It has nothing to do with forgiveness, you jackass. I just don't want you. I don't love you."

Knox slanted a look at Daniel that was so knowing and smug that she wanted to scream. "I think she does."

Daniel replaced the lid back on his cup. "I see," he said, as though he did in fact see.

She reached for his arm. "Daniel, I'm so sorry. This is really embarrassing."

"No, not at all. This stuff happens. It took me a long time to get over my ex and be ready to even date." He pushed back his chair. "Clearly, you're not in a place where you're ready, Briar. Good luck." He glanced at Knox. "Nice meeting you."

Knox shook his hand again. "You, too."

"I trust you can see she gets back home."

"Not a problem."

Briar gaped and then dropped her head into her hands. "This isn't happening." She looked up and glared at the back of Daniel as he walked away.

"Nice guy."

She turned her wrath on Knox. "Yeah. He was. Thanks for screwing that up."

Knox helped himself to one of the scones on the table. "C'mon. That would have gone nowhere. You still want me."

"Stop saying that!" She grabbed her purse off the back of the chair. "I'm going home." He stood and fell into step beside her as she hurried over the plank wood floor of the coffeehouse. "Don't worry. I'll walk."

"Briar, it's not even close. Don't be so stubborn," he said as they stepped out onto the parking lot.

She started toward the sidewalk, not even caring that he was right. She would walk the seven miles in these boots. She didn't care. She was not climbing into his truck with him.

She kept moving, passing a group of three preppy-looking young men heading to the coffeehouse. One of them elbowed another one and nodded at her and Callaghan.

They just cleared the three men when one called out, "Callaghan!"

Knox stopped and turned. Curious, she stopped, too, and looked back.

The three men stood side by side, legs braced apart, anger bristling off them like wild dogs. "They let you out?"

Briar looked up at Knox. He was tense, the brackets around his mouth drawn tight. He immediately understood what this was. And so did she. These guys knew who he was and they clearly had an ax to grind. "That's right."

"We played football with Mason. They should have given you the death sentence for killing him."

"Nope. Just eight years," Knox returned, his bland voice in direction opposition to the tension radiating from him. He touched her arm and pulled her behind him.

"You with him?" one of the guys called out to her, his gaze direct and piercing. "You know he's a murderer?"

Knox squeezed her arm, advising her to say nothing.

"We don't want any trouble. We're just leaving," Knox said, sounding so very un-Knoxlike. Usually he'd be kicking ass by now.

"What the hell world we living in when a man like you can walk the streets free?"

Knox turned then, keeping her in front of him and guiding her toward the truck. She wasn't about to argue with him about walking home anymore. She just wanted to get away from these men with violence in their eyes.

Then Knox's hand was wrenched off her arm. He went down with a grunt. She spun around, watching in horror as two of them men started beating him.

"Knox!" she screamed, lunging forward, but the

other man caught her up and held her back, one arm locked around her waist.

The two continued to beat on him, but he did nothing. Simply took it. He made it back up to his feet, and they let him, panting and grinning, enjoying every moment of it.

"What are you doing? Knox, fight!" she pleaded. His gaze found hers, and what she saw there was like a knife in her heart. He wouldn't. He wouldn't fight because of her. He was showing her he could restrain himself even under provocation.

"That's right!" One man punched Knox in the face and sent his entire body spinning. He collided with a parked car and clung to it to keep from falling. "Fight back, you bastard."

But he didn't. He wouldn't lift a finger.

"Knox," she whimpered. She felt like she was dying, unable to catch her breath.

A man stepped out of the coffeehouse and shouted in their direction. "Hey! I'm calling the cops!"

"Hear that?" she shouted. "The cops are coming! You better go!"

The man holding her laughed. "We'll probably get a medal." They kept pounding on him. Over her screams.

"He won't fight you! Just stop! Stop it!" Briar shouted at them.

"Prison turned you into a pussy," one of the guys

said, and spat in Knox's bleeding face. "C'mon. Let's go."

Just then a police cruiser turned the corner and whipped into the parking lot with a brief blare of its siren. The two men hitting him stood back. Knox dropped to his knees, then to his side, dead weight, as the two officers hopped out of the vehicle, taser guns at the ready.

The man holding her released her and she rushed to Knox's side, tears streaming hotly down her face. She ignored the policemen and three guys, her only thought for Knox. She wrapped an arm around him and gingerly touched the eye already swelling shut. "Why? Why did you let them do this to you?"

He looked out at her with his one good eye. "I told you. *You* make me stronger."

She shook her head, bewildered. "You make no sense. They hurt you." She was sobbing now.

An officer approached them. "Ma'am, are you all right?"

She turned on him, wiping at her tears. "Yes. These men attacked my boyfriend."

"I'm a felon," Knox admitted, wincing as he spoke. "They took exception to the fact that I was granted parole."

The officer nodded, eyeing Knox up and down, not missing the fact that he had been beaten within an inch of his life. Behind him, his partner had the three men face down on the asphalt with their hands behind their heads. "I'll call an ambulance to—"

"That's not necessary—" Knox started to say.

"It's necessary," Briar cut in.

The policeman was moving away, already speaking into his radio.

"They're going to look you over. What they did to you needs to be documented."

"Boyfriend, huh?" He attempted a smile and winced at the effort.

Her cheeks warmed.

"I like that," he murmured.

She took the edge of her shirt and rose on her knees to gingerly wipe his face. "You should have defended yourself." Tears threatened again, making her voice crack.

"Sssh." He stroked her face, his thumb tracing her bottom lip. "This is nothing. I'll heal. But if I fought them and got in trouble, got my parole revoked . . . then I go back. I lose you." His voice choked up a little then. "I would never heal from that. I can't lose you, Briar."

She threw both arms around him, mindful not to squeeze him too tightly, convinced that he was the strongest man she had even known. "You're not going to lose me. You won't," she vowed, pressing her lips to wherever she touched skin. His neck, cheeks, lips. "You're never going to lose me, Knox. I love you."

He grinned against her lips. "Told you so."

She laughed harshly against his mouth. "Is that all you have to say?"

He sobered instantly. "No." He cupped her head in both hands and looked steadily into her eyes. She gazed back at his battered face, waiting. "I love you, Briar, and I want to be with you. Always. I don't want to go to bed a single night without you next to me. I want to marry you. I want to have kids with you. The whole thing." He inhaled a broken breath just as an ambulance sounded in the distance, growing closer. "Please say you'll have me."

Her heart pounded so hard that she couldn't say anything for a moment. She reached up and covered his hands where they held her face. "Yes. Yes, to all of that. I'll have you, Knox. For always."

With a short exultant cry, he covered her mouth with his own, muttering against her lips, "I can't wait to get you home."

EPILOGUE

Four months later . . .

BRIAR LET THE door slam behind her, anxious to leave the bitter cold of the February night behind. Immediately the aroma of rich tomato sauce hit her nose.

Textbooks littered her kitchen table alongside Knox's open laptop, but the sound of a knife on the cutting board carried from the kitchen. "I'm home," she called, unwinding the thick scarf from her neck.

Knox stepped out of the kitchen wearing a smile. "Hey, how was work?" He pulled her into his arms, and she smelled all the ingredients that went into his delicious sauce in the fabric of his snug-fitting thermal shirt.

"Good. How was your day?"

He kissed her long and hard before answering, "Good. I'm making spaghetti." His lips drifted from her mouth to nuzzle at her neck. "But it's on a low simmer. We can disappear into the bedroom for, oh . . . an hour . . ."

"An hour?" she laughed as he wrapped his arms around her waist and lifted her off her feet, carrying her into her bedroom.

"An hour," he repeated. "At least."

"Don't you have a test tomorrow?" In addition to still working at Roscoe's, Knox had just started two courses at the local college.

"I'm ready," he replied, lowering her to the bed and coming over her. Straddling her, he reached behind him and pulled his shirt over his head. Her hands drifted down the flat expanse of his stomach, her blood heating to a simmer that was probably hotter than that sauce on the stove.

He seized her wrist and positioned her palm on the bulge of his erection. "See? Ready." He winked down at her and she giggled.

He sighed and leaned over to kiss her again. "I love the sound of your laugh."

"It's because of you. You make me happy."

He stared at her solemnly for a moment. "I love you, Briar."

"I love you, too."

"We're going to have a good life together," he said with resolve, his eyes glittering with emotion. Almost as though a lingering part of him would always doubt that possibility.

She brushed a hand over his bristly jaw reassuringly and stared into his eyes. "I know, Knox. That's why we're going to move in together."

He stilled. "We are?"

She shrugged, trying not to feel suddenly insecure. "You're here almost every night . . ."

"Briar, my uncle needs someone with him out at the farm. I can't just—"

"I'm moving in with you both at the farmhouse," she clarified.

He stilled. "You want to live with me and Uncle Mac? I can't ask you to—"

"I know you'll never leave him. That's who you are. The kind of man you are. Loyal and kind and devoted. It's why I love you. So yeah, if we're going to live together, it's going to be with Uncle Mac. At the farmhouse."

He expelled a breath and pulled her tightly into his arms. "Finding you, being with you . . . you make everything that's ever happened to me worth getting to this moment."

She hugged him back, her arms looped around his big shoulders, shivering a little as he spoke into her ear. "Except . . . we can't move in together, Briar."

She pulled back, looking at him in alarm. "What do you mean?"

"Not without an understanding between us first," he added. She blinked, shaking her head, utterly bewildered. His cobalt gaze flicked over her face. "Marry me."

Those two words speared her in the chest, robbing her of breath. There was a shadow of uncertainty as he stared at her, waiting for her to say something. Something good. Something like *yes*.

She swallowed, fighting for her voice. "Yes," she said hoarsely. "Yes, yes, yes, I'll marry you."

His face broke into a smile. Then she couldn't breathe again because they were kissing. And loving. There were no more words. Their sighs and moans and reverent touches said everything.

It wasn't until later that either one of them could speak.

An hour at least.

ACKNOWLEDGMENTS

THANK YOU TO my fabulous editor, May Chen, and the team at Avon for taking a chance on this book. I've been itching to write the Devil's Rock series for a long time—even before I knew what it was called. As someone who has been writing for over ten years, it's sometimes hard to stay excited about every project. It means the world to have a team that gives me the support and encouragement to write books that continuously excite me.

Additionally, this book wouldn't be what it is without the keen insight of Stacey Kade, Sarah MacLean and my lovely Kiawah Island retreaters: Ally, Carrie, Monica and Rachel—thanks for listening to me wax on about this book and inspiring me through a wonderful week crammed full of blackberry pie and writerly magic. And lastly, a great thank you to Lisa

Dess. Who knew when you worked as a corrections officer you would one day have an author pelt you with question after question regarding prison life? Thank you for your input. I hope you approve of any liberties I may have taken.

Look for Reid and Grace's story in

HELL BREAKS LOOSE

the second book in

New York Times best-selling author

SOPHIE JORDAN'S

Devil's Rock series.

Coming August 2016 from Avon Books

At Avon Books, we know your passion for romance—once you finish one of our novels, you find yourself wanting more.

May we tempt you with . . .

- **Excerpts** from our upcoming releases.

- Entertaining **extras**, including authors' personal photo albums and book lists.

- Behind-the-scenes **scoop** on your favorite characters and series.

- **Sweepstakes** for the chance to win free books, romantic getaways, and other fun prizes.

- Writing **tips** from our authors and editors.

- **Blog** with our authors and find out why they love to write romance.

- **Exclusive content** that's not contained within the pages of our novels.

Join us at
www.avonbooks.com

AVON

An Imprint of HarperCollins*Publishers*
www.avonromance.com

*G*ive in to your Impulses!

These unforgettable stories only take a second to buy and give you hours of reading pleasure!

Go to *www.AvonImpulse.com* and see what we have to offer.

Available wherever e-books are sold.

AVONIMPULSE